ALTER EGO, LIMITED

Earth took Cal Tremon, stripped away his self, and put the mind and personality of a solar agent into him. Then they sent him on a one-way trip to Lilith. All he had to do was conquer the whole damned planet, execute the Overlord, and report mind-to-mind with the agent he had become but who still remained at home!

Lilith, unfortunately, was one of the four worlds of the Warden Diamond, where a symbiotic bug invaded every living cell—and from which no infected life could escape and live.

If he failed, Earth would find a way to kill him. If he should succeed, probably they would kill him for knowing too much. And meantime, naked and a slave, he had to survive—survive despite the mutated witches and all the feudal hell of a planet gone mad and a people without hope.

Cal Tremon meant to survive—and to hell with Earth!

Also by Jack L. Chalker
Published by Ballantine Books:

AND THE DEVIL WILL DRAG YOU UNDER

A JUNGLE OF STARS

THE SAGA OF THE WELL WORLD

Volume 1: *Midnight at the Well of Souls*

Volume 2: *Exiles at the Well of Souls*

Volume 3: *Quest for the Well of Souls*

Volume 4: *The Return of Nathan Brazil*

Volume 5: *Twilight at the Well of Souls:
          The Legacy of Nathan Brazil*

LILITH:

A Snake in the Grass

Book One of
THE FOUR LORDS OF THE DIAMOND

JACK L. CHALKER

A Del Rey Book

BALLANTINE BOOKS • NEW YORK

For Lou Tabakow,
a great unsung friend
of science fiction for
almost fifty years and a man
whose kindness and
friendship I will always
treasure

A Del Rey Book
Published by Ballantine Books

Library of Congress Catalog Card Number: 81-66665

ISBN 0-345-29369-X

Manufactured in the United States of America

First edition: October 1981

Cover art by David B. Mattingly

Contents

Prologue:	Background to Trouble	1
Chapter One:	Rebirth	29
Chapter Two:	Transportation and Exposure	42
Chapter Three:	Orientation and Placement	48
Chapter Four:	Zeis Keep	58
Chapter Five:	Village Routine	66
Chapter Six:	Ti	75
Chapter Seven:	Father Bronz	83
Chapter Eight:	Social Mobility on Lilith	93
Chapter Nine:	The Castle	102
Chapter Ten:	Dr. Pohn and Master Artur	108
Chapter Eleven:	Choosing a Different Road	118
Chapter Twelve:	Too Dangerous to Have Around	135
Chapter Thirteen:	Some Interested Parties	152
Chapter Fourteen:	Savages and Amazons	158
Chapter Fifteen:	A Dialogue	162
Chapter Sixteen:	Sumiko O'Higgins and the Seven Covens	177
Chapter Seventeen:	I Do Believe in Witches— I Do, I Do!	187
Chapter Eighteen:	Moab Keep	200
Chapter Nineteen:	The Wizards of Moab Keep	206
Chapter Twenty:	Council of War	216
Chapter Twenty-One:	The Battle of Zeis Keep	223
Chapter Twenty-Two:	First Lord of the Diamond	232
Chapter Twenty-Three:	A Little Unfinished Business	242
Epilogue		246

THE WARDEN DIAMOND

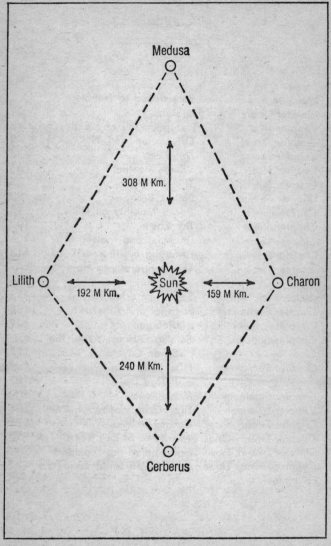

Background to Trouble

1

The little man in the synthetic tweed jacket didn't look like a bomb. In fact, he looked much the same as most of the other clerks, junior computer operators, and political men on the make in Military Systems Command. Two beady little brownish eyes set a bit too far apart by a hawk nose, a twitchy little mouth above a lantern jaw—the kind of nebbish nobody ever looked at twice. That's why he was so dangerous.

He wore all the proper entry cards, and when handprints and retinal patterns were taken at doors that could trap or even destroy if the slightest thing was wrong he was passed without so much as an electronic pause. He carried a small briefcase, unusual only in that it was merely clasped and not chained to him or attached in some other way. Still, that caused no notice or alarm—it was probably tuned to his body, anyway.

Occasionally along brightly lit halls he'd meet another of his apparent ilk, and they'd pass, perhaps nodding as if they knew each other but more often simply ignoring one another as they would in a crowd or on any street corner. There was nothing exceptional about them, nothing to mark them as something apart from the common herd, because, except for their jobs and job location, there *wasn't* any real difference. Except for this one little man. He was definitely exceptional, being a bomb.

Finally he reached a small room in which a single computer access element was placed in front of a comfortable-looking chair. There were no warning symbols, no huge guards or robot sentinels about, even though this particular room was the gateway to the military secrets of an interstellar empire of vast proportions. There was no need. No single individual could activate that access element; doing so required the combined and nearly simultaneous consent of three different human beings and two robot backups, each of whom received a different coded order from a different source. Any attempt to use it without the actions of all the others would result not only in a dead computer and blank terminal but also in a warning flashed to security.

The little man sat down in the chair, adjusted it for proper operating position, then leaned over and casually opened his briefcase. Removing a small crystalline device, he idly flicked it on with a thumb motion and then it set against the activation plate of the terminal.

The screen flickered, came to life. Printed on it were all the access codes as if it had received them and the question of whether the user preferred voice or CRT communication. There was no question of a print-out. Not with *this* computer.

"CRT only, please," the little man idly said, in a thin, dry, nasal voice that bore no trace of accent. The machine waited. "Defensive files C-476-2377AX and J-392-7533DC, please, at speed."

The computer seemed to blink at that last; at speed would be at roughly four hundred lines a second, the limit of the CRT to form the images in the first place. Nonetheless, the computer went to work. Both plans were delivered up and snapped past the little man in less than a second.

He was pleased. So much so that he decided then and there to press his luck a little and ask for more. "Run the master defense emergency plans, please, at speed, in order," he told the machine casually.

The machine obeyed. Because of the volume of material it took almost four minutes.

The little man glanced at his watch. It was so tempting to continue, but every second he was here increased his chances of somebody just looking in or some random check. That wouldn't do, not at all.

He placed his device back in his briefcase, snapped it closed, stood up, and walked out. At that point he made one minor mistake, one he would not be expected to know. You had to tell the damned thing to clear and reset the codes. If you didn't, this computer didn't react like all others and simply stay on—intolerable, with access to such secrets—or shut itself down. When it "saw" that the operator had left the room without resetting it, the machine advised control personnel of that fact, then locked in emergency shutdown until reset.

As the little man reached the first checkpoint door on his way out, things were already starting to crack around him.

The young woman glared for a moment at the red alert light that had flashed on her console. She ran a quick check to make sure there was no internal malfunction, then punched up the trouble—the Eyes Only Storage Computer.

Although she was one of those with part of the code that would activate the computer, she could not ask it any questions on its information storage from where she was—but she could get *security* information. She knew she had given no access so far today, so she punched two buttons and instructed, "Run tape last operation."

The little man's face showed clearly. Not only his face, but his retinal pattern, thermal pattern, everything about him that could be read by remote sensors and recorded. She brought in the rest of the computer net. "Identify!" she commanded.

"Threht, Augur Pen-Gyl, OG-6, Logistics," came the computer's reply.

Before her hand could hit the alarm it had already been hit by two of her associates.

No alarms sounded, no flashing lights and whistling bells that would panic or tip off a spy. Instead, as Threht reached the third and last security door, peered into the oculator, and pressed his palm on the identiplate, it simply refused to open.

He realized at once that security, both human and robotic, was already closing in on him from all sides, and decided in a flash that the least security would be on the other side of the door. He raised his left hand, paused for a moment, frozen, as if marshaling all he had, then struck the door near its locking mechanism. The area buckled, and he leaned forward and without seeming effort pushed until the door slid back enough for him to squeeze through.

Once he was inside, the door slammed shut behind him, and he could hear the secondary seals slide into place. It formed an effective trap, between the inner and outer door. The chamber itself was airtight; so if someone got this far, the air inside the chamber could be rapidly withdrawn. No chances, not with somebody this good.

The vacuum hardly bothered him. He kicked at the outer door once, twice; on the third try, it gave. He leaned forward with all his might, opening a crack and holding the door open against the massive inrush of air until the pressure equalized. At that point he threw it open and strode through into the main entrance hall.

His guess had been correct; security forces were only now reaching the hall area, and stunned personnel throughout the hall prevented a quick shot. Four sleek black security robots sped toward him. Apparently unafraid, he let them advance. Then, just before they reached him, he suddenly ran right at the two in the lead, pushing one into the other and spilling both to the floor. The scene was incredible: a tiny, ordinary-looking fellow tumbled four tons of animated metal without so much as recoiling.

He moved quickly now, directly for the clear windows at the front of the hall. He moved with such tremendous speed, speed beyond human and most robots, that when he reached the windows he leaped straight into them. The panes were tremendously thick, able to resist even conventional bombs hurled against them, but they cracked and shattered like ordinary glass as he sailed through; he then dropped the twelve meters to the ground, landing on his feet with perfect balance, and started to run across the broad courtyard.

By then he had lost the element of surprise. Realizing from the point at which he'd battered in the first door that they were dealing with some clever sort of robot, the security forces had assumed the worst and were ready for him with killer robots, human troops, even a small laser cannon.

He stopped in the center of the grassy knoll and looked around, sizing up the situation but appearing cool and efficient. Then, suddenly, turning to look at the massive amounts of firepower trained on him, he grinned; the grin became a laugh, a laugh that rose in pitch until it became eerie, inhuman, maniacal, echoing back from the building's walls.

The order was given to open fire, but as the beams tore into the spot on which he stood he just wasn't there any more. He was going up, rising into the air silently and effortlessly at a tremendous rate of speed.

Automatic weapons tried to follow him but couldn't match his rate of climb. One officer stared up into the empty sky, laser pistol drawn. "The thing that pisses me off most is that he didn't even tear his pants."

Control shifted instantly to Orbital Command, but they weren't prepared for the suddenness of the little man's departure, nor could they be certain of how high he would rise or to where. Thirty-seven commercial and sixty-four military ships were in orbit at that point, plus over eight thousand satellites of one sort or another—not to mention the five space stations. Sophisticated radar would spot him if he changed course or attitude and decided to land elsewhere on the planet, but while he remained in space they would have to wait until he did something to draw their attention. There were simply too many things in orbit, and he was too small to track unless first spotted so they could lock onto him.

So they waited patiently, ready to shoot the hell out of any ship that made a break for it or simply decided to change position. And they closely monitored each ship; should someone try to board from space they'd know it.

The robot played the waiting game for almost three full days. By then its primary mission was a total failure—the plans it had stolen were now known, so quite obviously obsolete at that point—but what it had stolen was of some value, since they revealed strengths and current positions, and when analyzed by a specialist in military affairs would show a prospective enemy how the thinking of the Military Command and its bosses ran. Still, it couldn't wait forever —the force positions could not be so easily or quickly changed, and any contingency plan for their dispersion must be a variation of the original. For the present, their range of options was narrowed, but the options would increase geometrically with each elapsed hour. The robot had to make its move, and it did.

A small planetary satellite officially on the records as an obsolete weather-control monitor station came within three thousand meters of a small corvette. The ship, a government courier boat, would ordinarily be unmanned while keeping station, but no ships were left unguarded at this point.

The robot, still looking like the perfect clerk, emerged from the satellite through a hatch that should not have been there. But, then, the satellite was only superficially what it appeared to be, having long ago been copied and replaced with something infinitely more useful.

With seeming effortlessness, the robot sped to the corvette and stuck to the outer hull. It reached to its belt and pulled off a small weapon whose dangling line it attached to a small terminal that was otherwise invisible under its left arm. The robot had spent the past three days drawing enormous energy reserves to itself with the devices in the satellite; now, at capacity, it discharged through the weapon. A strong beam emerged from the thing, quickly cutting a hole the size of an orange in the corvette's hull. It had chosen its spot well: there were only two guards, one human and one robot, on the ship, and both were in the compartment directly under the point at which the beam went through the elaborate triple hull and into the opening. No one would ever know if it was decompression or the beam that killed the unlucky human guard; the robot, obviously, was shorted out by the sudden dispersion of energy within the compartment.

The enemy robot then tripped the airlock in the forward compartment and entered effortlessly, finding no apparent alarms and no opposition. The instant acceleration from a standing start would have killed any living thing on board.

2

The young man sat in absorbed silence, listening to the taped narrative. He was in much the same mold as most of his fellow humans at this point in human history, the perfection of the physical body. From the viewpoint of earlier times he was almost a superman; genetic engineering had made that possible. But every man and woman these days was at this peak of perfection, so among his fellow humans he was merely average-looking, somewhere around thirty with jet-black hair and reddish-brown eyes, at the legal norm height of 180 centimeters, and the legal norm weight of 82 kilograms. But he was neither average nor normal in more than one specific area, and that was why he was here.

He looked over at Commander Krega as the narrative stopped at the fleeing ship. "You had all the available ships under close watch and trace, of course?" It wasn't a question, merely a statement of fact.

Krega, an older version of the norm himself in whom the experience of an additional forty years' service showed on his face and particularly in his eyes, nodded. "Of course. But merely to have destroyed the thing at that point, when he'd already come so far and done so much, would have been a waste. We simply placed a series of tracers on everything that could conceivably move in orbit and waited for him . . . it . . . whatever. It was just a robot, after all, albeit a striking one. We had to know whose. At least who it worked for. You know something about subspace ballistics, I take it?"

"Enough," the younger man admitted.

"Well, once we had his angle and speed—and *what* speed from a standing start!—we knew where he'd have to come out. Fortunately, tightbeams can outrun any physical object, so we had someone in the area when he emerged a few subjective minutes later. Close enough, anyway, to get his next set of readings. That much wasn't difficult. He made seven blind switches, just to try to throw us off the track, but we never lost him. We were able to move in within a few minutes of the point in time at which he began transmitting the data—a safeguard just in case we were as efficient as we actually are. We closed in immediately then, though, and fried him and the ship to atoms. No other way around it. We'd seen firsthand just some of the things that baby could do."

The younger man shook his head. "Pity, though. It would have been interesting to disassemble the thing. It's certainly not any design I know of."

The commander nodded. "Or any of us, either. The fact is, the thing was just about at the limits of our own technology, if not a bit beyond. It fooled x-ray scanners, retinal scanners, body heat and function sensors—you name it. It even fooled the friends of the poor civil servant it was pretending to be, imply-ing memory and possibly personality transfer. At any rate, even though its clever little orbital base blew up after it departed, there was enough left to piece to-gether some of its insides—and I'll tell you, it's not ours. Not anything close. Oh, you can deduce some of the functions and the like, but even where the func-tion is obvious, it isn't done the way *we'd* do it, nor are the materials similar to ours. We have to face the ugly fact that the robot and its base were built, de-signed, and directed by an alien power of which we are totally ignorant."

The young man showed mild interest. "But surely you know something about it now?"

The commander shook his head sadly. "No, we don't. We know more than we did, certainly, but not nearly enough. These bastards are wickedly clever. But I'll get to that in a minute. Let's first look at what we do know, or can deduce, about our enemy." He turned in his desk chair and punched a button. A blank wall blinked and became a visor screen showing an enormous collection of stars, thousands of which blazed a reddish color.

"The Confederacy," the commander stated needlessly. "Seven thousand six hundred and forty-six worlds, by last count, over a third of a galaxy. Quite an accomplishment for a race from a single planet out there on that one little arm. Planets terraformed, planets where the people were adapted to the place, even planets with sixty other intelligent native life forms on them, all now nicely acculturated to our way of doing things. We own it, we run it our way, and we've always had our own way. Not a single one of those other races was ever in any position to challenge us. They had to accept us and our way, or they died in much the manner our own native world was pacified so many centuries ago. We're the boss."

The young man didn't respond. He felt no need to. Born and raised in this culture, he simply took what Krega was saying for granted, as did everyone else.

"Well, we've now met our technological equals, perhaps even slight technological superiors," the commander continued. "Analysis made the obvious deductions. First, we're always expanding. Obviously there is another dominant race and culture doing the same from some other point in the galaxy. They discovered us before we discovered them—bad luck for us. They scouted, probed, and analyzed us, and came up with several facts. Second, our ultimate collision is unavoidable. We're starting to compete for the same space. Third, they are probably smaller than we, numerically weaker, as it were, but with a slight technological edge. They assume war, but they are not certain they could win it. If they *had been* sure they'd have attacked by now. That means they need information—lots of it. How our military organization is set up. How our defenses are established and would be used. And most important, how we think. A total understanding of us while we remained in ignorance of their ways would give them and their war machines a tremendous edge, assuming equal firepower. Fourth, they've been at this for some time, which means our collision is still way off, perhaps years. Finding us was probably accidental, some scout of theirs who got overextended, lost, or just overly ambitious. They've been around long enough, though, to make robots that pass for humans, to put spy stations in orbit around Military Systems Command, of all things, and to work out a deal with some of our own to help sell us out."

The young man suddenly looked interested. "Ah," he breathed.

"Exactly," the commander grumbled. "The last deduction is that they themselves are physically so alien to us that there is simply no way in hell they could move among us undetected, no physical disguise even possible. That leaves human-mimicking robots—who knows how many? I'm getting so I suspect my own staff—and human traitors. That last becomes the province of this office, naturally."

In earlier times the Operational Security Office might have been referred to as a secret police, which it most certainly was. Unlike the earlier models, though, it had little to do with the day-to-day life of the citizenry in the specific sense. Its mandate was broader, more generalized.

Mankind had perfected a formula long ago, one that worked. It was neither free in a libertarian sense nor in a personal sense, but it was efficient and it worked—not just for one world but for every world, across an interstellar empire so vast that only total cultural control could keep it together. The same system everywhere. The same ideas and ideals, the same values, the same ways of thinking about things— everywhere. Flexible, adaptable to different biomes and even, with some wrenching adjustments made mercilessly, adaptable to alien cultures and life forms.

The formula was all-pervasive, an equalizing force in the extreme, yet it provided some play for different conditions and a measure of social mobility based on talent and ability.

There were of course populations that could not or would not adapt. In some instances, they could be "reeducated" by means of the most sophisticated techniques, but in others they could not. These were not merely alien worlds where the formula simply couldn't be tried because of their very alienness—those were ruthlessly exterminated as a last resort. Every system also bred individuals who could circumvent it and had the will and knack of doing so. Such people could be extremely dangerous and had to be hunted down and either captured for reeducation or killed outright.

"In the early days, however, the powers that be were much softer on those who couldn't otherwise be dealt with," Commander Krega told him. "They had not yet reached the absolute perfection of our present system. The result was permanent exile in the Warden Diamond, as you know. We still send a few there—the ones with particular talents and abilities we need or those who show potential for some great discovery. It's paid off, too, that policy, although we ship barely a hundred a year out there now."

The young man felt a nervous twinge in his stomach. "So that's where your alien race went for help. That's where your robot fled—the Warden Diamond."

"You got it," Krega agreed.

In a galaxy whose system was based on perfect order, uniformity, harmony, and a firm belief in natural laws, the Warden Diamond was an insane asylum. It seemed to exist as a natural counterpoint to everyplace else, the opposite of everything the rest of the Confederacy was or even believed in.

Halden Warden, a scout for the Confederacy, had discovered the system nearly two hundred years earlier, when the Diamond was far outside the administrative area of the Confederacy. Warden was something of a legend among scouts, a man who disliked most everything about civilization, not the least other people. Such extreme antisocial tendencies would have been dealt with in the normal course of events, but there was an entire discipline of psychology devoted to discovering and developing antisocial traits that could benefit society. The fact was, only people with personalities like Warden's could stand the solitude, the years without companionship, the physical and mental hardships of deep-space scouting. No sane person in Confederation society, up to Confederation standards, would ever take a job like that.

Warden was worse than most. He spent as little time as possible in "civilization," often just long enough to refuel and reprovision. He flew farther, longer, and more often than any other scout before or since, and his discoveries were astonishing in their number alone.

Unfortunately for his bosses back in the Confederacy, Warden felt that discovery was his only purpose. He left just about everything else, including preliminary surveys and reports, to those who would use his beamed coordinates to follow him. Not that he didn't make the surveys—he just communicated as little with the Confederacy as possible, often in infuriating ways.

Thus, when the signal "4AW" came in, there was enormous excitement and anticipation—four human-habitable planets in one system! Such a phenomenon was simply unheard of, beyond all statistical probabilities, particularly considering that only one in four thousand solar systems contained anything remotely of use. They waited anxiously for the laconic scout to tell them what he would name the new worlds and to give his preliminary survey descriptions of them, waited anxiously not only in anticipation of a great discovery, but also with trepidation at just what Crazy Warden would say and whether or not his message could be deciphered.

And then came the details, confirming their worst fears. He followed form, though, closest in to farthest out from the sun.

"Charon," came the first report. "Looks like Hell.

"Lilith," he continued. "Anything that pretty's got to have a snake in it.

"Cerberus," he named the third. "Looks like a real dog."

And finally, "Medusa: Anybody who lives here would have to have rocks in his head."

The coordinates followed, along with a code confirming that Warden had done remote, not direct, exploration—that is, he hadn't landed, something that was always his option—and a final code, "ZZ," which filled the Confederacy with apprehension. It meant that there was something very odd about the place, so approach with extreme caution.

Cursing Crazy Warden for giving them nothing at all to go on, they mounted the standard maximum-caution expedition—a full-scale scientific expedition, with two hundred of the best, most experienced Exploiter Team members aboard, backed up by four heavy cruisers armed to the teeth.

The big trouble with Warden's descriptions was that they were almost always right—only you never figured out quite what he meant until you got there. Appearing out of hyperspace, the follow-up party gazed upon a strange sight—a hot, F-type star, with a huge solar system containing ringed gas giants, huge asteroids, and numerous solid planets. But in the midst of it, close to the sun, were four worlds with abundant oxygen, nitrogen, and water, four jewels that screamed "life." Although the four planets were in far different orbits—from a little more than 158 million kilometers from their sun to 308 million kilometers out—when the party first encountered them, they were in a rare configuration. For a brief period, the four were at almost exact right angles to one another. Although that configuration was a fluke and rarely observed since, the system's four worlds became known as the Warden Diamond. And diamonds they were despite the orbital coincidence at their discovery —sparkling gems with potential untold riches.

Still, even some of the most materialistic among the observers took the diamond configuration as some sort of omen, just as Warden himself might have. And so, like Warden, they didn't land immediately. They poked and they probed and they analyzed, but found nothing at all suspicious. There was no evidence of supernatural meddlings here, despite the incredible impossibility of four worlds so closely matched to permit life. So they laughed at themselves for their foolishness, their superstition, their sudden infusion with primitive fears they all believed themselves well beyond, and they relaxed a little. Some suspected that the Warden Diamond was the result of some ancient civilization terraforming to suit—but if it was, there was no sign of that now.

They moved cautiously in on the planets. Charon was hot and steamy, closest of the four to the sun. It rained much of the time there, and the small, nasty dinosaurlike saurians that lived there seemed formidable, perhaps even dangerous—but not unmanageable. There might be more dangerous stuff in the seas that covered much of the world, but only a permanent expedition could find that out. In the meantime, this jungle world, with an axial tilt of under 6 degrees, had a temperature range of from roughly 28 to 60 degrees centigrade. Thanks to the land distribution it was habitable and usable—but not inviting.

Charon did indeed look like Hell.

Next out was Lilith, almost a textbook perfect world. Slightly smaller than Charon, it was roughly 70 percent water but far more temperate and far gentler in its landscape. Mountains were low, and there were broad plains and swamps. A nice variety of landforms without serious extremes or violence, and an axial tilt of 84 degrees—almost a world on its side, which meant little seasonal variation. It was very hot all over, with days of 40 degrees centigrade or more, with 20 to 25 considered absolutely frigid.

Its junglelike forests were the most verdant green, and though the foliage was alien, it wasn't all *that* alien, bearing large amounts of fruits and other products that proved edible by humans. The dominant animal life was apparently exclusively insects, from giant behemoths down to tiny creatures smaller than the head of a pin. It was the kind of world Confederacy terraformers aimed for and rarely achieved artificially; now, here it was, apparently natural, the beautiful Edenlike paradise of Lilith. And not a snake in sight—yet.

Cerberus was harsher. Its 25-degree axial tilt gave it extreme seasonal variations that ranged from its frozen polar caps to a hot 40-degree Centigrade at the equator. The oddest thing about Cerberus was its land surface, which appeared almost covered with enormous varicolored forests. It took the actual landing to discover that Cerberus in fact had no land area at all, but was almost covered by enormous plants growing up from the ocean bottom, some many kilometers, so tremendously dense in many places that they formed an almost solid surface. On the tops of these great waterlogged forests whole new varieties of plants grew, forming a unique botanical ecosystem. The visible wildlife seemed to be birdlike in appearance, although there were some insects as well, but animal life was sparse on Cerberus, it seemed—unless it lay beneath the omnipresent waters of the surface. Still, so dense and enormous were the plants of this water world that men could live there, perhaps even build cities in the trees—an alien but not impossible world. With no apparent natural resources beyond wood and no way to bring in a truly modern lifestyle, settlement there would be precarious. Inhabitable, yes, but from the standpoint of modern man it *was* something of a dog.

Last and least pleasant of all was Medusa, a planet with frozen seas, blinding snow, and jagged, towering peaks. Its 19-degree axial tilt gave it seasons, all right, but it was a bad to worse situation, with summer in the tropics averaging 20 degrees centigrade or less and going to the impossibly cold polar regions. Although in heavy glaciation, it was the only one of the four Warden worlds with signs of volcanic activity. There were some forests, but mostly tundra and grasslands, although it had what appeared to be mammalian life in the form of herds of odd grazing animals and some very fierce and nasty carnivores. It was a harsh, brutal world that could be tamed and lived on; still, the Exploiter Team had to agree with Warden—to *want* to go and live there, you'd have to have rocks in your head.

Four worlds, from a steaming hell to frozen tundra. Four worlds with temperature extremes that could be borne and air and water that could be used. It was incredible, fantastic—and true. And so the Exploiter Team went in, set up its main base just off a tropical lagoon out of the most romantic travel poster—on Lilith, of course. Smaller expeditions went from there to the other three worlds for preliminary testing, poking, and probing.

Warden had been right about three of them, but his suspicion of Lilith seemed to be just the natural suspicion of somebody who sees something too good to be true. Or perhaps it was some sixth sense, developed from so many years in isolation and poking and probing into so many alien systems. Perhaps it was . . .

Once down, the Exploiter Teams were in effective quarantine from the military and from all commerce with the Confederacy. The initial exploration would take at least a year, during which they would be both scientists and guinea pigs, poking and probing one another as much as they poked and probed each planet. They had shuttlecraft capable of traveling between the planets if necessary and ground and air transportation to carry on their own work, but nothing interstellar. The risk was too great. Man had been burned too many times before to take such chances.

It took Lilith's snake about six months to size up the newcomers.

By the time all their machinery ceased to function it was already too late. They watched first as all the power drained out of the machinery and equipment as if being drunk by an eager child. Within forty-eight hours the machinery, the equipment—in fact, all artifacts—started to break up into so much junk. Four died as a result, and the rest watched in helpless horror as their corpses, too, rapidly began to decompose.

Within a week there was simply no sign that anything alien had ever landed. Cleared places seemed to grow over almost overnight; metal, plastics, organic and inorganic compounds—everything rotted, dissolved, and eventually was nothing more than a fine powder quickly absorbed by the rich soil. There was nothing left—nothing but sixty-two stunned, stark-naked scientists both bewildered and scared, without even the most rudimentary instruments to help explain what the hell had happened to them.

Just a week earlier direct contact between the parties on the four planets had been resumed. A small group from each of the other three worlds had come to Lilith to share their findings and decide what to do next. They had come, talked, analyzed, filed preliminary reports with the guardian cruiser still in space nearby, then returned to their own planets, unknowingly taking with them the snake.

The science section on the cruiser immediately jumped on the problem. And with remote robot-controlled labs they finally found the one thing everybody but Warden's sixth sense had missed. The snake was an alien organism, microscopic beyond belief and acting in colonies within the cells. It was not intelligent in the sense that it possessed anything humans would recognize as thought processes, but it did seem to have an amazing set of rules it enforced on an entire planet and an incredible capacity for adjusting to new conditions and bringing them to heel. Though its life span was a sparse three to five minutes, somehow this microorganism operated at a time rate hundreds, perhaps thousands, of times faster than anything around it. On Lilith, it still had taken the organism six months to adapt to these new things that had been introduced to its world, and it had finally evolved enough to adapt the aliens to its comfortable, symbiotic system.

But the other planets were different—different atmospheric balances, different gravity, different radiation intensities, all sorts of great differences. It could not adapt such alien environments to its system, so it adapted to them instead. In some cases—Medusa, for one—it adapted the host organism, the people, and quickly, the animals and plants. On Charon and Cerberus it struck a balance in the hosts that was to its liking; this produced by-products of physical change not relevant to it but rather resulting from where, in those bodies, it was most comfortable.

The Warden Diamond was, sadly, quarantined while scientists looked for a cure. Removing some of the unlucky victims in isolation chambers did not work: something linked the organisms to the Diamond, and they died when removed from the system, killing their hosts in the process, since the organisms resided in the hosts' cells and took over, really, rearranging things to suit themselves. Without their managers, the cells rapidly went berserk, causing an ugly and painful, although mercifully swift, death.

Oddly, those on one of the planets could still move in-system to the others, the organism having mutated so much inside them that it no longer even recognized Lilith as its home and, having struck a comfortable balance, having no further reason to change.

Humans *could* live and work and build on the Warden Diamond, but once there they could never leave.

That did not stop the scientists, of course, and they came and set up their colonies, although doing so was difficult on Lilith, where nothing not native to the planet seemed to be allowed. They came prepared and they came to study and uncover the secrets of the Warden Diamond. After two centuries their descendants were still at it, joined occasionally by others—but very little progress had been made. The planets, the organism, even the changes defied them. That only spurred them on all the more.

But it wasn't the scientists who were to settle the Diamond, but the antisocials. Early on, when the magnitude of the problem was realized, came the idea of setting up the four worlds as the perfect prison.

The misfits were sent there in droves—all those whose connections could avoid the psych boys, who had genius or some sort of talent that would be destroyed by reeducation, political prisoners from countless worlds—all sent there rather than killed or mentally altered in the hope that some future successful rival would remember they didn't kill or psych the deposed but exiled them. Male, female, it didn't matter. The best antisocials, the political-criminal elite. And there they lived and bore their children and died, and their children lived and bore *their* children, and so on.

So these worlds were run, dominated in fact, by a criminal elite imprisoned forever and with little love for or feeling of kinship with the masses of the Confederacy. Nonetheless, they had commerce. The organism could be killed, sterilized out, in a complex process, on unmanned ships. So other criminal geniuses, those not yet caught or in charge of governments, could establish caches of money, jewelry, precious art, and stolen goods of all types on the Warden worlds with no fear that the Confederacy could touch them.

At the same time the strongest, the smartest, the most ruthless of the exiles clawed their ways to the top of these four strange worlds, until they controlled them and their own trade. Lilith, where nothing physical could be stored, was the perfect place for storing such information as special bank account numbers, official secrets even the Confederacy had to be kept ignorant of, things of that sort—the kind of information one never put into a computer because all computers are vulnerable to a genius technician. No matter how foolproof the machine, the foolproof system was devised by someone and could therefore be broken by someone else.

So these great criminal kings—the Four Lords of the Diamond, alien now from their ancestral race, geniuses all yet bitterly exiled nonetheless—had the secrets, the stolen goods, the blackmail of the Confederacy, and their influence extended throughout the Confederacy even though they were forever barred from seeing it.

"Then the Four Lords are selling us out," the young man sighed. "Why not simply destroy all four worlds? Good riddance anyway, I'd say."

"So would I," Commander Krega agreed. "Only we can't. We let them go on too long—they're politically invulnerable. Too much wealth, too much power, too many secrets are there. There is simply no way to get them any more—they have the goods on just about anybody who would be high up enough to make those decisions."

The young man cleared his throat. "I see," he responded a little disgustedly. "So why not place agents on those worlds? Find out what's what?"

"Oh, that was tried from the first," Krega told him. "It didn't work, either. Consider—we're asking someone to exile himself permanently and allow himself to be turned, equally permanently, into something not quite human. Only a fanatic would agree to that—and fanatics make notoriously poor spies. The Four Lords are also not exactly easy marks, you know. They keep track of who's coming in, and their own contacts here tell them just about everything they want to know about any newcomers. We might sneak one agent, one really good agent, in on them—but a lot? Never. They'd quickly catch on and just kill the lot, innocent and guilty alike. They also are supremely confident of human psychology—the agent is going to have to be *damned* good to get away with such an assignment. Anybody with that much on the ball is also going to realize that he is trapped there and that he'll have to live there, on the Four Lords' worlds, until he dies. Loyalty comes hard, but even the most loyal and committed agent is going to have to have the brains to see which side his future bread will be buttered on. So he switches sides. One of the current Lords is in fact a Confederacy agent."

"Huh?"

Krega nodded. "Or was, I should say. Probably the best infiltrator in the business, knew all the ins and outs, and found the Diamond not threatening but fascinating. The Confederacy bored him, he said. We dropped him on Lilith just to worm his way into the hierarchy—and he sure did. In spades. Only we received almost no information from him while feeding him a great deal—and now he's one of the enemy. See what I mean?"

"You have a tough problem," the young man sympathized. "You don't have any reliable people on the Warden worlds, and anybody capable of doing what has to be done winds up on the other side. And now they're selling us out to an alien force."

"Exactly." Krega nodded. "You see where this puts us. Now, of course, we *do* have some people down there. None are a hundred percent reliable, and all of them would slit your throat in an instant if doing so was in their best interests. But we find occasional inducements—small payoffs of one sort or another, even a little blackmail on ones with close relatives back in the Confederacy—that give us a little edge. A little, but not much, since the Four Lords are pretty ruthless when it comes to what they perceive as treason. Our only advantage is that the worlds are still fairly new to us and so therefore relatively sparsely settled. There is no totalitarian control on any of them, and there are different systems and hierarchies on each."

The young man nodded. "I have the uneasy feeling that you are leading up to something—but I must remind you of what you told me about past agents, and also that, even kicking and screaming, I'd be but one man on one world."

Commander Krega grinned. "No, it's not quite like that at all. You're a damned good detective and you know it. You've tracked down and upset rocks in places nobody else looked at twice; outmaneuvered and outguessed sophisticated computers and some of the best criminal minds ever known, even though you are still quite young. You are the youngest person with the rank of Inspector in the history of the Confederacy. We have two different problems here. One, we must identify this alien force and trace it back to its origin. We must find out who they are and where they are and what their intentions are. Even now it may be too late, but we must act as if it were not. Two, we must neutralize their information conduit, the Four Lords. How would you do it?"

The young man smiled thoughtfully. "Pay the Four

Lords more than the aliens do," he suggested hopefully. "Put 'em to work for us."

"Impossible. We already thought of that," the commander responded glumly. "It's not profit—they have more than they need. And it's not power—that, too, they have in abundance. But we have cut them off forever from the rest of the universe, trapped them there. Before, they could do nothing—but now, with an alien force as their ally, they can. I'm afraid such people are motivated by revenge, and *that* we cannot give them. We can't even commute their sentence, short of a scientific breakthrough—and nobody has more people working on that angle than they do. No, making a deal is out. We have no cards."

"Then you need somebody good down there on each world, looking for clues to the aliens. There has to be some sort of direct contact: they have to get their information out and their little play-toys, like that fancy robot, programmed and in. An agent might turn traitor, but if he was a volunteer he wouldn't be motivated by revenge and would sure as hell feel closer to humanity than to some aliens of unknown appearance and design."

"Agreed. And it would have to be the very best for all four. Someone who could survive, even prosper under their conditions while having the ability to collect enough data and get it out. But how do we buy the time we also need?"

The young man grinned. "Easy. At least easy to say—maybe nearly impossible to do. You kill all four Lords. Others would take their places, of course, but in the interim you'd buy months, maybe years."

"That was our thinking," Krega agreed. "And so we ran it through the computers. Master detective, loyal, willing to volunteer, and with an Assassin's License. Four needed, plus a coordinator, since they all would have to be put to work simultaneously and would obviously have no likely reason or means to contact one another. Plus for insurance, of course, spares that could be sent in if something happened to one or more of the originals. We fed in all these attributes and requirements and out you popped."

The young man chuckled dryly. "I'll bet. Me and who else?"

"Nobody else. Just you."

For the first time the man looked puzzled. He frowned. "Just me?"

"Oh, lots of secondaries, but they were slightly less reliable for one reason or another, or slightly weaker in one or another way, or, frankly, were engaged on other vital business or located halfway around the Confederacy."

"Then you've got two problems," the young man told Krega. "First, you have to figure out how the hell I'd volunteer willingly for an assignment like this, and, second, how you're going to make . . ." His voice trailed off and he suddenly sat up straight. "I think I see . . ."

"I thought you would." Krega sounded satisfied and confident. "It's probably the most guarded secret in the Confederacy, but the Merton Process works now. Almost a hundred percent."

The other nodded absently, thinking about it. When he'd received his promotion to Inspector over a year ago, they'd taken him into an elaborate and somewhat mystifying laboratory and put him into some sort of hypnotic state. He was never quite sure what they had done, but he'd had a headache for three days and that had aroused his curiosity. The Merton Process. The key to immortality, some said. It had taken a hell of a lot of spare-time detective work to come even that close to it, and all he'd been able to determine in the end was that the Confederacy was working on a process wherein the entire memory, the entire personality, of an individual could be taken, stored in some way, and then imprinted on another brain, perhaps a clone brain. He had also learned that every time it had been tried, the new body either had become hopelessly insane or had died. He said as much.

"That used to be the case," Krega agreed, "but no more. The clone brains just couldn't take it. Raised in tanks, they had developed different brain patterns for the autonomic functions, and those were always disrupted in the transfer. Still, we had been able to remove all the conscious part of the brain from someone and then put it back just the way it was in the original body while also keeping the original information on file. That led, of course, to trying it with other bodies —remove the cerebral part, as it were, just like erasing a recording, then put someone else's personality and memories in there. It's a ticklish business—only works once in a while, when loads of factors I don't understand very well, and maybe Merton doesn't either, match. The new body has to be at least two years younger than the original, for example. On the other hand, some important factors like sex or planetary origin seem to be irrelevant. Still, we get a perfect transfer about one in twenty times."

He stirred uneasily. "What happens to the other nineteen?"

Krega shrugged. "They die, or are nuts and have to be destroyed. We use only minor antisocials anyway, those who would have to be psyched and programmed or simply eliminated. We took your print fourteen months ago—you must know that. Now we can make four of you. Different bodies, of course, but you inside in every single detail. More than four, if necessary. We can drop you on all four planets simultaneously, complete with criminal record and past history. We can drop you on all four and still keep *you* here, as you are, to correlate the data from the others."

The young man said nothing for almost a minute, then: "Well, I'll be damned."

"Four times damned, yet also not damned at all," the commander came back. "So you see, there's no risk. We already *have* your imprint."

He considered the facts. "Still, there'd have to be a more recent one," he noted. "It wouldn't do to have four of me wake up en route to the Warden Diamond in different bodies with no knowledge of the last fourteen months, not to mention this conversation."

Krega nodded. "You're right, of course. But I have mine updated annually, anyway. Except for the headache, if the process worked the first time it'll work ever after."

"That's reassuring," the man replied uncomfortably, considering that they had done it to him without his knowledge before—and the commander's words implied that sometimes it *didn't* work. Dismissing that idea from his mind, he asked, "But how do I get the data to correlate? Even supposing that these four versions of me are able to ferret out everything you want to know—how do *I* know it?"

Krega reached into a desk drawer and pulled out a small box. He opened it gingerly and pushed it over to the young man. "With this," he said flatly.

The man looked at the object. "This" turned out to be a tiny little bead of unknown substance so small it could hardly be seen with the naked eye even in its black velveteen setting.

"A tracer implant?" The young man was skeptical. "What good does that do us?" The device was familiar to all cops; it could be implanted anywhere on a body with no chance of detection and with no operation necessary. Once in place, someone could follow its signal to just about anywhere—a common police tool.

"Not a tracer," the commander told him. "Based on it, I'll admit, but more a by-product of the Merton researches. It is implanted directly into a specific point in the brain—I'm sorry I don't have enough technical biology to explain further. You'll get one, too. It only works when two bodies have exactly the same brain pattern; otherwise you get gibberish. Using the tracer part, a special receiver can locate the wearer anywhere on a planet, then lock onto him, receive, and enormously amplify what it receives, which then is fed to a Merton recorder. From that another imprint can be made, a 'soft' one, that will give its matched mate a record of just what happened after the new body awoke until we took the readout. It's soft—they tell me the sensation is kind of like seeing a movie all at once. But it's a record of everything your counterpart said and did. We'll put you on a guard picket ship, very comfortable, and take almost continuous soft imprints using monitor satellites. You'll have your information, all right. And the thing's actually a quasi-organic substance, so even on Lilith, which hates everything alien, it will continue to function as part of the body. We know. We have a couple of people with tracers down there now—they don't know it, of course. Just a test. Works fine."

The young man nodded. "You seem to have thought of everything." He paused a moment. "And what if I refuse after all this? Or to put it another way, what if I say to go ahead and my, ah, alter egos decide once down there not to cooperate?"

Krega grinned evilly. "Consider what I'm offering. We have the capacity to make you immortal—if you succeed. If you succeed, no reward would be high enough. You are an atheist. You know that when you go, you go forever—unless you succeed. Then you, and because of the soft imprints, your alter egos as well will continue to exist. Continue to live on. I think that is quite an inducement."

The young man looked thoughtful. "I wonder if *they* will see it that way?" he mused, only half aloud.

Four Lords of the Diamond. Four enormously powerful, clever people to kill. Four keys to an enigma that could spell the end of humanity. Five problems, five puzzles.

Krega didn't really have to offer a reward. The assignment was irresistible.

3

The base ship was seven kilometers long. It floated there off the Warden system, about a quarter of a light-year from the sun. Designed as a floating base, almost a mini-world, the ship was completely self-contained, and were it not for the feeling of isolation all around, a pretty comfortable duty.

From its lower decks sped the picket ships: one-man or often totally automated vessels that encircled the Warden system and kept the base ship in constant touch with every section of space around and inside the solar system itself. All commerce had to come here first, then be transferred to automated craft for an in-system run. No one but the military was allowed beyond the perimeter the picket ships established, and even military personnel never landed. The penalty for any violation was simple—capture if possible, elimination if not possible. Between the automatic guardians and the manned patrols a violator might get by one or two, but he would have to run a gauntlet of several hundred to get anywhere meaningful—and do so against the best defensive computers known.

For this reason, the pinpointing of the Warden Diamond as the center of some alien conspiracy was met with a great deal of skepticism by the organized military forces, most of which believed that the alien robot had simply practiced misdirection in desperation after being discovered.

The analytical computers and strategic specialists thought otherwise. At least, they couldn't afford *not* to think otherwise, which explained the arrival of a very special man at the base ship. They all knew he was special, and rumors abounded as to who he was, whom he worked for, and what he was doing there; but no one, not even the commanding admiral, really knew for sure.

With the man came a complete module that interlocked to the building-block nature of the base ship in the security control section. From here the mysterious man would do whatever he was doing, away from all others, surrounded by security guards who had no idea who he was or what he was doing—and who could not enter the module any more than the admiral could. It was keyed to the man's own brain waves, voice print, retinal pattern, gene structure, and just about everything else any paranoid security division had ever figured out. Anyone else attempting entry would be instantly stopped and neatly packaged for security. Any nonliving thing that tried would be instantly vaporized.

Although the man had been there for months, not a soul even knew his name. Not that he was totally withdrawn—on the contrary, he joined in the sports games in Recreation, ate his meals in the Security Mess, even wined and dined some female soldiers and civilians aboard, many of whom were simply intrigued by this man of mystery. He was likable, easygoing, relaxed. But in all those months he had not revealed the slightest thing about himself, not even to those with whom he'd been most intimate—although, security officers noted, he'd had a positive knack of finding out the most private things about the people with whom he'd come in contact. They admired him for his total self-control and absolute professionalism, and even the highest-ranking of them were scared stiff of him.

He spent several hours most days in his little cubicle, and always slept there. They all wondered and guessed at what was inside until they were almost crazy with curiosity, but they never guessed the truth.

He heard the buzzer sounding as he entered the command module and for the first time felt genuine excitement and anticipation. Long ago he'd accomplished all he could with the physical data, but for too long now it had been a boring exercise. The computer filed what it could from the memory traces but gave him a picture that was too emotional and incomplete when examined in his own mind to make much sense. Hoping this time would be different, he headed for the master command chair and sat comfortably in it. The computer, sensing its duty, lowered the small probes, which he placed around his head, then administered the measured injections and began the master readout.

For a while he floated in a semihypnotic fog, but slowly images started forming in his brain as they had before. Only now they seemed more definite, clearer, more like his own thoughts. The drugs and small neural probes did their job. His own mind and personality receded, replaced by a similar, yet oddly different pattern.

"The agent is commanded to report," the computer ordered, sending the command deep into his own mind, a mind no longer his own.

What would happen, or so the techs had advised him, would amount to a sort of total recall from the mind of his counterpart down below, information his own mind would sort, classify, and edit into a coherent narrative.

Recorders clicked on.

Slowly the man in the chair cleared his throat several times. It still took more than three hours to get him to do anything beyond mumbling some odd words or sounds, but the computers were nothing if not patient, knowing that the man's mind was receiving a massive amount of data and was struggling to sort and classify it.

Finally the man began to speak.

Chapter One

Rebirth

After Krega's talk and a little preparation to put my own affairs in order—this would be a long one—I checked into the Confederacy Security Clinic. I'd been here many times before, of course, but never knowingly for this purpose. Mostly, this was where they programmed you with whatever information you'd need for a mission and where, too, you were reintegrated. Naturally, the kind of work I did was often extralegal, a term I prefer to illegal, which implies criminal intent—and much of it was simply too hot ever to be revealed. To avoid such risks, all agents had their own experience of a mission wiped from their minds when it involved sensitive matters.

It may seem like a strange life, going about not knowing where you have been or what you've done, but it has its compensations. Because any potential enemy, military or political, knows you've been wiped, you can live a fairly normal, relaxed life outside of a mission structure. No purpose is served in coming after you—you have no knowledge of what you've done, or why, or for or to whom. In exchange for those blanks, an agent of the Confederacy lives a life of luxury and ease, with an almost unlimited supply of money, and with all the comforts supplied. I bummed around, swam, gambled, ate in the best restaurants, played a little semipro ball or cube—I'm pretty good, and it keeps me in shape. I enjoyed every minute of it, and except for my regular requalification training sessions—four- to six-week stints that resemble military basic training, only nastier and more sadistic—I felt no guilt at my playboy life. The training sessions are to make sure that your body and mind don't turn soft from all that good living. Permanently implanted sensors constantly monitor and decide when you need a good refresher.

I often wondered just how sophisticated those sensors were. The thought that a whole security staff might see all my debauchery and indiscretions used to worry me, but after a while I learned to ignore it.

The life offered in trade is just too nice. Besides, what could I do about it? People on most civilized worlds these days had such sensors, although hardly to the degree and sophistication of mine. How else could a population so vast and spread out possibly be kept orderly, progressive, and otherwise peaceful?

But when a mission came up you naturally couldn't forgo all the past experience you'd had. A wipe without storage simply wouldn't have been very practical, since a good agent gets better by not repeating his mistakes.

So the first thing you did was go to the Security Clinic, where they stored everything you ever experienced, and get the rest of you put back so you would be whole for whatever they'd dreamed up this time.

It always amazed me when I got up from that chair with my past fully restored. Even the clear memories of the things I'd done always amazed me, that *I,* of all people, had done this or that. The only difference this time, I knew, was that the process would be taken one step further. Not only would the complete "me" get up from that table, but the same memory pattern would be impressed on other minds, other bodies—as many as needed until a "take" was achieved.

I wondered what they'd be like, those four other versions of myself. Physically different, probably— the kind of offender they got here wasn't usually from one of the civilized worlds, where people had basically been standardized in the name of equality. No, these people would come from the frontier, from the traders. and miners and freebooters who existed at the edge of expansion, and who were necessary in an expanding culture, since a high degree of individuality, self-reliance, originality, and creativity was required in the dangerous situations in which they lived. A stupid government would have eliminated all such, but a stupid government degenerates or loses its vitality and potential for growth by standardization.

That, of course, was the original reason for the Warden Diamond Reserve. Some of these hard-frontier types are so individualistic that they become a threat to the stability of the civilized worlds. The trouble is, anybody able to loosen the bonds that hold our society together is most likely the smartest, nastiest, meanest, cleverest, most original sort of mind humanity can produce—and therefore not somebody who should be idly wiped clean. The Diamond could effectively trap people of this sort forever, allowing them continued creative opportunities which, when properly monitored, might still produce something of value for the Confederacy—if only an idea, a thought, a way of looking at something that nobody else could come up with.

And the felons down there were naturally anxious to please as well, since the alternative was death. Eventually, such creative minds made themselves indispensable to the Confederacy and ensured their continued survival.

The damned probe hurt like hell. Usually there was just some tingling followed by a sensation much like sleep, and you woke up a few minutes later in the chair once again yourself. This time the tingling became a painful physical force that seemed to enter my skull and bounce around, then seize control of my head. It was as if a huge, giant hand had grabbed my brain and squeezed, then released, then squeezed again in excruciating pulses. Instead of drifting off to sleep, I passed out.

I woke up and groaned slightly. The throbbing was gone, but the memory was still all too current and all too vivid. It was several minutes, I think, before I found enough strength to sit up.

The old memories flooded back, and again I amazed myself by recalling many of my past exploits. I wondered if my surrogate selves would get similar treatment, considering that they couldn't be wiped after this mission as I could. That realization caused me to make a mental note that those surrogates would almost certainly have to be killed if they did have my entire memory pattern. Otherwise, a lot of secrets would be loose on the Warden Diamond and many in the hands of people who'd know just what sort of use to make of them.

No sooner had I thought of that than I had the odd feeling of *wrongness*. I looked around the small room in which I'd awakened and realized immediately the source of that feeling.

This wasn't the Security Clinic, wasn't anyplace I'd ever seen before. It was a tiny cubicle, about twelve cubic meters total, including the slightly higher than normal ceiling. In it was a small cot on which I'd awakened, a small basin and next to it a standard food port, and in the wall, a pull-down toilet. That was it. Nothing else—or was there?

I looked around and spotted the most obvious easily. Yes, I couldn't make a move without being visually and probably aurally monitored. The door was almost invisible and there was certainly no way to open it from inside. I grasped immediately where I was.

It was a prison cell.

Far worse than that, I could feel a faint vibration that had no single source. The sensation wasn't irritating; in fact it was so faint as to be hardly noticeable, but I knew what it was. I was aboard a ship, moving somewhere through space.

I stood up, reeling a little bit from a slight bout of

dizziness that soon passed, and looked down at my body. It was tremendously muscular, the body of a miner or some other sort of heavy laborer. There were a few scars on it that obviously had been treated by someone other than a meditech, and I recognized two of them as knife wounds.

My entire body was almost covered in thick, coarse, black hair—more hair on my chest, arms, and legs than I'd ever seen on anything but an animal. I couldn't help noticing, though, that I was better endowed sexually than I had believed humanly possible. I just stood there, stunned, for I don't know how long.

I'm not me! my mind screamed at me. *I'm one of them—one of the surrogates!*

I sat back down on the cot, telling myself that it just wasn't possible. I knew who I was, remembered every bit, every detail, of my life and work.

My shock gave way after a while to anger—anger and frustration. I was a copy, an imitation of somebody else entirely, somebody still alive and kicking and perhaps monitoring my every move, my every thought. I hated that other then, hated him with a pathological force that was beyond reason. He would sit there comfortable and safe, watching me work, watching me do it all—and when it was over, he'd go home for debriefing, return to that easy life, while I . . .

They were going to dump me on a world of the Warden Diamond, trap me like some kind of master criminal, imprisoned there for the rest of my life—of this body's life, anyway. And then? When my job was done? I'd said it myself upon awakening, passed my own sentence. The things I knew! I would be monitored at all times, of course. Monitored and killed if I blew any of those secrets. Killed anyway at the completion of the mission just for insurance.

My training came into automatic play at that point, overriding the shock and anger. I regained control and considered everything I knew.

Monitor? Sure—more than ever. I recalled Krega saying that there was some sort of organic linkup. Are you enjoying this, you son of a bitch? Are you getting pleasure from vicariously experiencing my reaction?

My training clicked on again, dampening me down. It didn't matter, I told myself. First of all, I knew just what he must be thinking—and that was an advantage. *He,* of all people, would know that I would be a damned tough son of a bitch to kill.

It was a shock to discover that you were not who you thought you were but some artificial creation. It was a shock, too, to realize that the old life, the life you remembered even if you personally didn't experience it, was gone forever. No more civilized worlds, no more casinos and beautiful women and all the money you could spend. And yet as I sat there, I adjusted. That was what they picked men like me for from the start: we had the ability to adjust and adapt to almost anything.

Although this was not my body, I was still me. Memory and thought and personality made up an individual, not his body. This was no more than a biological disguise, I told myself, of a particularly sophisticated sort. As to who was really me—it seemed to me that this personality, these memories, were no more that other fellow's than my own. Until I got up from that chair back in the Security Clinic I had really been somebody else anyway. A lot of me, my memories and training, had been missing. That old between-missions me was the artificial me, the created me, I thought. He, that nonentity playboy that currently did not exist, was the artificial personality. The real me was bottled up and stored in their psychosurgical computers and only allowed to come out when they needed it—and for good reason. Unleashed, I was as much a danger to the power structure as to whomever they set me against.

And I was good. The best, Krega had called me. That's why I was here now, in this body, in this cell, on this ship. And I wouldn't be wiped and I wouldn't be killed if I could help it. That other me, sitting there in the console—somehow I no longer hated him very much, no longer felt anything at all for him. When this was all over he'd be wiped once more—perhaps killed himself if my brother agents on the Diamond and I found out too much. At best he'd return to being that stagnant milquetoast.

Me, on the other hand . . . Me, I would still be here, still live on, the *real* me. I would become more complete than he would.

I was under no illusions, though. Kill me they would, if they could, if I didn't do their bidding. They'd do it automatically, from robot satellite, and without a qualm. *I* would. But my vulnerability would last only until I mastered my new situation and my new and permanent home. I felt that with a deep sense of certainty, for I knew their methods and how they thought. I'd have to do their dirty work for them, and they knew it—but only until I could find a way around it. They could be beaten, even on their own turf. That was why they had people like me in the first place: to uncover those who expertly covered over their whole lives and activities, who managed to vanish totally from their best monitors—to uncover them and get them.

But there'd be no new expert agent sent to get me if *I* beat them. They'd just be putting somebody else in the same position.

I realized then, as they had undoubtedly figured, that I had no choice but to carry out the mission. Only as long as I was doing what they wanted would I be safe from them while still in that vulnerable stage. After that—well, we'd see.

The thrill of the challenge took over, as it always did. The puzzle to be solved, the objectives to be accomplished. I like to win, which is even easier when you feel nothing about the cause, just the challenge of the problem and the opponent and the physical and intellectual effort necessary to meet that challenge. Find out about the alien menace. It no longer concerned me either way—I was trapped on a Warden world from now on anyway. If the aliens won the coming confrontation, the Wardens would survive as allies. If they lost, well, it wouldn't make a damned bit of difference, only continue the current situation.

That meant the alien problem was purely an intellectual challenge, which made it perfect.

The other objective created a similar situation. Seek out the Lord of that particular Diamond world and kill him if I could. In a sense accomplishing that would be more difficult, for I'd be operating on totally unfamiliar ground and would therefore require time and perhaps some allies. Another challenge. And if I got him, it could only increase my own power and position in the long term. If he got me instead, of course, that would solve everybody's problem—but the thought of losing is abhorrent to me. That set the contest in the best terms, from my point of view. Track down assassination was the ultimate game, since either you won or you died and did not have to live with the thought that you lost.

It suddenly occurred to me that the only real difference between me and a Lord of the Diamond was that I was working *for* the law and he—or she— against it. But no, that wasn't right, either. On his world *he* was the law and I would be working against that. Fine. Dead heat on moral grounds.

The only thing wrong at this point, I reflected, was that they were starting me at a tremendous disadvantage. The normal procedure was to program all pertinent information into my brain before setting me off on a mission—but they hadn't done that this time. Probably, I thought, because they had me once on the table for four separate missions, and the transfer process, to a new body, was hard enough without trying to add anything afterward. Still, this method put me in a deep pit. I thought sourly that somebody should have thought of that.

Somebody did, but it was a while before I discovered how. About an hour after I had awakened a little bell clanged near the food port and I went over to it. Almost instantly a hot tray appeared, along with a thin plastic fork and knife I recognized as the dissolving type. They'd melt into a sticky puddle in an hour or less, then dry up into a powder shortly after that. Standard for prisoners.

The food was lousy, but I hadn't expected better.

The vitamin-enriched fruit drink with it, though, was pretty good; I made the most of it, keeping the thin, clear container (not the dissolving type) in case I wanted water later. Everything else I put back in the port, and it vaporized neatly. All nice and sealed.

About the only thing they couldn't control was bodily functions, and a half-hour or so after eating my first meal as a new man, you might say, nature called. On the far wall was a panel marked "toilet" and a small pull ring. Simple, standard stuff. I pulled the ring, the thing came down—and damned if there wasn't a small, paper-thin probe in the recess behind it. And so I sat on the john, leaned back against the panel, and got brief and relief at the same time.

The thing worked by skin contact—don't ask me how. I'm not one of the tech brains. It was not as good as a programming, but it enabled them to talk to me, even send me pictures that only I could see and hear.

"By now I hope you're over the shock of discovering who and what you are," Krega's voice came to me, seemingly forming in my brain. I was shocked when I realized that not even my jailers could hear or see a thing.

"We have to brief you this way simply because the transfer process is delicate enough as it is. Oh, don't worry about it—it's permanent. But we prefer to allow as much time as possible for your brain patterns to fit in and adapt without subjecting the brain to further shock, and we haven't the time to allow you to 'set in' completely, as it were. This method will have to do, and I profoundly regret it, for I feel you have the most difficult task of all four."

I felt the excitement rise in me. The challenge, the challenge . . .

"Your objective world is Lilith, first of the Diamond colonies," the commander's voice continued. "Lilith is, scientifically speaking, a madhouse. There is simply no rational, scientific explanation for what you will find there. The only thing that keeps all of us from going over the brink is that the place does have rules and is consistent within its own framework of logic. I will leave most of that to your orientation once you make planetfall. You will be met and briefed as a convict—along with the other inmates being sent there with you—by representatives of the Lord of Lilith, and that will be more effective than anything I can give you secondhand.

"Though the imprint ability of this device is limited," he continued, "we can send you one basic thing that, oddly, you will not find on Lilith itself. It is a map of the entire place, as detailed as we could make it."

I felt a sharp back pain followed by a wave of dizziness and nausea; this quickly cleared and I found that in fact I had a detailed physical-political map of the entirety of Lilith in my head. It would come in very handy.

There followed a stream of facts about the place not likely to be too detailed in any indoctrination lecture. The planet was roughly 52,000 kilometers around at the equator or from pole to pole, allowing for topographic differences. Like all four of the Warden Diamond worlds, it was basically a ball—highly unusual as planets go, even though everybody including me thinks of all major planets as round.

The gravity was roughly .95 norm, so I'd feel lighter and be able to jump further. That would take a slight adjustment of timing, and I made a note to work on that first and foremost. It was also a hair higher than the norm for oxygen, which would make me feel a tad more energetic but also would make fires burn a little easier, quicker, and brighter. Not much, though. The higher concentration of water than normal combined with its 85-degree axial tilt and slightly under 192,000,000 kilometer distance from its sun—made this world mostly hot and very humid with minimal seasons. Latitude and elevation would be responsible for the main temperature variations on Lilith, not what month it was. Elevation loss was a near-standard 3 degrees centigrade per 1,800 meters.

And even latitude wasn't all that much of a factor. Equatorial temperatures were scorchers—35 to 50 degrees centigrade, 25 to 34 or so in the midlatitudes, and never less than 20 degrees even at the poles. No ice caps on Lilith. No ice, either, which in itself might explain why there was only one enormous continent on Lilith, along with a bunch of islands.

A day was 32.2 standard hours, so it would take some adjusting to the new time rate. A lot, I thought. That was over 8 hours more than I was used to. But I'd coped with almost as bad; I could cope with this one, too. A year was 344 Lilith days. So it was a large world, as worlds go, but with low gravity, which meant no metals to speak of. Pretty good prison, I thought.

"The Lord of Lilith is Marek Kreegan," Krega continued. "Most certainly the most dangerous of the Four Lords, for he alone is not a criminal or convict but instead was, like you, an agent of the Confederacy, one of the best. Were he able to leave the Warden system, he would probably be considered the most dangerous man alive."

I felt a thrill go through me for more than one reason. First, the absolute challenge of tracking down and hitting one like myself, one trained as I was and considered the most dangerous man alive—it was fantastic. But more than that, this information offered me two rays of hope that I'm fairly sure Krega hadn't considered. If this man was a top agent sent down on a mission, he'd have been in the same position as I would be upon its completion—and he hadn't been killed. There could be only one reason for that: they had no way of killing him. He'd figured the way out and taken it. Perfect. If Kreegan could do it, so could I.

And he'd worked himself up to being the Lord of Lilith.

The logic still held. If he and I were judged at least equal, then that meant that I potentially have the same powers as he has—greater powers than anyone else on the planet or somebody else would be Lord. And what he could do, *I* could do.

"Still, to find Kreegan, let alone kill him, could prove to be an almost impossible task," Krega continued. "First of all, he rarely makes an appearance, and when he does, he is always concealed. Everyone who discovers what he looks like is killed. He has no fixed base, but roams the world, always in disguise. This keeps his underlings on their toes and relatively honest, at least toward him. They never know who he might be, but fear him tremendously, as he can kill them and they can do nothing to him. At last count there were a little over 13,244,000 people on Lilith —that's a rough estimate, of course. A very small population, you'll agree—but Kreegan can be any one of them."

Well, actually he couldn't, I noted to myself. For one thing, Kreegan was a standard from the civilized worlds. That meant he was within fairly definite physical limits, thus eliminating a lot of people. Of course, since I knew he was male that eliminated close to half the population right there. He was also seventy-seven, but he'd been on Lilith for twenty-one years, which would change him a great deal from any picture of him as a younger man. Still, he'd be an older man, and on Lilith older men would stand out anyway—it would be a rough world. So we call him middle-aged, standard height and build, and male. When you were starting with 13,000,000, that narrowed the field down more than, I suspect, Krega himself realized.

A challenge, yes, but not as impossible as it sounded. Even more important, as the Lord and administrator there would be certain places he'd have to hit, and certain functions he'd have to attend. Still more narrowing down, and I wasn't even on the planet yet.

The rest of the briefing was pretty routine. After it was over I simply got off the john and pushed it back in the wall. I heard a flushing sound and, the next time I used it, discovered that my waste wasn't the only thing that had disappeared. Because it had been a direct neural transmission, less than a minute was needed to get all the information they could pack into it, too.

Extremely efficient, the security boys, I told myself. Even my ever-vigilant jailers on the other end of those lenses and mikes would have no idea that I was anybody other than who I was supposed to be.

As to who that was, I'd gotten my first mental picture of myself from the briefing. Brutish, my old self might have said, but in many ways I was not all that bad-looking and definitely oversexed—something I really didn't mind at all.

I was Cal Tremon, a lone-wolf pirate, murderer, and all-around bad boy. Over two meters tall, 119 kilos of pure muscle and gristle. My face was square and tough-looking, with a shock of coal-black hair fading into a beard that framed it like some beast's mane, with a big, bushy mustache that connected to the sideburns. A broad mouth, thick-lipped, atop which sat a slightly flattened but very large nose. The eyes were large and a deep brown, but what made the effect so menacing was the bushy black eyebrows that actually connected at the bridge of the nose.

I looked and felt like some primordial caveman, one of our remotest ancestors. Yet the body was in good condition, tremendously powerful and formidable—far more powerful than my own had been. The muscles bulged. It would take some getting used to, this huge, brutish body, but once fine-tuned it would, I was certain, be an enormous asset.

On the other hand, the one thing Cal Tremon had never been and never would be is a cat burglar. He was about as petite as a volcano.

He. I, my mind corrected. Now and forever after *I* was Cal Tremon.

I lay back down on the cot and put myself in a light trance, going over all the briefing information, filing, sorting, thinking. The data on Tremon's own life and colorful, if bloody, career was of particular import. Although he didn't seem like the kind of guy who would have any friends, there was a world full of crooks down there. *Somebody* must have known him.

Chapter Two

Transportation and Exposure

Except for regular meals I had no way to keep track of time, but it was a fairly long trip. They weren't wasting any money transporting prisoners by the fastest available routes, that was for sure.

Finally, though, we docked with the base ship a third of a light-year out from the Warden system. I knew it not so much by any sensation inside my cloister but by the lack of it—the vibration that had been my constant companion stopped. Still, the routine wasn't varied; I supposed they were waiting for a large enough contingent from around the galaxy to make the landing worthwhile. I could only sit and go over my data for the millionth time, occasionally reflecting on the fact that I probably wasn't very far from my old body (that's how I'd come to think of it). I wondered if perhaps he didn't even come down and take a peek at me from time to time, at least out of idle curiosity—me and the three others who probably were also here.

I also had time to reflect on what I knew of the Warden situation itself, the reason for its perfection as a prison. I had not of course swallowed that whole—there was no such thing as the perfect prison, although this one had to come close. Shortly after I was landed on Lilith and started wading in and breathing its air I would be infected with an oddball submicroscopic organism that would set up housekeeping in every cell of my body. There it would live, feeding off me, even earning its keep by keeping disease organisms, infections, and the like in check. The one thing that stuff had was a will to live, and it only lived if you did.

But it needed something, some trace element or

42

some such that was only present in the Warden system. Nobody knew what and nobody had been able to do the real work to find out, but whatever it needed other than you was found only in the Warden system. Whatever it was wasn't in the air, because shuttles ran between the worlds of the Diamond and in them you breathed the purified, mechanically produced stuff with no ill effect. It wasn't in the food, either. They'd checked that. It was possible for one of the Warden people to live comfortably on synthetics in a totally isolated lab such as a planetary space station. But get too far away, even with Warden food and Warden air, and it died; and since it had modified your cells to make itself at home, and those cells depended on the organism to keep working properly, you died, too —painfully and slowly, in horrible agony. That distance was roughly a quarter of a light-year from the sun, which explained the location of the base ship.

All four worlds were more than climatologically different, too. The organism was consistent in what it did to you on each planet, but—possibly because of distance from the sun, since that seemed to be the determining factor in its life—it did different things to you depending on which world you were first exposed to it, and whatever it did stuck in just that fashion even if you went to a different world of the Diamond.

The organism seemed somehow to be vaguely telepathic in some way, although nobody explained how. It certainly wasn't an intelligent organism; at least it always behaved predictably. Still, most of the changes seemed to involve the colony in one person affecting the colony in another—or others. You provided the conscious control, if you could, and that determined who bossed whom. A pretty simple system, even if nobody had yet been able to explain it.

As for Lilith, all I would remember was that it was some sort of Garden of Eden. I cursed again not having been fed the proper programming to make me fully prepared. Learning the ropes there would take time, possibly a lot of it.

About a day and a half—five meals—after I'd arrived at the base ship, a lurching and a lot of banging around forced me to the cot and made me slightly seasick. Still, I wasn't disappointed. No doubt they were making up the consignments and readying for the in-system drop of these cells. I faced the idea with mixed emotions. On the one hand, I wanted desperately to be out of this little box, which provided nothing but endless, terrible boredom. On the other, when I next emerged from the box it would be into a much larger and probably prettier box—Lilith itself, no less a cell for being an entire planet. And what it would make up for in diversion, challenge, excitement, or whatever, it would also be, unlike this box, very, very final.

Shortly after the banging about started, it stopped again, and after a short, expectant pause, I again felt a vibration indicating movement—much more pronounced than before. Either I was on a much smaller vessel or located nearer the drives. Whatever, it took another four interminable days, twelve meals, to reach our destination. Long, certainly—but also fast for a sublight carrier, probably a modified and totally automated freighter. The vibration stopped and I knew we were in orbit. Again I had that dual feeling of being both trapped and exhilarated.

There was a crackling sound, whereupon a speaker I'd never even known was there suddenly came to life. "Attention, all prisoners!" it commanded, its voice a metallic parody of a man's baritone. "We have achieved orbit around the planet Lilith in the Warden system," it continued, telling me nothing I didn't know but probably informing the others, however many there were, for the first time. I could understand what they must be going through, considering my own feelings. A hundred times mine, probably, since at least I was going in with my eyes open even if no more voluntarily than they. I wondered for a fleeting instant about Lord Kreegan. *He* had gone in voluntarily, the only one I ever knew about. I couldn't help but wonder why. Perhaps there were things about the Warden Diamond that were outside the knowledge of the Confederacy.

"In a moment," the voice continued, "the doors to

your cells will slide open and you will be able to leave. We strongly recommend you do so, since thirty seconds after the doors open they will close again and a vacuum pump will begin sterilization operations within the cells. This would be fatal to anyone who remains."

Nice touch, I thought. Not only did their method ensure against breakouts en route, you moved or you died on their schedule. I couldn't help wonder whether anybody chose death.

"Immediately after you enter the main corridor," the voice continued, "you will stand in place until the cell doors close once again. Do not attempt to move from in front of your cell door until it closes or automatic guard equipment will vaporize you. There will be no talking in the corridor. Anyone breaking silence or failing to obey orders precisely will be dealt with instantly. You will receive further instructions once the doors close. Ready to depart—*now!*"

The door slid open and I wasted no time in stepping out. A small white box, complete with marks for feet, indicated where you were to stand. I did as instructed, galling as all this was. Being totally naked and isolated on a ship controlled only by a computer humbled you more than was right, gave you a sense of total futility.

I could still look around and saw that I'd been right. We were standing in what was basically a long, sealed hall, along the sides of which were attached the little cells. I looked up and down and counted maybe a dozen, certainly no more than fifteen. The cream of the crop, I thought sourly. A dozen men and women —about half and half—naked and bedraggled, beaten prisoners about to be dropped and left. I wondered why these had been selected for transport rather than wiped, considering the transportation expense alone. What had the computers and psych boys found in these dejected specimens that dictated that they should live? *They* didn't know, that was for sure. I wondered who did.

The doors snapped shut. I waited expectantly, listening perhaps for the scream of somebody who didn't move fast enough as the air was pumped out, but there was no hint of melodrama. If anybody had taken that way out, the fact was not evident.

"At my command," the voice barked from speakers along the ceiling, "you will turn right and walk slowly, in single file, as far forward as you can. There you will find a special shuttle that will take you to the surface. You will take seats from the front first, leaving no empty seats between you. Immediately strap yourselves in."

"Sons of bitches," I heard a woman ahead of me mutter. At once a brief but very visible spurt of light from a side wall hit with an audible hiss just in front of her foot. She started in surprise, then muttered, "All right, all right." She was silent once more.

The voice had paused, but now took up its instructions with no reference to the incident. "Right turn— *now!*" it commanded, and we did as instructed. "Walk slowly forward to the shuttle as instructed."

We walked in silence, definitely in no hurry. The metal floor of the corridor was damned cold, though —in fact, the place wasn't any too comfortable as a whole—and this made the shuttle at least preferable to this damned refrigerator.

The shuttle itself was surprisingly comfortable and modern, although the seats weren't made for naked bodies. I found a seat about four rows back and attached the safety straps, then waited for the rest to enter. My first impression had been close, I noted. The shuttle itself could seat twenty-four, but there were only fourteen of us, eight males and six females.

The hatch closed automatically, and I heard the hiss of pressurization. Then, without further fanfare, there was a violent lurch and we were free of the transport and on our way down.

The shuttle was much too modern and comfortable for mere prisoner transport, I told myself. This, then, had to be one of the interplanetary ships regularly used for transportation between the worlds of the Warden Diamond.

The overhead speakers crackled, and a much nicer female voice that actually sounded human came on. It was a great improvement.

"Welcome to Lilith," the voice said, sounding for all the world as if it meant it. "As has no doubt been explained to you, Lilith is your final destination and new home. Although you will be unable to leave the Warden system after debarking, you will no longer be prisoners but citizens of the Warden Diamond. Confederacy rule ended when you entered this shuttle, which is owned in common by the Warden Worlds, one of a fleet of four shuttlecraft and sixteen freighters. The System Council is a corporate entity fully recognized as internally sovereign by the Confederacy and even with a seat in the Confederation Congress. Each of the four worlds is also under separate administration, and the governments of each planet are unique and independent. No matter who you were or what you might have been or done in the past, you are now citizens of Lilith and nothing more. You are no longer prisoners. Anything done prior to now is past history that will not be remembered, filed, or referred to ever again. Only what you do from this point on, as citizens of Lilith, Warden System, will matter."

It—or she, I really wasn't sure—paused for that piece of information to sink in. The contrast between the attitude and tone taken now and the one we'd all just been subjected to was enormous.

"Because of the unique properties of Lilith," the voice continued, "the shuttle cannot remain long or it might become disabled. Furthermore, it has a schedule to keep, and others need to use it. We therefore would appreciate your debarking as soon as the hatch opens. Someone will be there to meet you, answer your questions and assign you to your new homes. Please cooperate with this individual, as Lilith is a primitive world and extremely dangerous to newcomers. We will arrive in approximately five minutes."

Although the lid was off, nobody really said anything for the rest of the ride—partly because we were still conditioned by our recent imprisonment; the rest was nerves, me included. This was it, I told myself. Here we go.

A sudden sensation of falling as if we'd hit an air

pocket in some flying craft was followed by the reim-
position of weight and a hard thump. They had come
in as fast as was safely possible, and I wondered for a
moment what their hurry was. Then the hatch hissed
and opened; to my surprise, a sudden rush of tremendously warm, moist air hit us.

We lost no time doing as instructed—no use in alienating our new lords and masters before we even
got the lay of the land—and debarked quickly. I was
surprised to find a moving walkway extending from
the shuttlecraft itself down to the bare ground. No
spaceport, nothing. In a matter of moments we were
standing, naked and disoriented and already beaded
with sweat from the heat, on a grassy plain or
meadow.

We had arrived on Lilith—and even as that first
warm rush of native air had hit us our bodies were
being systematically invaded.

Chapter Three

Orientation and Placement

I was aware of others around now—not the mechan-
ics and service personnel one would expect but just
other people—passengers for the outbound, I realized.
A half-dozen or so wearing loose-fitting skirts or even
shiny robes but not looking very different from the
run-of-the-mill frontier individual I knew well. Not
very different from us, really. After the last of us
emerged, they moved quickly to replace us on the
craft, a sleek, saucerlike vessel. The ramp retracted
and the hatch closed almost immediately.

"They sure don't waste any time, do they?" a man
near me remarked, and I had to agree.

Reflecting for a moment on the passengers I *did*
realize one odd thing about them that separated them

from any passengers on any interplanetary craft I'd ever known. None of them, not one, carried any sort of luggage—and there certainly had not been time to load any before we got off. In fact, none of them had anything at all except the flimsy-looking clothes they had worn.

We were well clear of the craft and watched it come to life, then rise very quickly. The ship was gone in an instant, yet all of us followed it with our eyes, continuing to stare at the exact spot where it had vanished into the deep blue sky. It was as if that shuttle represented our last link with the old culture, our last line to the places we'd been and the people we'd known—and the people we had been, too.

I was among the first to look down and spotted a very attractive woman approaching us. Wearing only one of those flimsy but colorful skirts and what looked like a pair of flat sandals, she was extremely tall—almost 180 centimeters, surely—with long black hair, her skin tanned very dark, almost black.

"Hello!" she called out in a deep, throaty, yet pleasant voice. "I am your orientation guide and teacher. Will you all please follow me and we'll get you settled in?"

A few of the others continued to look skyward as if spellbound or hypnotized for a few moments, but eventually all of us turned and followed her. We were all survivors and life went on.

The Garden of Eden description of Lilith I'd heard was mostly an impression of a warm, resort-type world. At least that had been how I'd pictured it. But nearly naked women and grass huts were a bit more primitive than I'd imagined—or been used to.

Yet grass huts they were, with yellow reed walls and thatched roofs. I could see the others having thoughts similar to my own. We'd been prepared for almost anything, but we'd grown up in a slick, automated world. Even those in the lowest classes were used to glancing at their watch for time, date, and whatever; to lights turning on when you entered rooms; to having food ready to be ordered when you were hungry with a command and a touch of a wall plate.

A primitive place was one where the weather wasn't always controlled and buildings might be made of stone or wood, things like that—and a place with grass and trees. But *this*—not only did I now look like some prehistoric man, but I was living the part.

We all sat down in front of one of the huts and the woman introduced herself to us. "I am Patra," she told us, trilling the *r* sound slightly. "Like you, I was a convicted felon sentenced here about five years ago. I won't reveal what my offenses were, nor my old name—such things are not asked on the Warden worlds, although the information is sometimes freely given. It remains your choice to tell as much or as little about your past as you wish, and to whomever you wish. It is also your choice to use your old name or to choose any new one you like, as I did."

There were murmurs and nods at that, and I liked the idea myself. Barring a chance meeting with someone who had known the old Cal Tremon, I'd be spared the embarrassing questions and consequent chances of being tripped up somewhere.

"You will stay here a few days," Patra continued. "For one thing, you are now on a new and very hostile world. I realize that many of you have been on new and hostile worlds before, but never one quite like this one. In the past, you've had maps, charts, reference computers, all sorts of mechanical aids—not to mention effective weapons. There is none of that here, so you will have to get your information from me. Furthermore, as you are no doubt aware, the Warden organism invades our bodies and lives within us, and during the first few days, that process can have some unpleasant side effects. I don't want to alarm you—mostly some dizziness, disorientation, stomach upset, things like that. You won't be really sick, just a little uncomfortable from time to time. The discomfort passes quickly, and you'll never even think about it again. And it has some advantages."

"Yeah, keeps us planeted on this rock," somebody muttered.

Patra just smiled. "Not exactly, although it keeps us in this solar system. It's a fact of life, so accept that fact. Don't even think about escape, beating *this* system. Not only can't it be done—and some of the best minds in the galaxy have tried—but the death it brings is the worst, most horrible sort imaginable."

She paused to let that sink in, knowing it probably wouldn't, then continued. "The advantage of the organism is that you'll never have to worry about even the slightest ailment again. No toothaches, no colds, no infection, nothing. Even pretty large wounds, if not fatal or of an extremely critical nature, will heal quickly, and tissue regeneration is possible. There has never been a need for any doctor on Lilith, nor will there be. In other words, the Warden organism pays for what it takes."

She went on for a while, detailing some of the basics of the planet that I had already gotten from the briefing; then it was time for food. That took the most getting used to. The cuisine of Lilith seemed to consist of cooked insects of all sorts and lots of weeds, sometimes mixed with a grain of some sort that was a very unappetizing purple in color.

There were a few of my group who just couldn't manage the food for a while, but of course everybody would come around eventually. For a few it might be really tough going, or prove to be a very effective form of dieting.

Getting used to insect stews and chewy purple bread was going to be tough, I told myself, but I would have to learn to eat it and like it or else. Over the next few days I did manage to adjust to eating the food and to crapping in the bushes, using leaves instead of automatic wipers, and all the rest. As I said earlier, we were chosen for our ability to adapt to just about anything—and this was the "just about" the training manuals had implied.

Patra was also right about the side effects of the organism's invasion. I experienced strong dizziness, some odd aches and pains, and a feeling of itching all over inside—damned unpleasant, but I could live with it. We all had the runs, too, but I suspect that was mostly due to the food, not to the organism.

So far, though, Patra's orientation lectures had

mostly covered things I already knew about, and
though they went into greater detail than any I'd had
before and were therefore welcome, she hadn't covered the facts I needed so far. On the fourth very long
day—it was hell sleeping in that climate as it was,
without the days and nights being so much longer—
she finally got around to material of more interest.

"I know a lot of you have been wondering and
asking why there are no machines, no spaceport, no
modern buildings or conveniences here," she began.
"So far I've put you off, simply because this was important enough for me to want you all to be through
most of the ill effects of arrival. The reason is easy to
explain but damned difficult to accept, but it's the explanation for everything you've seen around here."
She seemed to look at each of us in turn, a half-smile
on her face.

"Lilith," she said, "is alive. No, that doesn't make
sense—but none of the Wardens do. I am going to
tell you what *is* in terms that can only be approxima-
tions of what is going on.

"I want you to imagine that every single thing you
see—not just the grass and trees, but *everything*:
rocks, the very dirt under your feet—is alive, all cells
of a single organism, each of which has its own Warden organism inside it in the same symbiotic relationship as it is establishing in your bodies. That organism
likes the world *exactly* the way it is. It maintains it.
Chop a tree down and another grows from its stump
in record time. Meanwhile the original starts decaying
with equal speed—in a full day it's started to decompose; within three it's completely gone, absorbed into
the ground. Same for people. When you die you'll be
completely gone to dust in under three days. That's
why our food is what it is. It's what can be caught,
killed, and prepared within a day. You probably have
noticed that people arrive with our rations every
morning."

There were a few nods, but I frowned. "Wait a
minute. If that's true, then how do these grass huts
stay up? They're dead matter."

She smiled again. "A good question. The truth is,

they *aren't* dead. They're single living *bunti* plants, related to those yellow stalks you see growing here and there in the woods."

"You mean they obligingly grow into houses for us?" a woman asked skeptically.

"Well, not exactly," came the reply. "They grow into houses because they were ordered to do so."

Eyebrows shot up at this. "Ordered by whom?" somebody else asked.

"Life is a contest of wills everywhere," Patra responded. "On Lilith, it is more so. That is at the heart of the culture we've built here. You see, though the Warden organism isn't intelligent, at least as we understand such things, it is a truly alien organism that more or less becomes an integral part of whatever it lives in—and it lives in everything. You are no longer human beings. You are something else now—alien creatures, really. If you master your own body and if your mind is strong enough and has enough natural ability and sheer willpower, you can sense the Warden organism in all things around you. Sense it, and in a way talk to it. Somehow, nobody knows how, all Warden organisms are linked together. You might think of them as single, independent cells of a great creature. Unlike our cells, they don't adjoin, but like our cells, they are linked together somehow in a manner we don't yet understand. They communicate. You can make them communicate. You might, if strong enough and powerful enough, instruct Warden organisms not a part of you to do just about anything."

A sense of stunned unbelief swept over the group, but I was a little better prepared. Even so, I found the idea hard to visualize.

"The power of the individual over the organism," Patra explained, "varies wildly. Some people never get much of anything—the majority, I'm afraid, remain as you are now—and thus are at the mercy of more powerful minds that have more control and thus can control Warden organisms necessary to you—for food, for shelter, even within your own bodies. There are also those wild talents with the ability to exercise power, sometimes considerable power, but not under any sort of control. Like the majority, they are essentially powerless—but they get a little more respect, particularly if their wild talents are dangerous or deadly. The degree of control you have is fixed. We have no idea why some have it and others don't. But I *can* tell you that for some reason non-natives in general tend to possess a higher level of power than those born here. Perhaps this is because the Warden organism remains alien, something we are always aware doesn't belong in us. If you have the power, it'll show up on its own. Once it does, though, training and practice are required to bring you up to your full potential—and that's when you'll find out where you fit in this world."

It was something to think about, and worry about —a wild-card factor beyond my control, and I felt more than a little nervous. Whether or not I'd go far around here depended on how well I got along with the little buggers in my cells.

"Lilith is divided into political regions," she explained. "These areas, or districts, are based on population. As of this moment, each District contains roughly twenty-eight thousand people and there are a total of four hundred and seventy of them, each headed by an official called a Duke. They are enormously powerful, having the ability to stabilize dead matter. As a result, they live in fine mansions and often have art, dinnerware—all the finer things you can think of. And weapons, too.

"The Duke of a District is the most powerful Knight in his District. Therefore the officials below him are called Knights, and each Knight rules an area called a Keep. Knights also have some control over dead matter, but nothing like on the scale of a Duke—there's really no difference in power between Dukes and Knights with regard to the rest of the population. A Duke is only the most powerful of Knights. The Keeps, by the way, vary in size from very small to huge, depending on the number of people living in them. The more powerful the Knight, the more people he or she controls and the larger the Keep. The Duke, also being a Knight, has the largest Keep, of course."

I nodded to myself. Knights and Dukes had their way around here. The place was beginning to sound like a monarchy, but one determined by some indefinable natural ability, not heredity. Well, at least it kept dynasties down.

"Keeps," Patra went on, "are administered by Masters. Think of them as department heads. Each runs a particular area of Keep administration. Masters can control living things, but their ability to stabilize dead matter is very, very limited. A Master could make these *bunti* grow into a house, though, to his or her particular design.

"Below Masters are Supervisors, who are just what the term says. They manage the actual work. Their ability to stabilize dead matter is limited to usually a few articles of basic clothing, but they still have power over living things—mostly destructive. However, they can regenerate parts of themselves, even whole limbs, and can cause regeneration in others— as can, of course, Masters, Knights, and Dukes. I must warn you, they can also do the opposite—cause a limb to wither, inflict pain by sheer will."

"Which are you?" a man asked.

"None of the above," she laughed. "I am a Journeywoman. Basically my power is similar to a Master's, but I don't belong to a Keep. Dukes need people to travel between Keeps, to carry messages, to work out commerce, to—well, give orientation talks to newcomers. We're salespeople, ambassadors, couriers, you name it—answerable only to our Dukes. It's mostly a matter of temperament whether you're Journey or Master class. There are pluses and minuses for both jobs, and the fact that I'm a Journeywoman now doesn't mean I might not take a Master's position sometime."

"You've covered all the high spots," I noted. "You've accounted for maybe several thousand people, but you said there were more than thirteen million on the planet. What about the rest?"

"Pawns," she answered. "They do the work. In fact they do just about anything they're told to do. Consider—pawns need those more powerful to feed them, to provide shelter, to protect them against the savage beasts of the planet. They are in no position to do anything else."

"Slaves," the man next to me muttered. "Just like the civilized worlds, only reduced to the lowest common denominator."

I didn't agree with the man's comparison at all, but I could understand him completely now and why he was there.

"You've left somebody out," a woman—I think the one who was defiant back on the prison ship—spoke out. "The guy who runs the place. What kind of power does it take to be the Lord?"

Patra appeared to be slightly embarrassed by the way in which the question was put, but she answered it anyway. "There's only one Lord," she pointed out. "Right now it's the Lord Marek Kreegan. He got there because he challenged the previous Lord and killed him, thereby proving his power. Lords, of course, have all the powers of Dukes plus one extra ability that almost no one has—the ability to stabilize alien matter. They can possess a device that is not of this world. All alien matter except that stabilized by the Lord or his almost-as-powerful administrative aide, Grand Duke Kobé, decomposes. As well as undergoing extreme decontamination procedures, our two shuttles were stabilized by Lord Kreegan. If that weren't so, even the shuttles would decompose here."

Well, there it was: the unbelievable reality of the pecking order on Lilith and what individuals could—and could not—do, and the reason those folks didn't have any luggage. This also explained the clothing, and lack of it, seen around. Since your ability to "stabilize dead matter" was what counted, the more clothes you could comfortably wear, the higher your rank. I wondered idly if Dukes wore so much clothing they looked like moving clothes racks; if so, there would be disadvantages to higher rank, which would seem to *require* that outer badge of office. No wonder Lord Kreegan wanted to remain anonymous. The ceremonial robes of office alone would probably suffocate him.

On Lilith, clothes made the man or woman—and the man or woman made the clothes. That meant that because we remained naked, we all started out as low rank on the social scale. Well, at least on Lilith one wouldn't freeze to death. However, a certain sense of social modesty had been ingrained in me—not that I really minded here, surrounded by a lot of new prisoners in the same state. But in a strange land and civilization I knew I was going to feel more than a little self-conscious, particularly around the midsection.

Later that afternoon small blood samples were taken from each of us. I had no idea how they could analyze it, but apparently the results were satisfactory to everyone. Later that evening, Patra called us together for the last time as a formal group.

"Tomorrow," she told us, "the shuttle will return for you and take you to widely scattered Keeps. From then on you will be on the rolls of a specific Keep—I have no idea which—and will be assigned work. Your first few weeks will be an education, I think, in the powers of this world and the way it operates. Whether you remain pawns or whether you rise will depend on you. You *will* rise to your proper level—you won't be able to avoid it, really—but the timing will vary from weeks to months to years. Just remember that almost three million on Lilith came here as you did; the rest are native born to the generations past and present that came here. You have the same potential as they."

There were murmurings from the group. This seemed to be the worst kind of culture to enter: a totally combative one that relied on powers the strength of which was totally beyond the individual's control.

I slept very little that evening. I suppose few of us got much rest, considering the new day. As for me, I was feeling several emotions I had not experienced in a very long time and facing a situation I felt uncomfortable about. I felt doubt within me, and a sagging confidence in myself and my abilities. And there was still so much I didn't know about this world—things I *had* to learn, even as I learned where this odd sys-

tem would place me. The only thoughts that consoled
me were that Marek Kreegan had come here from the
same background as me and that he had risen to rule
it. Most importantly, he was a man like me, a person,
a human being. He had enormous power, it was said,
but he was mortal, and he could die.

Besides, I already knew an awful lot about him. I
knew his age, sex, and general appearance, and I
knew that he had a passion for anonymity and disliked the soft life. That meant he had to masquerade
as a Journeyman, in order to be able to travel about
and observe both great and small. Naturally others
would also have figured this out, so he obviously had
extra tricks up his sleeve to preserve his disguise. But,
I realized, though Journeymen might have only the
power of a Master, they would have a more exalted
position, particularly the middle-aged men. Not even
the greatest Duke could avoid being paranoid about
such people. Journeyman would be the rank I'd find
best suited to my own purposes, I decided—but that
was a factor beyond my control.

That idea brought the depression back once again,
and I consoled myself with the thought that, here only
a few days and having seen almost none of this
strange world, I had already narrowed my suspects
down to a mere handful, perhaps less than a thousand.

Yeah, sure. The assignment was becoming simple.

Chapter Four

Zeis Keep

The shuttle that had brought us to the orientation
point—I was never sure where that was on Lilith—
had been silver; although the one that took us to our
new homes was a dull rusty-red color, it looked like
the first on the inside. I wondered whether it was the

same one. Maybe it got a new paint job every time it reached orbit, to replace what was lost. Undoubtedly the schedule for the shuttle, which had to operate from an orbital base, had to be carefully worked out in advance. Somebody had to do it without benefit of transceivers—that meant a representative of all the Dukes and the Lord of Lilith, since the schedule would have to be coordinated well in advance, yet be available as need arose.

I still hadn't much of a clue as to what this special "power" might be like, either in execution or from the standpoint of just seeing it work. Nothing had dissolved around me, nobody had shot thunderbolts from their fingertips, nothing like that. If I never saw the power in operation, I didn't know how I could find out whether I had it myself. If I didn't, and in sufficient quantity, I'd lose before I had really started. I had to have some faith in Security there. Their computers had carefully selected me for this job, and that would have been one of the prime considerations—factors favorable to great power. But those same computers and the best scientists in the galaxy had absolutely no nice, normal, and natural physical explanation for the Warden phenomena, either.

I kept coming back to Kreegan. He'd known what he was getting into, and he'd voluntarily and confidently consigned himself to Lilith. Obviously the man had a strong reason to expect gaining great power or he wouldn't have done it.

Before it was my turn we landed four times, picking up and discharging not only those from my party but regular passengers as well. It was not wasted on me that we newcomers were the only passengers without clothing. Then we landed once again—the shuttle made orbit between stops to cleanse itself, which meant a slow journey—and the speaker called my seat number. The hatch hissed and opened, the ramp extended, and I walked out once more onto the surface of Lilith.

The scene was incredible. It was a beautiful valley surrounded by tall mountains, some of which had slight traces of snow on them. The valley itself was out of some children's fairy tale: broad fields in which long, leafy plants grew up to three meters in the air, all in nice, neat rows; a few small lakes that looked shallow enough to be paddies of some sort; and a meadow where really hideous-looking livestock grazed. This was my first look at the kinds of things that went into those stews, and my stomach automatically recoiled. Giant insects that resembled monstrous roaches except for their enormous, glittering, multi-faceted eyes on stalks and their thick, curly brown fur. I'd seen an awful lot of alien life in my travels, including some creatures even more repulsive than those, but I'd never eaten them.

To one side stood groves of fruit trees. The fruit was unfamiliar but large and of different varieties. Another area seemed to be devoted to bushes covered with berries. They all at least looked comfortably edible.

But what made the pastoral scene so unreal was the castle in the middle, set against the mountains and built on a possibly man-made ledge right into the mountainside at an elevation of perhaps a hundred meters. The stone building came complete with towers, parapets, and battlements; it was the kind of place found *only* in fantasy.

Below the castle, in the valley itself, was what looked like a complex of straw huts much like those we'd used for orientation but a lot denser. That, then, was where the common folk lived, or at least the area around which their lives centered. I did note that there were other clusters of huts in various parts of the valley.

I heard a rumbling and turned to see a very plain sledlike wagon made of some thick plant material. It was being pulled by a large green thing with a shiny, almost round shell and who knew how may legs underneath. The tiny head, which seemed to be a horn-like snout atop which sat two dim little red dots and a couple of thin antennae, was all that was visible.

The man sitting on a crudely fashioned seat behind the creature was a large, dark, nasty-looking fellow, but that didn't really bother me—after all, I was now a large, dark, nasty-looking fellow myself. It did, however, seem interesting that he had no reins, no steering or other controls in his hands or attached to his body at all. He was just sitting there looking bored, letting the green beast pull him.

I realized in an instant that I was seeing the first demonstration of this mysterious power. He *was* controlling that thing, but not with any mechanical apparatus.

The wagon came up to me and stopped, whereupon the man rose to his feet and just stood there, staring down at me. He was an imposing figure—solid muscle, a weightlifter's physique—yet he wasn't really a big man. His squat build and muscles just made him seem so. He wore what appeared to be a yellow jockstrap, around which, oddly, was a wide belt of some pliable dark-brown material, from which a nasty-looking coiled whip hung at his side.

"Well?" he growled. "You just gonna stand there gawking or are you gonna get aboard?"

Welcome to your new home, I thought sourly as I climbed up and sat next to him on the bench. It was, like a lot on this world, made from some kind of thick, hard plant material, possibly bark. Without another word the huge green creature started off again, almost knocking me off the seat.

The other man chuckled. "Yeah, it's a rough ride," he commented, "but you get used to it. Not that you have to worry much—pawns don't do much ridin'." He paused a moment, giving me a good look. "Nice muscles, good build. We can use you, all right. You got any skills from your old life that maybe would make you a little more useful? Carpentry? Masonry? Animal care?"

I almost laughed at the question. The concept of anybody from the civilized worlds even knowing the meaning of those terms was ridiculous. I checked my reaction because I remembered that this was not my old body, but that of a frontiersman from a rough life, an impression I wanted to maintain as long as possible.

So I just shook my head and replied, "No, sorry,

nothing I can think of. Electrical and power systems, weapons, things like that."

He snorted. "Electrical! Haw! Around here that don't mean shit. You're just a common laborer now. The only electricity we got on Lilith is lightning from the thunderstorms, and the only power is what some people got. Nope. Best forget the old comforts—you're a pawn of Zeis Keep now. I'm Kronlon, work supervisor for this section. You'll be workin' fer me. You call me 'sir' and you obey orders from me, nobody else."

"I'm not used to taking orders," I muttered, low and deep but deliberately loud enough for him to hear. I expected this to provoke him and gain his measure, but he laughed instead. The wagon stopped in the middle of a field about halfway to a group of huts to the left of the castle.

"Get down," he ordered, his tone more casual than menacing, gesturing with a beefy hand. "Go ahead. Get down."

I shrugged and did as instructed. Ordinarily I'd have expected a menacing tone or perhaps a swing, but if this was any kind of fight preparation he was definitely the cool one.

He jumped down after me, then walked right up to me. I towered over him, but that seemed to increase his pleasure. "Okay, go ahead. Take a swing at me. Go on—swing!" He thrust out his jaw. So it *was* a showdown after all.

I shrugged again, then hauled off and punched as hard as I could. Only I couldn't. My arm was suddenly stopped in midswing, fist tightly clenched. I couldn't move it, not forward, back, up, or down. I felt my muscles, tensed for the punch, start to hurt from the unreleased tension, but I could do nothing to release that energy. The fist was only a few centimeters from his out-thrust jaw.

He hauled off and hit me in my midsection with a blow that seemed designed to shatter ribs. I went down hard, with a groan and yelp of surprise and pain. Lying there on my back, gasping for breath, I realized that my right arm was still stiffly clenched.

He walked over and grinned. "See? Kind of hard to believe, isn't it?" He was clearly enjoying himself.

I felt my arm suddenly unfreeze, and lying there on the road, I completed the swing, almost rolling over in the process.

Kronlon laughed derisively, then turned and started to walk back to the wagon.

Marshaling my strength, I leaped up and rushed his back, attempting to tackle him. He might have heard me, but there was no way he could have seen me, and the combination of my new body and the low gravity gave me both force and speed. Suddenly, just a few meters from him, my legs seemed to turn to rubber. I stumbled, cried out, and crashed to the ground once again.

He stopped and turned to look down on me, grinning like mad. "See? You can't even sneak up on me. Listen—I got your number, see? I got your pattern inside my skull." He tapped it for emphasis. "You don't make a move against me I don't know it ahead of time and tell your body to screw up. Okay, get up. You ain't hurt."

I got slowly to my feet, starting to feel a few slight bruises. My mind raced, first in frustration and fury that this man had me completely at his mercy, and second, because now that I'd seen this power in operation I still knew nothing about how it worked. And this guy was the lowest rung on the power structure!

He unhooked his whip from his belt and for a moment I was afraid he was going to use it on me—but to my surprise, he tossed it to me.

"Here, catch. Uncoil it. You know how to use one of these? All right, use it, then. Whip the living shit out of me!"

I was mad enough to do it, and though the whip was crude and fashioned out of some sort of shiny braided material, it was well balanced and long. I snapped it a few times, getting the feel of it, then took him at his word.

He just stood there and laughed. Try as I might, I could not make any part of that whip touch him. I could, after a little bit, pick up a stone or cut grass with it, but no matter how dead on my aim, the whip always seemed to miss him just slightly. I couldn't believe it and kept at it for several minutes while he just stood there, laughing and taunting but not flinching.

"Okay, fun's over," he said at last, seeming bored with it all. "Now you see your problem. Drop a twenty-kilo boulder on my head from a fall of less than a meter and it'll still miss me. *But not the other way around!*" He reached out and the whip seemed almost to leap from my hand to his, then coil back into its storage position. To my relief, he replaced it on his belt loop.

The grin grew wider. "I know what you're thinkin'. I can see it on your face. You're glad I didn't use the whip on you. Want to know why? It's just a badge of office—all supervisors carry 'em. I got it from Boss Tiel himself, matched to me, and I don't like it to get mussed up or broke." The grin vanished, and so did the casual tone. Menace now dripped from his lips.

"Now, you got two choices and that's all," Kronlon growled. "You obey orders. You listen, you live, for my orders, and then you obey 'em. You don't ask no questions, you don't wonder why or figure anything out. You just do it. Do that and you live. The other choice is you kill yourself. *I* won't kill you. I don't hav'ta. I can do much worse."

Suddenly my whole body was consumed with the most horrible, agonizing pain I had ever known. I cried out and fell, senseless to anything but the pain, rolling about the grassy earth in sheer agony. I could not bear it; the pain was so intense, so all-encompassing. Almost immediately I longed for death, for anything to give me release.

And just as suddenly the pain was gone. The relief was tempered by echoes of the agony in my nervous system and the burning memory in my brain. I just lay there face up on the grass, panting.

"Get up!" Kronlon ordered.

I hesitated, still in shock and unable to get my bearings fully. Instantly the pain was back, if only for a fleeting second that seemed like an eternity. I turned,

I crawled, I scrambled to my feet, still trembling and gasping.

Kronlon watched, a look of amused satisfaction on his face. He had done this many times before. I hated him worse than I ever hated anyone in my life.

But he still wasn't through.

"What's your name?" he asked.

"Tre—Tremon," I gasped. "Cal Tremon."

The agony was back, knocking me down again; then it was released.

"Get up!" the supervisor commanded. I tried to get back to my feet once more, making it on the second try. He waited patiently until I succeeded.

"Now, you'll address me as 'sir' always," he warned. "You will put 'sir' at the beginning of every statement to me, and you will put 'sir' at the end of it. You will stand straight when I am around and face me always, and when you are given an order you will bow slightly and then do it. You will speak to anyone not of your class only when spoken to, and only in reply to their questions or commands. Understand that?"

I was still gasping for breath. "Yes . . . sir," I responded. The pain returned.

"Not what I ordered, Tremon! What kind of a dumb shit are you? Now get up, you bastard, and we'll try it again."

For a moment I was confused, hesitant, until I realized he was deadly serious. The pain and agony he could inflict without moving a muscle was horrible, intense. By now I feared that more than anything, the memory so vivid that I would do almost anything to avoid it. It was horrible to know that I had been so easily humbled and beaten, so quickly broken—but broken I was. I wasn't even thinking straight any more. I just wanted to avoid that pain.

We spent what felt like hours out in that field, with quick applications of the pain followed by increasing demands, over and over again, a terrible torturer's delight. It was a process not unfamiliar to me, but one in which I'd never participated on the receiving end. Keep at the victim: administer pain, then demands, then pain again. Never be pleased, never be satisfied.

Agents were trained to black out after a certain threshold was reached, but I found even that suddenly beyond my power. Agents could also will themselves to death, of course, but that was the one point at which he was not going to win, not yet.

If I were being interrogated about a mission, or jeopardizing a mission, other people, anything, I would not have hesitated to take the death-wish route —but such was not the case. Nor was any torture mechanism being used—just one short, squat, brutish man standing there in a field, doing nothing at all.

As Kronlon had warned, there were only two routes for any thinking human being to take in this situation —death, or absolute, unquestioning obedience. My ego shattered in the waning sun, and my will seemed to recede into nothingness. Before sunset I was, on command, licking his stinking, dirty feet.

As we rode into the small village, me sitting dully at his side, a small corner of the old me, all that seemed to remain on the conscious level, kept saying over and over, "And a Master is ten times as powerful as a Supervisor and a Knight is ten times a Master and a Duke is ten times a Knight and a Lord is like a god. . . ."

I don't even remember entering the little village of straw and mud huts. It was nearly sunrise when I awoke.

Chapter Five

Village Routine

The pawns lived a miserably primitive life, I soon discovered, sleeping crammed into those huts with only more of the strawlike *bunti* plant that formed the hut covering the floor so deeply that it actually gave slightly under the weight of human bodies.

For several days I remained in nearly complete withdrawal, going through the motions like an automaton, thinking little and feeling nothing. The other pawns seemed to understand what a newcomer went through, even though most of them were native-born and had been raised on this horrible system and probably hadn't gone through quite what I had. There was no attempt to rush me, or to establish normal contact with me. They seemed content to wait until I snapped out of it, if I ever did, and initiated the contact myself.

We were routed out at dawn, and everybody crowded into a huge communal eating area in the center of the "village," as it were, where food-service pawns put out enormous, mostly tasteless rolls and a fair supply of good-tasting pulpy yellow fruit. Then the supervisor arrived; actually, he lived right there, in a hut just like the rest of us, only privately. But his food, the same as ours, was served to him by the food-service pawns in his hut—and someone would clean the place while work was being done.

Incredibly, despite the enormous power Kronlon possessed, on Lilith he was only a slight notch, just a hair really, above us, the lowest of the low. Just one look at his modest *bunti* hut and that castle up on the mountain told of the gulf separating him from his own bosses.

The work consisted mostly of loading and hauling. How soft mankind has become, even on the frontier. On Lilith, life was frozen in the stone age: all labor was manual; all tools were crudely fashioned and usually temporary.

Two rivers flowed from the mountains down to those small lakes, causing the twin problems of flood control and irrigation. It rained heavily at some point almost every day, yet the duration was short, the run-off quick. The mountains clearly absorbed the brunt of the storms on their other faces and allowed only the worst to get over to Zeis Keep. Therefore irrigation canals had to be dug by hand; the mud and muck was carried out by hand to carts, then hauled by men pulling those carts to fill areas near the lakes, where the silt would be formed into crude earthen dikes. Hundreds of kilometers of drainage and irrigation canals were constantly silting up; so when you finished the whole route, it was time to start again.

Men and women worked equally in the fields and in those jobs. Of course the strongest and hardiest took on the heaviest labor, and job assignment was clearly based on physique, age, and the like. Children—some as young as five or six I guessed—worked along with their elders, doing what they could under the watchful eyes of the oldest and most infirm. The social system was crude and primitive but well thought out. It worked, on the most basic, tribal level. Once, when mankind evolved on its mother world into what we now know as human beings, all people must have lived something like this.

Days were long, punctuated regularly by very short breaks and by four food breaks during the sixteen-hour work cycle. When darkness finally fell across the valley and the distant castle blazed with light was there rest. But the nights, too, were long. Zeis Keep was only 5 degrees south of the equator, which made the periods roughly equal all year.

Social time for the pawns was at night, and it was as basic and primitive as everything else. They had some dances and songs, for anybody who was in any condition to join in, and they talked and gossiped in an elementary way. They also made love then, seemingly without regard for any family unit or other permanent attachments. Marriage and such seemed alien concepts to these people, though if both partners felt like it, they married.

They were a lively, yet somewhat tragic group, largely ignorant of anything beyond their own miserable existence, which they accepted as normal and natural because they knew nothing else. So thoroughly ingrained was the system that I cannot recall a single instance in which a supervisor had to exercise his or her terrible powers.

As for me, I was in a curious state of mental catalepsy. I functioned, did my job as ordered, ate and slept, but basically didn't think. Looking back on the period now, I can see the reasons and understand, although I can't really forgive myself. It was not the defeat at Kronlon's hands or the crushing blow to my ego and pride that was inexcusable. What bothers me, really, is that I retreated into being a mental vegetable at the end of the contest.

I don't know how long I remained that way—days, weeks; it was hard to be sure, since there are no watches or calendars on Lilith. Still, slowly my mind struggled for some kind of control, some sort of reassertion of identity—first in dreams, then in fleeting memories. The real danger in this situation was that I could have gone mad, could have retreated into some sort of fantasy world or unreal existence. I realize now that the inner struggle was caused by compulsions placed on me by the Security Clinic programmers. They were not ones to take chances, and they could always program another body—but once a body was programmed and sent to the Warden System, they had to make sure it would remain true to them.

Find the aliens . . . kill the Lord. . . .

These commands echoed in my dreams and became the supports to which other parts of my shattered ego could cling.

Find the aliens . . . kill the Lord. . . .

Slowly, very slowly, night after night another fragment would return and coalesce around those deeply hidden commands, commands I might never have known were there had this not occurred.

Find the aliens . . . kill the Lord. . . .

And rationality finally returned to me. In the evening hours and just before falling asleep, I was able to try to sort out just what the hell had happened to me, to regain some of my confidence. I needed hope, and the only hope I could have was in reasoning a way out of my predicament.

The logic chain I forged may have been faulty, but it worked, and that alone was important. First and foremost was the realization that everyone who came here had undergone substantially the same treatment I had. It *had* cowed them all, driven them into some sort of grudging submission from which they'd had to learn to cope. Was that insanity, or perhaps a fatalistic acceptance?

Patra, that Knight up there in his fairyland castle, even Lord Marek Kreegan. There were no inherited positions or titles on Lilith, except perhaps for those skilled in things useful to the rulers. No political position, no position of authority, was hereditary or elected, either. All those positions, from Supervisor up to Lord, had been taken, won in a contest of power.

Find the aliens . . . kill the Lord. . . .

Everyone on this world who rose at all from the muck of pawn slavery rose from the bottom through the ranks. Everyone.

How did this power operate? How did you find out if you had it?

I felt ashamed of myself for my reaction to Kronlon. I had been in bad situations before, situations in which the enemy had all the power, and I had been stalled only temporarily by those conditions. The only difference between those situations and this one was that in this one I had looked at the lay of the land and the forces of the enemy, and instead of considering the problem and working out how to beat the enemy—or at least die trying—I had instead meekly surrendered. The day I faced and accepted the fact that I had run across a tremendously powerful obstacle, not an impassable barrier, was the day I rejoined the human race.

I started talking to people, although that was a pretty limited thing. Few topics for small talk were available—the weather was always hot and humid, for example—and it was difficult to talk down to people who might be bright and alert but whose whole world was this primitive, nonmechanized existence. What could you say to· people whose world view, if they had one, was that the valley was the world and the sun rose and set around it? Oh, they knew there were other Keeps, but they saw them all as being just like this one. And as for mechanization, they had seen the shuttle come and go, but that was as far as it went —after all, they were familiar with large flying insects.

The concept of any machine not powered by muscle was simply beyond them.

That was the core of my problem. I didn't know enough, not by a long shot, but I knew a hell of a lot more than these natives. Also, now that I'd pulled myself together, I craved some kind of intelligent conversation. I'd always been a loner before, but there is a difference between being alone by choice and being alone by force. Conversation and diversion had always been available when I had needed it. Everything seemed stacked against me. I hadn't gotten a single break on this whole mission since waking up. But I did get one now.

Her name was Ti.

A few days after my recovery I encountered her in the village common one evening, after the last meal of the day. I had seen her a few times before, and once you saw her you couldn't forget her.

She was about 160 centimeters tall and very thin, particularly at the waist, but she had large breasts and nice buttocks and sandy brown hair—unusual in itself—down to those buttocks. A pretty, sexy young woman, you might say—except that her face was amazingly young and innocent, the kind of face not seen on a body like that in my experience. It was a pretty face, all wide-eyed and innocent. But it was the face of a child, one no more than eleven or twelve, atop that well-developed body. Though the two would eventually reconcile, the body seemed to be developing several years ahead of that face.

I could have understood the contrast more if such a thing had been common on Lilith, but it was not—at least not from this pawn sample. Here was one minor mystery that perhaps I could learn something about, and I asked a couple of my co-workers about her.

"Oh, that's Ti," one explained. "A chosen of the Bodymaster. He'll pluck her in a little while, I'd say. Only thing that's slowed it is that she's got some wild talent in her and they want to see what it'll do."

Several items of new data. I felt like I was on to something new, something that would be of value.

"What do you mean, a chosen of the Bodymaster?" I asked. "Remember, I wasn't born here."

The question got me one of those looks of incomprehension I was becoming used to, since the natives just couldn't picture any other place as being any different than Zeis Keep. But the man shrugged and answered anyway. They had reconciled themselves to me by convincing themselves that the shock to my system, which they *could* comprehend, had made me funny in the head.

"Boss Tiel, he breeds women like he breeds *snarks*," the laborer explained. *Snarks* were those hairy monsters in the pasture that were raised for their highly prized meat. "When a child, particularly a girl child, is born with looks or something else special, well, she gets marked by the Bodymaster in charge of the breeding. He brings 'em along 'til they're the way he wants 'em, then he breeds 'em with selected boys. See?"

I *did* see, sort of, although the concept repelled me more than anything yet about this foul world. Repelled, but didn't surprise.

"But her—ah—development isn't natural, is it?" I prompted.

He chuckled and held up an index finger. "See this finger? I lost it—got chopped clean away—in an accident a while back. Bled like mad. They took me to the Bodymaster, who had only to look at it to stop the blood. Then he looked at it, touched it, and I came back. It grew back out in time, good as new. Look." He wiggled it for emphasis.

"But what does that . . . ?" I began, then realized what he was saying and shook my head in wonder. He caught my look and grinned.

"Breed stock needs to make lotsa babies, needs to want to make lotsa babies," the man noted. "You see?"

I saw, all right. Slowly, to make certain her cells and nervous system were capable of standing it, this Bodymaster was somehow reaching inside her with his power, in the same way as he had ordered the finger regenerated and as Kronlon had inflicted paralysis and pain. Subtle alterations were being made, had probably been made from the point of puberty, which could only have taken place a year or so ago. Hormones stimulated, body chemistry subtly altered, so that actually he was making her unnatural, his exaggeration deforming her somewhat—but all for his purposes. Breeding stock he wanted, not show stock. For what? The beautifully colored hair, perhaps? Possibly as little as that, although another thought came to me.

"Hogi?" I prodded my laborer companion once again.

"Uh?"

"You said she had some wild talent. What kind? What can she do?"

He shrugged. "Don't know. Might not understand it, anyway. I *do* know that none of the Supers bother her much, not even Kronlon. A little scared, maybe, which may mean she's got really great power—but it's wild. Comes and goes. No control."

I nodded. That would explain why the powers that be had left her here a while after puberty instead of taking her into the main village or perhaps to the castle grounds. They weren't quite sure what her powers were, either, or whether she might not someday learn to control them. They wanted to see more, first, to ascertain what she could or could not do. They were afraid of her potential, which indicated great power. If it stayed wild, well, she'd become a breeder and that was that. But if she gained control, she could threaten them.

I suspected that that was the real reason for this breeding program. It must frustrate that upper class to see their own children wind up as pawns, to have to pass on their splendor and holdings to some stranger or subordinate who would take it from them. For the first time I thought I understood people like the Masters and Knights. How galling, how frustrating it must be to be like a god and know that you can't pass it on, leave it to anyone. Genetic manipulation was out, as were all the scientific tests and lab procedures of the civilized worlds. What bestowed and regulated that mysterious and terrifying Warden power had eluded technological science and would elude them as well. They would have no choice but to try and breed for it. First among themselves, of course, but that hadn't worked.

It struck me that, except for Patra, virtually all the powerful people I'd heard about were male. That might be a misleading statistic, based as it was on so small a sample, but if it held, even partly, it would mean even more problems in pure inbreeding.

Hogi at least knew enough to answer that. "Well, yes, more men than women, but lots of women have it," he assured me. "No, I hear tell that when a woman like a Master or a Duke gets with child, she loses control, becomes a wild talent while carrying the child. During that time somebody could steal her job, see?"

I *did* see. With only a few thousand positions near the top and only 471 really at the top, people in those positions were always on the spot, always being challenged by newcomers—and to put yourself in the position of being wide open to challenge for nine months would be unthinkable.

"You mean the big people don't have sex?" I asked incredulously.

"Haw. Sure. When you got the power it's easy," Hogi responded. "You get cut, you just tell your body not to bleed. You also just tell your body not to get pregnant. See?" This was all said in the boy-are-you-dumb tone he usually used when talking to me.

It all fit, though. They were breeding with the strong wild talents that occasionally cropped up among the pawns' children. Trying for power *and* control—and perhaps the key to breeding power in their own young.

But this young girl had the power, even if it *was* wild, and that was the most important thing to me. I had to know a lot more about that power, and since she was the only one around who had it that I could talk to as an equal, I determined to get to know her.

Ti

The next evening, I sought her out, trying to appear as casual as I could. I had been warned that she was hard to approach and difficult to talk to, but I had no problems. Sitting on a rock off by herself and out of the torchlights, she was fanning away the ever-present swarms of tiny bugs and idly chewing on a piece of *gri,* a melonlike fruit with an odd sweet-and-sour taste.

There wasn't really too much I could do without being either corny or obvious, so I just walked up close to her and said, "Hello, there."

She looked up with those huge, little girl's eyes and smiled. "Hi. Sure. Have a seat."

"My name is—" I began, but she cut me off. "Your name's Caltremon, and you come from Outside," she shot, catching me a little off-guard. Her voice, still a youthful one, more matched her face and true age than her body.

I laughed. "And how do you know all that?"

"I seen you lookin' at me," she responded playfully. "O'course, all the men look at me, but I 'specially noticed you. They say you's sick in the head. That right?"

I found myself instantly warming to her. "I was," I told her, "but I'm better now. This is not like the place I came from, and it took a lot of getting used to."

She tossed the rind back into the bushes and shifted around, pulling her knees up against her bosom and putting her arms around her legs, rocking slightly. "What's it like—Outside, I mean?" she wanted to know.

I smiled. She was so damned cute. "Nothing like here," I replied, trying to find terms she could understand. "Not at all. For one thing, it's cooler. And there aren't any pawns or supers or knights."

I could see that this was hard for her to digest. "If there ain't no pawns, who does the work?"

A fair question. "People who want to do it," I tried carefully. "And it's a different kind of work than we do here. Machines do all the really heavy stuff."

"I heard 'bout 'sheens," she said knowingly. "But somebody gotta raise 'em and breed 'em, right?"

I sighed. The usual dead end. How could you explain machines to somebody who was born and raised on a world where nothing worked and practically nothing lasted? I decided this could be used as a back way into the subject that really interested me.

"Where I come from nobody has the power," I told her. "And when a place doesn't have the power, you can change things, make things that last. Some of those are machines, and they do what the power does here."

She mulled this over, trying to sort it out, but didn't seem to understand. That was about as far as I'd gotten with anybody else, though, which indicated she had some brains.

"Why don't they have the power?" she asked.

I shrugged. "I don't know. I don't know why some people do. I don't really understand what the power is even now." Watch it, I warned myself. Be very careful. "I hear you got the power. Is that right?"

"Well, yeah, I guess so," she admitted. "Don't do me no good, though. Y'know, like you can *feel* it inside but can't talk to it. I guess that's what them others can do. They can talk to it, tell it to do things."

"But you can feel it," I prompted. "What's it feel like?"

She unclasped her arms and slid down from the rock, stretching and rubbing her behind. She slithered over and sat right next to me. "I just can feel it, that's all," she replied. "Can't you?"

I shook my head. "Nope. Either I don't have it or I don't know how to look or what to feel."

She shrugged. "Ever look?"

I considered that, and filed it for reference.

I tried to press the subject, but she'd become bored with it and didn't want to talk about it any more. I decided not to push her. I'd made an easy friend here, and I didn't want to blow my advantage all at once. There would be other nights.

I was suddenly aware that she was sitting *very* close to me, and for the first time I realized why she was attracted to me and had noticed me before. My most outstanding outsized feature would be an almost irresistible magnet to somebody being manipulated as she was. And for the first time in this body, I did start feeling the urge, but something stopped me. She was so very young, damn it all, and for her the word "pawn" took on an even greater meaning.

After a little small talk elicited no response from me she sat up and looked at me strangely. "You ain't one of them man-lovers, are you?" she asked, genuinely perplexed.

I had to laugh. "No, not that," I replied carefully. "I—well, it's just that, where I come from, somebody my age feels funny with somebody your age." *I could have a child your age,* I added to myself.

She gave me a disgusted look. "That's what I thought," she pouted. "I dunno why that's a big deal. It ain't like I never *done* it, you know. I do it lots since I come out. Master Tang said it was good to do it." She stood up, looking miffed. "Guess I'll go up to the Super, then. He don't mind."

I sighed. This combination of child-woman was hard for me to accept, let alone cope with. I was also torn by my desire not to alienate her and my mental reaction to her as a child. How can I explain it? It was as if an adolescent who was very desirable had said, "If you don't make love to me I'll hold my breath until I turn blue, so there!" The contrast between willing and sensuous woman and small child was just something I couldn't figure out how to handle, particularly when I knew that her avid sexuality was induced by cold, uncaring men who saw her as an animal, some kind of domesticated beast. It seemed, damn it, somewhat *incestuous* to take advantage of that sort of situation.

I'd like to think that the reason I gave in that night had to do with my fear of alienating her and thus jeopardizing my only avenue of gaining knowledge.

The body Security had given me was, of course, a body of opportunity. Krega had said that they went through a lot of bodies before an imprint "took," so it was pure chance that I wound up with this one—yet it proved to be my real break. Its primitive, throwback nature gave me size and great strength, and its oversexed development had attracted Ti. In the days that followed she stayed with me and near me, at least in the evenings. On size alone I seem to have made, in her mind at least, the other men around seem inadequate. Furthermore, a playboy learns just about every variation, and variety wasn't well known on Lilith.

I kept after her, subtly and without boring her, about this power she felt and its nature. Slowly, considering her fairly short attention span, I got what I could. Late at night, with Ti lying at my side, I tried to shut out everything and everybody else and see if I, too, could "feel it."

It was an internal process, somewhat a mental process, but there was no real guide to it. Ti had been born with the power, had grown up with it, and therefore wasn't the best person to tell me exactly what to look for. The best would have been a super or higher, and they weren't going to reveal anything.

Kronlon was the key to my persistence. The man was a sadist, a petty little godlet without the brains he was born with. Yet somehow *he'd* found it, learned to use it. I will never understand the selection process for Warden worlds, I'm convinced, if a Kronlon could have been sent here instead of wiped. And sent here he'd been—or so Ti assured me. A long time ago now, of course, but that bastard had been spawned in *my* space, not here on this primitive and brutal planet.

What had he done to awaken those powers? I wondered each night. What did he feel?

Sometimes, on the border of sleep, I thought I *could* feel something stirring, something strange; but it was elusive, beyond my grasp. I was beginning to worry that it was denied me. Or perhaps the fact that this was not my body was the blocking factor. It was said to be a sense of alienness. To my mind, anyway, this body I wore, former property of the late and unlamented Cal Tremon, was alien, too—though becoming less and less so. I was not really aware of it at the time, but now, looking back, I can see more clearly.

My memories and personality were intact, but there is a biological side to us as well, one involving enzymes, hormones, and secretions. It is as if the individual, the personality, is a particularly vivid black-and-white photograph and those physiological elements add the color, the shading, the nuance. Even your sexual preferences are determined mostly by a small cluster of cells deep in the cerebrum. Such cells aren't transferred in the process with the personality; you inherit the body you get with all its physiological and chemical properties, and they change you.

Tremon's body was particularly sensitive to that sort of thing, since it was an unregulated one from the frontier. On the civilized worlds such physical and chemical properties are carefully regulated. But Tremon, the result of a random coupling of two unregulated people, was subject to all the ancient genes and the variations spawned not only by evolution but also by mutation, something spacers were particularly prone to.

Personality is built on these properties, not the other way around. Tremon was violent, aggressive, and amoral; he simply couldn't be more of the brutish male, with all that implies than he was. All these physical factors now worked on me as they had on him, and were tempered only by my own memories and personality, my old ingrained habits and cultural inhibitions. Tempered, but not damped out. Of course the longer I remained in the **body,** the more completely these factors would come to dominate my behavior. Already I was beginning to look back on my old life and existence with more than a little wonder, trying in vain to understand how I could have acted this way or that, or done this or that, or enjoyed this rather than that. It was becoming more and more difficult to think of that old life as my own. Terribly clear and vivid and the only past I had, but increasingly I began thinking and acting as if I, Cal Tremon, had somehow inherited from Security the memories and knowledge of a total stranger.

Within a couple of weeks of first meeting Ti, I found it difficult to understand my earlier reluctance about her. I understood on an intellectual level, of course, but on the increasingly dominant emotional level it became harder and harder to believe that those objections mattered.

Then one evening, on my way back to the village after a long, tiring day, looking forward to food and Ti, I heard the grass talking.

It was an eerie, alien sensation like nothing I'd ever experienced before; it wasn't any kind of conversation we humans could comprehend. It was as if somehow the grass was suddenly filled with colonies of living things in contact with one another, even between blades and clusters of grass. I was aware of a discomforting protest when I trod down some of the grass, and of a tiny tickle of relief when I moved on. I don't think it was intelligence I was sensing, but it was awareness, life of some sort, on a very basic, emotive level. And yet it was communication of a sort. For after a bit of walking I could sense a distant feeling of tension just ahead in the grass that I was about to step on.

It was a strange sensation, there and yet almost not there, sensed mostly because it was so pervasive, because there was just so damned much grass. The feeling excited me, even though I had to face the fact that I was tired, dirty, somewhat depressed, and just possibly was going nuts.

Ti, however, who joined me from her job at the nursery, seemed to sense something even before I told her about it. "You felt it today," she said, not asked.

I nodded. "I think so. It was—odd. Hearing the grass, sensing countless billions of tiny interconnected living things."

She didn't follow some of the big words but she knew what I meant and I saw an unexpected look of pity on her face. "You mean," she asked incredulously, "you couldn't hear it 'fore now?"

It was a revelation to her, as if suddenly discovering that the supposedly normal person she knew had been deaf all his life and had suddenly acquired hearing. It was that acute—almost like another sense, a sixth sense, one that grew and developed as the days went on.

Once I knew what to look for, I could find it everywhere.

The rocks, the trees, the animal life of this world, all sang with it over and above their existence as separate entities. It was an incredible sensation, and a beautiful one. The world sang to you, whispered to you.

People, too—although they were the most difficult partly because their own activities partially masked the effect, so quiet and subtle it was, and partly because it's almost impossible to observe a human being with the same objectivity as can be applied to a rock or tree or blade of grass. Yet each entity was also unique, and with a little concentration I could not only sense but actually mentally map a particular area with my eyes closed.

This, I realized, was the key to that mysterious power. My own Warden organisms, inside every cell, perhaps every molecule of my body, were in some way interconnected by some sort of energy to every other Warden organism. It was this interconnection I saw and felt and heard. It had to be what they all saw and felt and heard, all the ones with any vestige of the power.

A Supervisor sensed what I sensed and had the ability to send, through his own body's symbiotes, a message to yours—or to a rock's or to anything else's. A Master, then, could do it in more detail—could see the individual parts inside a human body and order changes in the way those cells operated.

When something died, or if it lost its primary form —such as when a rock was crushed—the Warden organisms died, and without them, the very structure of the thing became unstable and collapsed. A Knight, then, I realized, could somehow keep the Warden organisms alive under those conditions. But even then, the organism attacked and destabilized inorganic matter from outside its environment. Somehow I thought of antibodies, those substances in human blood that attack foreign substances such as viruses that invade our bodies. It seemed to me that the Warden organism acted much like an antibody on inorganic alien matter: it attacked, destabilized, and destroyed it.

Kreegan, then, could do the impossible—convince the Warden organism not to attack and destroy alien inorganic matter. And each rank could also keep lower ranks from communicating with the Warden organisms inside their own bodies, thus protecting them.

But what tuned you to your own symbiotes, allowed you to relay commands through them to others outside your own body? That I had yet to discover. The mere discovery that I could sense the communication while most pawns could not was the best thing that could have happened to me. I no longer felt tired or depressed. I had the talent. I needed to explore my powers, test them, learn how to use them, learn my own limits.

Perhaps I wouldn't equal the Lord; perhaps I'd need help, a valuable ally.

For now, though, it was enough to know, finally, what was what on this mad world—and to know, too, that my days of hauling mud for sixteen hours were numbered.

More than enough.

Chapter Seven

Father Bronz

Over the following days my increasing sensitivity to the silent communication absorbed me, and I tried to learn everything I could about it. None of the pawns were any help except Ti, who could feel the power but had never learned how to control or use it properly. Since one's position on Lilith was dependent on mastery of the power—and since social mobility usually led to the death of one of the contestants for a particular position—there were, needless to say, no instruction manuals.

Although I've lived with the sensation for quite some time now, it is still nearly impossible to describe. The best objective description I can give is a tremendously heightened sensitivity to an energy flow. The energy is not great and yet you can sense it, not as a static thing but as a continuous and pulsating energy flow from all things solid. Gases and water don't seem to be affected by the flow, although things living *in* the water, no matter how tiny, possess it.

The energy itself is of the same sort—that is, there's no difference between a flow from a blade of grass, a person, and the insects—and yet the patterns that it forms are unique. You can tell one blade of grass from another, a person from some other large creature; you even get different patterns from the billions of microbes we all carry inside us.

I was still experimenting when the stranger arrived in our little village. He'd apparently been there most of the day, walking around to different work parties and details, but hadn't yet reached mine. Early in the evening I finally saw him, relaxing in the common and eating some fruit.

He wore a toga of shiny white that seemed to ripple with his every move and a pair of finely crafted sandals that marked him as a man of extreme power. Yet he was sitting there at ease, eating with and socializing with us mere pawns. He was an elderly man, with a fine-lined face and carefully trimmed gray beard, but he was balding badly both in front, where only a widow's peak remained, and around the top of his head. He looked thin and trim, however, and was in good physical condition, as would be expected. His age could not be guessed, but he would have to have been at least in his seventies, perhaps years older.

For a fleeting moment the idea entered my naturally suspicious head that this might be Lord Marek Kreegan himself. Why he'd show up here at this particular time, however, was a mystery that pushed coincidence to the limit. Besides, Kreegan would be of standard height and build, as all the other people of the civilized worlds and I had been. This man seemed a bit too short and too broad to fit into that absolute category.

It was interesting to see the pawns' reaction to him. While they would not even address a supervisor and would treat such a person with abject servility, they freely approached this man and chatted with him, almost as equals. I found Ti and asked her who he was.

"He is Father Bronz," she told me.

"Well? What's that mean?" I responded, a little irritated. "Who and what is a Father Bronz?"

"He is a Master," she responded, as if that explained everything when all it did was state the obvious.

"I *know* that," I pressed bravely on, "but I've never seen pawns be so casual with anybody with the power before. They even steer a little clear of you because of your reputation. I mean, is he from the castle? Does he work for the Boss or the Duke or what?"

She laughed playfully. "Father Bronz don't work for nobody," she said scornfully. "He's a God-man."

That threw me temporarily until I realized that she wasn't referring to his power but to his job. Obviously, she meant he was a cleric of some sort, although I'd seen no sign of any real religion on Lilith. I knew clerics, of course; for some reason those cults and old superstitions still held a lot of people even on the civilized worlds. The more you tried to stamp 'em out, the more strength they seemed to gain.

I stared again at the strange old man. Odd place for a cleric, I thought. He must have some really weird religious beliefs if he's here on Lilith. Why condemn yourself here when you could be living the good life in some temple paid for by the ignorant? And, I wondered, how could a man of God, whichever one or ones it was, have risen to Master without blood on his hands?

I kept noticing the men and women going up to him, talking to him, in singles and small groups. "Why are they talking to him?" I asked her. "Are they afraid not to?" It seemed to me that if you were stumping for converts and had the power of a Master you could at least compel them to listen to your sermons—but he wasn't sermonizing. Just talking nicely.

"They tell him their troubles," Ti said, "and sometimes he can help them. He's the only one of them with the power who likes pawns."

I frowned. A confessor—or did he actually offer intercession? I considered it, but couldn't really figure out his function. More stuff to learn, I told myself. Though there was really only one way to do so, I hated even the thought of going up to someone with ten times or more Kronlon's powers.

I guess he noticed me standing there staring, for when the group thinned out, he glanced over in my direction and then gestured and called to me. "You there! You're a big, hairy fellow, aren't you? Come on over!" he called pleasantly, his voice rich and mellow. That was a charmer's voice, a con man's voice —the kind that could make a crowd do almost anything he wanted.

I had no choice but to approach him, although my nervousness must have showed.

"Don't worry," he assured me. "I don't bite, nor do I inflict pain on pawns or eat little babies for breakfast." He looked me over in the torchlight, and his eyes widened slightly. "Why, you must be Cal Tremon!"

I betrayed no outward emotion, but inwardly I tensed. I had a bad feeling about that recognition.

"I've heard much about you from, ah, other colleagues of yours who wound up here," he continued. "I was wondering what you looked like."

I didn't like the sound of *that* at all. It implied that a fair number of people around might know more about Cal Tremon's life and exploits than I did.

"Have a seat," he gestured at a small tuft of grass, "and for heaven's sake, relax! I am a man of God—you have nothing to fear from me."

I sat, thinking just how wrong he was. It wasn't his power I feared, but his knowledge that could expose me. Despite my misgivings, I loosened up a little and decided to talk to him. "I'm Tremon," I admitted. "What sort of stuff have you heard about me? And from whom?"

He smiled. "Well, all of the newer folk were to one degree or another in your former line of work. Reputations carry, you know, among people of like trades. You're a legend, Cal—I hope I may call you Cal. That Coristan raid alone guaranteed that. Single-handedly blowing the domes of the entire mining colony and making off with forty millions in jondite!" He shook his head in wonder. "With that kind of talent and those brains—not to mention money—I wonder they ever caught you."

"They put a Security assassin on my trail," I responded as glibly as I could, having never heard of Coristan and not having the slightest idea what jondite was or what it was used for. "They're the best at what they do and they rarely fail. The only reason I wasn't killed outright was that I'd had the foresight to stash the loot and have it wiped, so they needed me alive to get the key information and find it." That much was the truth; the briefing had been better on the latter-day career and psychoprofile.

The cleric nodded sagely. "Yes, the agents are almost impossible to avoid—and even if you get one, the rest are on you. You know the reigning Lord of Lilith was an agent?"

I nodded. "So I heard. Excuse me for saying so, but it's pretty odd to find a cleric out here, and particularly strange to find one who talks to thieves and murderers so matter-of-factly."

Father Bronz laughed. "No preaching, you mean? Well, I have my work and it's a little different. I *was* a preacher once, and a good one—the victim of my own success, I fear. Started with a tiny little church—perhaps twenty, thirty members—on a small frontier world, and it just grew until I was the dominant cleric of three worlds, two of them civilized!" His face turned a little vacant, his eyes slightly glassy. "Ah! The enormous sums pouring into the coffers, the cathedrals, the mass worship and blessing for a half million at a time! It was *grand!*" He sounded both nostalgic and wistful.

"What happened to bring you here, then?" I asked him.

He returned to the present and looked at me squarely. "I gained too much. Too many worshipers, too much money, which of course meant too much power. The church was uncomfortable; they passed me over for archbishop and kept sending in stupid little men to take charge. Then the congress and powers that be on a number of worlds we were just starting on got nervous, too, and started putting pressure on the church. They couldn't do anything, though—I'd broken no laws. They couldn't just demote me. I'd just pop up elsewhere, and my following and my order would have exerted their influence to return me. That would have been an unforgivable defeat, so they had the idea of posting me to missionary work in the Warden Diamond—the perfect exile, you might say. But I wouldn't go. I threatened to take my order and my following out of the church and form our own denomination. It's been done before when the church has become corrupt. Of course that's where they got me. They played a few computer games, got some trumped-up charges about misappropriation of funds and using religion for political influence, and here I am—exiled to the post I wouldn't go to voluntarily, transported like any common criminal."

I had the idea that nothing about Father Bronz was common. "And yet you still serve the church as a missionary here?" I asked incredulously.

He smiled. "My bookkeeping may have been lousy, but my motives were sincere. I believe in the religious part of my church's teachings, and I believe God uses me as His instrument in His work. The civilized church is as secular and corrupt as the governments— but not here. On Lilith it's back to basics—no ranks, no churches, just pure faith. Here I am with a large heathen population and no superior save God Almighty." He looked around at the pawns going about their evening routines and lowered his voice a bit.

"Look at them," he almost whispered. "What kind of life is this you are all leading? There's no hope here, no future, just a stagnant present. If you don't have the power you're a pawn in the literal sense of that term. But they're human beings all the same. They need hope, a promise of something better, something beyond this life. They'll not get it on Lilith, and they can't leave the place, so Eternity is their only hope of salvation. As for some—the criminal element, let's say—well, that's where people like me are needed most. Besides," he added, "they need me. Who else will hear their complaints, as pitifully small as they really are, and who else will speak for them with authority to their superiors? Just people like me. No more."

I had his number now, I thought. He was completely insane, of course, but in his tremendous guilt over his own criminality with his cult or whatever, he'd decided on reparation for that guilt. The martyr type. Save his own soul through saving others. Such men were dangerous, since they were far too fanatical to face reality, but they were useful, too. Useful in some way to these people, and perhaps a lot more useful to me.

Father Bronz looked over and saw Ti standing shyly nearby. He sighed sadly. "Oh, no," he murmured under his breath but I caught it.

My eyebrows rose in surprise. "What's the matter?"

He gestured at Ti. "It's a sin, what they're doing with her and with a lot of other fine girls. They're coming along too quick—and their fates once they're taken into the castles are even worse."

I felt a nervous tingling. I didn't like to think of that, and by common consent, the subject was never mentioned. Perhaps I didn't want to think of her leaving, at least not while I was here. She had helped pull me out of the black pit into which my mind had sunk and had provided me with a friend, a companion, a source of information and growth. We'd already been paired longer than anyone in the village could remember anyone else being. Though I didn't kid myself that it was more than my body and her body having stronger needs that only we two could fulfill, I still didn't like to think of the future. But I felt compelled to ask the questions.

"What will they do to her?" I found myself asking in spite of myself.

He sighed sadly again. "First they'll freeze her, so to speak," Father Bronze said slowly. "A growing, intelligent mind would be a liability to them, so they'll keep her in a state of perpetual childhood. Even worse than now. It's only a matter of finding the right part of the brain and carefully killing what's necessary. Most of the bodymasters are former physicians and can do it easily. Then they heighten the glandular secretions or whatever—I'm no doctor, I don't really know—and when everything's balanced, they'll stick her in a harem with similarly treated girls and experiment with baby after baby trying to find the key to the power and how to transmit it. It's almost a mania with the knights, and the bodymasters are happy to practice, to continue to experiment, in their chosen field."

I shivered slightly. "And they're doctors? I thought doctors *saved* lives and made bodies and minds whole."

He looked at me strangely. "What an odd sort you are, Tremon! Why, of course doctors are no more free from sin and corruption than you or I. There are good ones and bad ones, and most of the highly skilled bad ones wind up here, the better to test their grotesque theories. I've heard it said that the Confederacy encourages them in this, even provides offworld computer analysis of their work, in the hope they'll find out what makes the Warden organism tick."

I just shook my head, refusing to accept such a horrible thought. The Confederacy! It was crazy, insane, and perfectly logical, damn it. All other experiments had come to nothing, after all, and these were considered prison worlds. But Confederacy support or no, what Bronz was saying was bleak news indeed for poor Ti.

"How long before they—take her?" I asked, fearing the answer.

He looked carefully at her. "Well," he replied, "she's already had all the preliminary treatments. I'd say she would be overdue. You see, they can't let her go too long or she'll have to set an intellectual pattern for them to play with safely. In other words, she'd be too smart for them, too complicated. I suspect that you've accelerated their plans, if they're aware of the attachment you two have formed, since contact with an outsider like you would widen her world."

I started, not only because I might have speeded up this dread fate but also because Bronz had so easily noted that Ti and I had been having a relationship. "How'd you know about us?" I wanted to know.

He laughed. "A priest is many things, but an observer of human nature is one of the most important. I see the way she hovers there, the way she looks at you, like some eager puppy for her master. She's really smitten with you, whether you realize it or not. What are your feelings toward her?"

I thought about it. Just what *were* my feelings about Ti? I really wasn't quite sure myself. By no stretch of the imagination did I consider us mates, having any obligations for one another. I'd never found that sort of arrangement comprehensible anyway. But I *did* feel a great fondness for her, not only physically but because she had the potential of becoming a complete human being. She was bright and curious, and she picked up new concepts much more quickly than any of the other native-born of this crazy world. I wondered vaguely whether it was possible to feel paternal and lustful at the same time. That smacked of some sort of incest, even though we weren't in any way related, yet it summed up my feelings as much as anything, so I told Bronz as much.

He nodded. "I thought it might be something like that. Too bad, too, because with you she might have grown to be a hell of a woman."

I considered what he was saying. Potential, that *was* the word. Potential. That was what I'd found so attractive in her, in contrast to the milling pawns around. Yet it was her tragedy, too. I felt a sudden strong fury rising in me, which I couldn't quite understand or fully control. That potential was what they were going to take from her. So great a wave of anger swept through me that I almost trembled with raw, brutal emotion, and I had trouble controlling it.

Father Bronz just sat and watched me, a serious expression on his face. Finally, as I gained some control over myself and tried to relax, to beat down the alien emotional tide, he spoke.

"For the first time," he said softly, "I saw the real Cal Tremon there beside me; he was a frightening figure, fully as terrible as his legends. I felt it, too. Great power welling up inside, bubbling like molten rock almost to the surface. You are going to be a powerful man indeed one day, Tremon, if you learn how to channel and use that fury."

I just sat and stared strangely at him, a sudden awareness of myself and my own potential exploding in my mind. In that instant I knew Bronz, from the standpoint of a very powerful Master, had *felt* a surge in my Warden abilities. Now I understood why some would rise and some would not, and how it was done. The key was emotion—raw, terrible emotion. Up until that moment I had never suffered much from emotion, a weakness I could not afford in my old work as an agent. Here, though, the enzymes and hormones and all the rest that had made Tremon such a terror had come to the fore, almost consumed me. Bronz had felt it.

It wasn't just how much power you had, it was how much self-control went along with that power—the ability to take raw, unbridled emotion and channel it, control it, shape it with your intellect. That, possibly more than any gradations of power, was what separated the ranks on this world. That explained why Kronlon, with all his power, was such a little man and would always be. That also explained why Marek Kreegan had risen to become Lord. He had been a trained agent, at the absolute top of his profession, here, in this sort of situation.

It was growing late; most of the other pawns had already returned to their huts and were sleeping now. I was, for now, still a pawn, facing the usual long day of work. "Will you still be here tomorrow?" I asked Bronz.

He shook his head. "No, sorry. I have a long way to go and I've tarried too long here now. I'm due in Shemlon Keep, to the south of here. Still, it was good meeting you, and I've a premonition of sorts we'll meet again. A man of your power will rise quickly on this world, if properly trained and developed."

That remark was too important to pass up. "Trained," I repeated. "By whom? Who does the training?"

"Sometimes nobody, sometimes somebody who knows somebody," he replied enigmatically. "The best training, I have heard, is from the colony descended from the first scientists to visit this world, Moab Keep, but that's thousands of kilometers from here. Don't worry, you'll find somebody—the best always do."

I left him still sitting there and accompanied Ti to the hut. Even though the hour was late and it had been a long day I had difficulty getting to sleep. Thoughts of breaking free of this pawn life, with eventually finding and facing down Marek Kreegan filled my head. And I also thought of Ti, poor, naive little Ti and what they were doing to her. I had built up a whole army I wanted to get even with, many of whom I hadn't even met as yet.

Chapter Eight

Social Mobility on Lilith

I continued to practice as much as I could while continuing my menial labors. If nothing else, I told myself, these past weeks or months or however long it'd been had accomplished two things. One was to tone up and fine-tune Cal Tremon's body so that it felt not only totally natural but really mine. Furthermore, its —no, *my*—muscles developed to a degree I'd have thought impossible not so long ago. I was hefting three or more times my considerable weight without even thinking about it, the aches long gone. I had no doubt that I could easily bend solid steel bars.

But, oddly, it was the second thing that I, as a trained agent, appreciated the most. I had been humbled. I had been bent, then broken, with almost ridiculous ease, and the process had been humiliating.

Now, this might be a curious thing to say, but I badly needed to be humbled. I had been cocky, eager, too sure of myself when this escapade had started. Homo superior—never beaten in an assignment. I still believed that, but the place I was superior was now forever closed to me. This was a totally alien world, a world that operated on very different rules. I was out of my element here; so if I was going to win, I had to be brought down hard in order to build up again, almost from scratch. This fact, I'm sure, was the only reason I was still alive at this point. That and the fact that, though broken in the face of seemingly unassailable power, I had lost my sense of purpose but never my will to survive.

At the end of a day shortly after Bronz's departure, I walked back to the village for the evening meal with the others. I was already well into the food when I turned and looked at the faces of the others, the dirty and tired pawns of the village, and realized that something was not quite right.

Ti wasn't there. We almost always met here and ate together, and the composition of the Keep was so regular and unvarying that the few times when she'd had to be elsewhere I had always known in advance.

I started asking around, but no one had seen her. Finally I sought out some of the people she worked with at the nursery and they only said that Kronlon had come for her around the midday meal and she had gone off with him.

I frowned. Although Kronlon wasn't above taking those he was attracted to for a little fun, this was the wrong time. Kronlon, for all his power in relation to us, was just a shade higher on the scale than we pawns, and he had his own duties to perform. I had a really bad feeling about this. I stopped eating, stood up, and walked slowly through the crowd of pawns toward the supervisor's area. This wasn't an act rational people performed, but I wasn't about to let this go.

Kronlon was in. I could see him off in his little cubbyhole drinking something—probably local beer—out of a large gourd and puffing on what could have been anything from a stinkweed cigar to happy smoke. Pawns didn't get those luxuries, so I really couldn't be certain. Since it was so unusual for anyone to approach his quarters voluntarily, he noticed the movement out of the corner of his eye and turned in surprise. When he saw who it was, his face broke into an evil grin.

"Tremon! Well, well! I kinda expected you tonight!" he called out. "Come on in, boy!"

I approached, a little cautious, since even though I could sense, feel, hear, *see* the Warden organism in just about everything, including him, I hadn't had any success in actually making use of that sense. Kronlon, it seemed to me, burned a little more brightly than others whom I'd concentrated on—or was that just nerves? You never forgot the feeling he gave you, the incredible agony he could inflict merely by willing it.

I had the fleeting impulse to back out, but it was

too late and I knew it. He'd seen me, he'd invited me over—and that was a command. No matter what, I was stuck.

Kronlon sat back and eyed me with an amused smirk. "Lookin' for your little bitch, huh? Missin' your bed partner?" His eyes flashed with cruel amusement: I knew he was baiting me, the son of a bitch.

I felt a warm, uncharacteristic rush of anger rising within me, but it was partially canceled out by my fear of him. I just nodded and stayed silent.

Kronlon laughed, enjoying his power and position. Here I was a giant of a man who could physically break him in two and he was my master as surely as if I were tiny and weak, like Ti. He roared with laughter and took another gulp of his beer. "She's gone, boy!" he told me. "Gone forever. You better get used to an empty bed for a while, son, 'cause she ain't never comin' back and you may as well get somebody new. Poor big ol' Cal's just got screwed." He laughed again.

My fury and frustration was growing almost beyond my control. All this time I'd been bossed and terrorized by this moronic sadist and I was becoming fed up with it.

"Where has she gone—sir?" I managed, still held back by the threat of that terrible power within him.

My hesitant tone and manner caused him even more amusement. "You really feel somethin' for her, don't you?" he responded, as if this made his news all the more a cruel joke. "Well, boy, I got a message midmornin' to fetch her and bring her up to the Castle. She didn't wanta come, I'll tell you, but hell, she ain't got no choice." His stare suddenly became slightly vacant, his tone more serious. "Ain't nobody got any choice in anything," he added. I realized that Kronlon never liked to think along those lines. He covered his own fear and debasement by his cruelty and sadism, the only things his tiny ego really had.

I should have felt some pity for him, but all I could see was a petty little man who had neither the right nor the qualification to wash the feet of the people whom he terrorized from his position of power. I was starting to boil.

"You know what they're gonna do to her?" he taunted. "Turn her into a human cow, Tremon. You know what a cow is, don't you? Big tits, no brains!" He roared at his joke.

"You slimy son of a bitch," I said evenly.

He continued laughing for a moment, and I wasn't sure he had heard me, nor, at that point, did I even *care* if he had. I was mad, howling, seething mad, perhaps crazy mad, too. I no longer cared what this worm, this lowest of the low, could do, what pain he could inflict. Agony was a price I was suddenly willing to pay if I could just snap his slimy neck.

He had heard. "What's that you said, boy? Somethin' on your mind? Why, hell, I'll give you somethin' else to think about, by damn!" He was almost shouting now, and he stood up. There was no mistaking it now—that sense of the Warden organism within him was stronger, more intense, *brighter* somehow, now. It was rising within him.

"Hell, boy!" he roared. "Maybe I'll fix you so's you won't get so worked up no more about no women! How'd you like t'be a gelding, boy? I can fix it, I can! I can fix you!"

Then hit the force of that agony, that searing pain in every cell of my body. I reeled back, staggering, but this time that terrible pain only fueled my anger and resentment. I exploded, no longer a thinking being, but a mass of raw emotions, a hatred such as I had never known all concentrated on this one terrible little man.

I stumbled and fell to my knees; yet as that animal fury took complete control, I no longer felt the pain the way I had. It lessened, still agonizing but somehow no longer relevant.

Slowly, deliberately, I pulled myself to my feet and took a step toward him.

Kronlon's bushy eyebrows rose in surprise; his expression showed confusion, then concentration as he threw everything he had at me.

I bellowed, a ferocious primal roar of rage that echoed throughout the whole village, then charged the startled and suddenly very frightened supervisor.

He retreated a couple of steps, then came up against the table he was using and almost fell back onto it. I was on him in an instant, my huge hands around his beefy throat. Kronlon had taught me more than the true meaning of fear; he'd taught me absolute, single-minded hatred.

He struggled to pry my hands loose from his throat. Somewhere in the dim recesses of my mind I was aware that the pain, the agony, was fading now, fading fast. It didn't matter. It wasn't relevant.

I felt a surge of energy grow within me, a strange, tangible power like some terrible fist. But before I could even comprehend what was happening, the tension broke and flowed outward from me, outward to the man whom I had pinned against the table. There was a searing burst of light and heat so intense I let him go and reeled backward. I recovered quickly but was still stunned as my head came up to see the supervisor lit in a strange glow, like some eerie supernatural flame.

And then he started decomposing before my eyes.

It was a gruesome sight, but one that, given my mental state, I could view without thought and, suddenly, without feeling of any kind. His skin fell from him, then his tissues, and finally the skeleton itself, which first glowed with a terrible brightness, then faded.

As my senses started to return, I just stood there, gaping at the impossible scene I had just witnessed. Finally I approached the place where Kronlon had stood and stared at it in the near darkness.

Everything, literally everything that was solid or liquid on Lilith burned with the tiny glow of Warden organisms. Everything—the table, the grass, the dirt, the rocks, the trees, even the lamp post. Everything. Everything but the grayish powder that now coated part of the table and a little of the ground beneath it.

All that was left of Kronlon.

Intellectually I was aware that I had caused it, but deep down, I could not believe it. The truth was incredible, impossible. Somehow, in my animal fury, my own Warden organisms had picked up that emotional power and transmitted it to those in Kronlon's own cells. Burned them up. Killed them.

I turned, stunned, suddenly aware that I was not alone. A crowd of villagers stood just outside, gaping in shocked silence at the scene, scared but unmoving —almost, it seemed, afraid to breathe. As I walked toward them, they quickly drew back, their fear a real and tangible thing. Fear not of Kronlon or of retribution.

Fear of me.

"Wait!" I called out. "Please! Don't be afraid! I'm not—like him. I won't hurt you! I'm your friend. I'm one of you. I live among you, work among you."

My protestations were in vain. Clearly I was *not* one of them any more. I was a man with the power. I had separated myself from them forever, drawn an unbridgeable gap between my own existence and their eternal toil.

"It doesn't have to be like this," I almost pleaded with them. "It doesn't *have* to be a tyranny. Kronlon's gone, and I am not Kronlon."

Torlok, an elderly man in a village where most never survived that long, was something of an authority figure; he ambled forward. The others were shrinking from me as if I had some terrible disease. Even Torlok would only come so far, but he was old and experienced and past a lot of caring about men and women with the power.

"Sir, you must go now," he croaked. "You are no longer one of us."

"Torlok—" I began, but he put up a hand.

"If you please, sir. When Kronlon does not check in tomorrow morning they will send someone to see why. They will find out why and they will send us another Kronlon. Things have changed only for you, not for us."

"You could leave," I pointed out. "You have until at least midday."

Torlok sighed. "Sir, you think you understand, but you do not. You are still new on this world of ours. You say flee—but where to? To another Keep run the same? To the wild to live in near starvation with the savages, unprotected from the nobles and the wild's own beasts? Or perhaps to be hunted down like some sporting beast?" He shook his head. "No, there will be no change for us. You must go now. You must go to the Castle, tell them what you have done. You belong to their life now, not ours. You cannot go back. We cannot go forward. Go—before you unknowingly bring the wrath of the Masters upon us. If you feel anything at all for us, go—go now."

I stared at them for a moment, not quite believing what I was hearing. They were fools, I thought, who deserved their miserable lot. They actually preferred it to any sort of challenge!

Well, let them go back to their miserable lives, I told myself. This mention of the Castle reminded me that I had more than one good reason for going there. As Kronlon had said, we didn't have a choice, any of us, least of all me in this situation.

The adrenaline was ebbing, though, and I no longer felt as cocksure and all-powerful as I had only moments before. I turned and looked off into the distance, up at that fairy-tale place built into the side of the hill. Somewhere in there was Ti.

Without another word, I turned my back on the crowd that had disowned me and walked silently out of the village, out across the grassy fields toward the Castle.

Before I was halfway there I'd come down completely from the high that the power and emotional fury had given me. Now my intellectual self, my old self, was able to assume control once more—not necessarily for the better, I realized.

Up to that point I had never been anywhere near the Castle. The only people I knew who had were those like Kronlon who weren't exactly the chatty sort. I had no idea how many people were there, and of what potential power. The Knight and his family were there, of course, most of the time, and I already knew that I was no match for a Master, let alone a Knight. I wondered if I was even a match for a trained person of Supervisor rank. Kronlon was where he was because of the kind of person he had been—petty, mean, cruel, and stupid. I suspected that the first three might not matter so much, but the last was unforgivable.

I began to think that individuals like Kronlon, with a little power and small mind, were actually the sacrificial lambs. Somebody had to do that kind of work. But the risk always existed that one of the pawns who had been abused was potentially as strong or stronger than the Supervisor. When that happened, you'd probably scratch one Supervisor.

That observation led to a different line of thought. If I had been merely as strong as Kronlon, we'd have fought to a draw. If I had been *slightly* stronger, well, he'd be in terrible pain but probably alive. Master strength, at the very least.

Master strength . . . yes, but untrained. I was unable to muster that power on command, automatically, as even Kronlon could. More like Ti, I supposed, at least at this point. I wondered if that had been the reason for the caution about her. Had she at some point gotten mad and fried somebody to atoms? Somehow done so, and yet been unable to repeat the act.

I stopped in the darkened field. Was I in fact one of the elect, or, like Ti, merely a Wild Talent? That was the most sobering question I had asked myself on the journey and the most disquieting.

All those nights I had sat there, sensing the Warden organism even as I felt it now in everything around me, trying to make it do something, anything—just bend a blade of grass. I'd failed miserably, despite intense concentration and force of will. And yet I had willed a man to decompose into dust and he had done so. How? Why?

It wasn't the absence of thought, although that was certainly true in this case, since the rulers, even those like Kronlon, could accomplish such things effortlessly and at their command. Yet there was no communication with the Warden organism itself, not really. The little buggers didn't think, they reacted to stimulus. External stimulus. If the power didn't depend on thought, but could be consciously mustered, then what was it?

The answer was so obvious I had only to ask the question of myself in order to be able to answer it. It was emotion, of course. My hatred, my sheer contempt and loathing for Kronlon had triggered the Warden organisms in my own body to transmit that devastating energy signal to the organisms in his.

Hatred, fear, love . . . all these emotions triggered chemical actions in various parts of the body, including most particularly the brain. These chemicals, then, were the catalyst that the Warden organism, living symbiotically in each and every cell of my body, needed to trigger its own powers. Emotion, reduced to its chemical products and by-products, was what was needed—and that explained a lot. Training, then, in the use of these powers was really concerned with controlling areas of the brain and body normally beyond control, much as yoga and other disciplines.

The criminals who were sent here were a bundle of messed-up psyches and unbalanced, often uncontrolled emotions. In the main, those born here were more naturally balanced as a result of their static society. Furthermore they were born with the Warden organism already growing and multiplying with their cells, in a better balance with their host's bodies; thus they were more like the creatures of Lilith, in perfect balance with the organism rather than alien to it. Outsiders, then, would naturally have the edge in triggering these odd powers. Ironically, while my cold, trained, logical mind had been unable to do a thing with this power, Cal Tremon's emotional imbalances —that new part of me that made me alien from myself—had done the job so well.

I resumed walking, but slowly, reflecting on what I knew and still didn't know. It was perhaps two hours before I reached the carved stone stairs leading, in a series of switchbacks, up to the Castle itself. For the first time in a very long time I was aware of and a little ashamed of my nakedness, my dirt and grime, my wild and savage appearance that was unfit for civilized company. Those up there in the Castle were civilized, no doubt about that. Perhaps not sane by any known definition, but certainly civilized—perhaps even cultured.

I wondered what I was supposed to do now and cursed myself for not asking someone back in the village. Did you just go up and knock and say, "Hello, I'm Cal Tremon. I just killed Supervisor Kronlon and I want to join your club?" What were the procedures here?

There seemed nothing to do but climb the stairs and wing it.

Chapter Nine

The Castle

It was an imposing structure, I had to admit that. Nothing like it had existed in the civilized worlds for a thousand years or so, if then, except in children's fantasies.

And they lived happily ever after . . .

Towers rose on either side of the main gateway, a huge double door of some bronze-colored wood that filled a massive stone arch. Windows in various parts of the place, which looked big enough to house several hundred, were all of stained glass and alit with the varying colors of the artist's hand. Judging from the lights, I deduced that at least the inhabitants were still up and I wouldn't be waking anybody.

I looked around for some simpler entrance, but it seemed as if the huge wooden door was it. I wondered whether every knight on Lilith had such a building, or whether this was the aberration of Boss Tiel. Certainly on Lilith there was nothing that walls and gates would keep out to be feared by one of such power.

There being no bell, apparently, nor any other system for summoning those inside, I pounded on the great wooden doors as hard as I could without hurting myself.

I hardly expected an immediate response, and I didn't get one. Vaguely, through the thick stone walls and gate, I could hear the sound of a crowd and some music, which meant I had to compete with some interior function. Still, I kept banging away, resting a bit between tries, although I was beginning to think I might have to camp out on the Knight's doorstep until the Castle opened for business in the morning.

With all my muscles I could pound pretty good, and somebody did eventually hear the pounding. I heard a voice from above me call out. "Hey! You, there! What the hell do you want?"

I jumped slightly, then turned to locate the speaker. He was standing at one of the small tower windows. He was too far away for me to see his features and how he might be dressed, or to get any idea of his rank.

I shrugged to myself. What the hell. "I'm Cal Tremon, sir!" I responded in my loudest, boomiest voice. "I just disintegrated one of your supervisors and I was told in no uncertain terms to get my ass up here."

The man hesitated a moment, as if considering what to do. Finally he called, "Just a moment! I'll have somebody come down and take care of you!"

I shrugged again. I sure wasn't going anyplace until they came, having no place to go. I wondered what was going on inside. For all I knew I was speaking to the lowest servant in the place—or to the big boss himself.

After a few minutes the huge wooden doors creaked open a bit and a young woman emerged. She was tall and thin and had an almost aristocratic bearing about her. Years ago she'd probably been a really pretty woman, but she was now well into middle age and that usually didn't wear well on this kind of primitive world. Her hair was white and her face more wrinkled than even her age should have permitted.

What was important was that she was fully dressed in a long dress or robe of deep-purple silk embroidered with gold—an impressive uniform. At least a Master, I told myself, feeling even more helpless and not a little embarrassed by my appearances.

She approached me and walked around me, examining me as if I were some prize animal stock. Her nose twitched a bit, indicating that mingling with the common stock was not altogether to her taste. She smelled of perfumes too sweet to remember the time long ago when she must have been out in the muck herself.

Finally she straightened up, stood back, and took the overall view. I decided it was better to say nothing until she did. No use in blowing protocol.

Finally she said, "So you killed Kronlon, eh?"

I nodded. "Yes, ma'am."

"Gior said you claimed to have, ah, disintegrated him or some such term?"

I could only nod again. "That's true. He decomposed into dust at my touch."

She nodded back thoughtfully, more to herself than to me. "You use those cultured words freely," she noted, a trace of surprise in her voice. "Disintegrate. Decompose. And your speech is cultured. You are from Outside?"

I grimaced, knowing her thoughts on my filthy appearance. "Yes, ma'am. I've been here some time— how long I'm not sure."

She put her hand to her chin in a gesture of deep thought. "What were you when you were Outside, Tremon?"

I tried to look as innocent as possible. "I was a, ah, gentleman privateer, ma'am."

She snickered. "A pirate, you mean."

"For political motives," I replied. "The Confederacy had a basic concept that I disagreed with and I took action against it."

"Indeed? And what concept was that?"

"Why, this notion of equality," I responded, still sounding as innocently insincere as I could. This was far more my game. After all this time I was back in my own element. "The Confederacy attempts to make everyone equal in all things, and to have everyone share equally in all its wealth. I believe that some people are simply more equal than others and acted accordingly."

She was silent for a moment; then suddenly she broke into deep, throaty laughter. "Tremon, you *are* amusing," she said at last. "I do believe you will be a welcome addition to the Keep. Please come in— we'll see about making you look and feel a bit more in keeping with your background."

She turned and walked inside; I followed, feeling quite a bit better. After all this time of slavery and subjugation I was beginning to feel more like myself again.

The entry hall was alit with oil lamps of some sort, giving it a bright but flickering appearance. The place was damp and seemingly a lot chillier than anything I'd felt since arriving on Lilith. But the cold dissipated as we entered the main hall, actually something of an enclosed courtyard. It was large—perhaps forty meters square—and covered with an ornate floor made up of tens of thousands of tiny square tiles in different colors that formed a number of pleasing designs. In the center of the place was a waterfall, incredibly— not a big one, but a waterfall nonetheless. The water spurted from some fissure in the rock far above us and cascaded into a pool that frothed with the action of falling water but did not overflow, indicating an outlet or many of them. I gaped in wonder at such a thing, which was in many ways quite beautiful and impressive and, more interesting, highly creative. Whoever had designed this place really knew his stuff.

My hostess noticed my admiring gaze. "It *is* nice, isn't it?" she noted in a friendly tone. "Most impressive, really. I never quite tire of it. Under us the water is channeled into a number of different conduits, where it's stored for fresh water, boiled for steam power and hot water, sent through the Castle for use everywhere. The excess runs off into an underground stream." She laughed again. "All the comforts of civilization, my dear boy." She gestured as she walked, and I continued to follow her.

Occasionally we passed people in the stone tunnel-like corridors that fanned out from the central hall. I was conscious of a lot of side glances and outright stares from the men and women whom we passed, but nobody stopped or questioned us. Many of the people were simply dressed, often in nothing more than a simple kilt and sandals or grass skirt, occasionally topped by flowing robes of varying colors and designs. Others wore odd-looking shirts, pants, and heavy boots, indicating a variety of ranks. None, however, was naked. Simple innocence ended with the pawn world most of these people probably seldom, if ever, encountered.

But, simple or complex in dress and rank, they all looked clean, neat, well-groomed, and, well, *soft* compared to the people I'd known up to now. This was civilization indeed, and I felt like a barbarian crashing a formal party.

I was led finally to a modest room off one of the corridors; it came complete with wooden door and inside bolt. The room was certainly nothing fancy by any Outside standards, but was heaven to somebody who'd spent the past few months crammed into a communal tree hut. It was perhaps five by seven meters and contained a small table on which sat an oil lamp plus a closetlike recess with three deep drawers that rose from the floor before opening up into a reasonable hanging space. In the center stood a bed. A real bed, complete with silken sheets and fluffy-looking pillows. It had been an awfully long time since I'd seen a real bed.

The floor was carpeted with some sort of fur, possibly from the *nur,* the large spiderlike giants raised by one Zeis village. It felt really nice and cozy.

"This will be your room until you complete your tests and begin training," my hostess told me. "After testing and training we'll know just where you should be put." She looked at me, and her nose twitched a bit again. "However, before you make use of it we'll have to get that accumulated filth off you. Goodness! Don't pawns *ever* bathe any more?"

"They do," I assured her. "But under more primitive conditions—and their work load doesn't allow bathing on a regular basis."

She shrugged. "Well, *you* will bathe, Tremon, and tonight. Come along, I'll set you up for it. Then I've got to return to the Banquet Hall. It's not often we have a party here with so many guests, and I'm afraid you're not as important as that to me."

I took her comment without insult, since I could see her point. Comparative luxury or not, life in the Castle was probably as dull as everything else about this world, so social events would be like drugs to the addict for those born Outside who knew a better, more interesting life.

She took me to the Baths, a series of small recessed pools with steaming hot water in them. Like the entry hall, the Baths were well tiled and styled by someone more artist than architect; the combination of tiny tiles and the smallest bricks I'd ever seen made the place classically elegant.

Some young women of Supervisor rank, judging from their leafy skirts with little else adorning them, waited for us. My hostess quickly turned me over to them. It was one of the most unusual, though pleasant, baths I'd ever had. I'd have been somewhat embarrassed back in the civilized worlds or even on the frontier, but after months as a pawn being in a hot pool with a bevy of attractive young women was something I didn't mind one bit.

I was scrubbed all over by gentle, experienced hands using a frothy soap of some kind that was lightly scented; then I was given an expert rubdown and my nails clipped and trimmed, my beard and hair expertly cut and styled. If there was a more wrenching experience I'd never heard of it—from squalor to luxury in a matter of hours. I was enjoying the sensation thoroughly, feeling better and more relaxed than I'd felt since awakening aboard that prison ship. Even now, only an hour or two into this new life, those months of slave labor as a pawn seemed a distant nightmare, as if it had happened to someone else.

The women would answer no questions and seemed as expert in turning attempts at friendly conversation into inconsequential nothings as they were in bathing and giving manicures.

Finally I was led back to my room and left alone, the door closed behind me. I didn't lock it; there seemed no reason. I just flopped on that great bed—the most wonderful bed ever made, I quickly decided—and let myself relax completely. As I was drifting off to sleep, somewhere in a corner of my mind Ti's face and form seemed to peer out and look accusingly at me. I remembered no more.

Chapter Ten

Dr. Pohn and Master Artur

They let me sleep late and I did. I rarely if ever remembered my dreams, but that night was beyond all experience. I am convinced that to this day it was the deepest sleep I'd ever experienced. When I finally did awaken, it was as if a signal had been given by some means. More than likely somebody had been posted in some hidden recess to watch me throughout the night. That must have been boring as hell.

At any rate, I'd barely opened my eyes when a bell sounded somewhere far off and there was a knock on my door, which I answered with a dreamy "Enter if you will." I had overslept to extremes and felt that I'd never really wake up.

The door opened and a young boy, certainly no more than ten or eleven, stuck his head in. "Please remain here for a while," he said in a pleasant, boyish tenor. "Breakfast is being brought to you."

I just nodded, and the door closed again. I wondered whether it was a good idea to tell them that I couldn't go anyplace right now if my life depended on it. Every muscle ached, every part of my mind was filled with sponge and cobwebs. I had more than slept off my months of toil, I'd slept for the first time free of the constant and intangible tension and uncertainty that life had produced.

I lay there, occupying myself as I could by trying to locate the peephole, which wasn't difficult. In order to take in the entire room, it had to be above and probably opposite me as well. A cursory figuring of the proper angles led me to the small discolored brick niche that almost certainly had a human eye behind it.

Breakfast arrived shortly, and I struggled up to meet it. It was a relatively simple affair, true—just some wheat toast, jellies, a few small sweetrolls, and a glass of juice—but after the gruel I'd been fed the past few months, it looked like heaven. My greatest need was the mug of hot—well, I wasn't sure what it was, but it tasted something like mocha and was obviously a strong stimulant. Everything tasted simply wonderful and did the trick.

By the time young attendants of Supervisor rank had cleared my little portable breakfast table and taken it away, I felt ready for anything and anybody. The sight of people with the power acting as the most menial of servants fit my idea of what the Castle *had* to be like. From past experience in the service, I knew a general or admiral was boss, the authority figure to be feared and respected. But at Military Systems Command, for example, junior generals and admirals were only glorified messengers. Power wasn't just what you had, it was always what you had compared to those around you.

Still, the Supervisor class had it easy compared to the masses on Lilith. Their toil was dignified, civilized, and most of all, comfortable. Still, the youth of many of them marked them as native-born, and also reminded me that Ti, too, was somewhere here in the Castle. It would be delicate, but I had to see how she was faring and to help if I could. In a sense I owed all this to her.

All set for my introduction into society, I hadn't long to wait before my guide and evaluator appeared. He hadn't knocked, a sign of extreme rank, and he was something to see. Cal Tremon was a huge man, but this chap was equally large and as well proportioned, although a lot of his body was hidden by gold-braided clothing of the deepest black—a rather fancy shirt and tailored pants, the latter held up by a shiny, thick belt and tucked into equally shiny and impressive black boots.

The man himself was clean-shaven except for a thick and droopy mustache. He had a rough, experienced face, burned and etched by sun and wind. His imposing gray eyebrows set off the coldest pair of jet-black eyes I'd *ever* seen. His hair, carefully cut and manicured, was full and somewhat curly, the gray of it marking the type of man he was rather than his age —he might have been thirty or sixty for all anyone could tell.

I knew in an instant this was a dangerous man, one whose fierceness and aristocratic bearing made the late, unlamented Kronlon look as threatening as Ti. I stood up and bowed slightly, feeling we might as well get off to a good start.

"I am Master Artur," he said, in a voice so low and thunderous that it alone would be intimidating enough to make most people jump when it sounded. Worse, I was convinced that this was Artur's nice, *pleasant* voice. I really didn't want to see this old boy mad, at least not at me.

"I am Keep Sergeant-at-Arms," he continued, looking me over. I could not fathom what might be going through his brain.

"I am Cal Tremon," I responded, hoping that was sufficient.

He nodded. "So you fried old Kronlon, did you? Well, good riddance to the little rat anyway. I never did like him much, although he did his job well enough. Well, enough of that. I'm to take you over to Medical and then we'll put you through your paces. Feel up to it?"

I nodded, although still a little hung over from my long sleep. "Now is as good a time as any," I responded, and bowed again slightly.

"Come along." He gestured with his hand, and with that he turned and walked briskly out the door. I followed as best I could, noting the big man's proud, military-style gait. He was no native of Lilith, I decided, and I wondered just who and what he had been.

The Castle was far more alive during the day, with hordes of people all over, many on cleanup and maintenance errands, but a lot seemingly just milling around. They all seemed so neat and clean and civilized, though, that they produced an odd set of comparisons in my mind. What these people were to the civilized worlds, ancient Greece of our ancestral world must have been to those of the early industrial revolution. Technologically primitive did not mean truly primitive at all.

Still, the technology that was in evidence was shock enough. Since coming to Lilith I'd been conditioned to believe that such clothing and buildings and things of this nature just weren't possible here. That's why people slept inside *bunti* trees and wore nothing. Now I was beginning to appreciate the other side of the power the Warden organism could bestow—the power that was fundamental to civilized thought and society.

The power to alter one's environment for one's own ends—that was the key denied to the pawns, the element that kept them in abject misery and slavery. The capricious rules of the Warden organism said that such a power was reserved to a select few.

I *did* notice, though, the slight traces of fear in these people's faces as Artur passed, the sideward glances and forced attempts not to appear to be looking at us. No doubt about it—they were terrified of him, as were the few Masters we encountered.

Artur dropped me at Medical and told them where to find him when they were through. They just nodded respectfully and said as little as possible, but you could feel the relief when the big man left the room. They measured, poked, and probed as best they could, having no Outside instrumentation. They *did* have some clever substitutions, though, fashioned, apparently, out of things in the environment itself. A clinging sort of vine from which they appeared to be able to read my blood pressure; a small yellow leaf whose color change to red showed to experienced eyes my body temperature. All these and more were dutifully recorded with reed pens on some thin, leafy substance that served for paper.

All of these men and women were Supervisor class, though. Only after they were through with the preliminaries and satisfied did they call in their own chief. He was a small, pudgy, middle-aged man who had the look of the civilized worlds about him without the physical standards exactingly carried through. He wore a soft white satiny robe and sandals, apparently because that was what was comfortable.

"I am Dr. Pohn," he began in the usual medical manner. He picked up the sheets and glanced idly at them. "I see you're disgustingly normal. Believe it or not, just about everybody is, you know. That's the Warden organism's trade-off to us for living off our bodies. Damage almost anywhere except the brain itself is corrected, new limbs grown, and so forth. And the viruses here are too alien for any of us to have to worry about. Still, we go through the forms. You never know when you're going to find someone unusual. Besides, we're interested in comparative readings from people such as you who have demonstrated abilities with the power."

I nodded, remembering now that Tiel was obsessed with breeding a class with the power. This, then, would be the man in charge of the Knight's pet project.

"Were you a doctor—before?" I asked, both curious and trying to be friendly.

He smiled. "Outside? Yes, yes, of course. But it was a far different thing there, you know. All those computer diagnosticians, automatic surgery, and yes, despite all, some diseases to cure if we could. Here I give physicals and administer native-distilled medication when needed for minor aches and pains and nervous strain. Otherwise, I'm engaged mostly in research on the Warden organism itself."

That was interesting, even if I did think I knew

what he meant. "Have you found out anything new?"
I asked carefully.

He shrugged. "A little, but it's slow work. There *are*
certain physiological and chemical factors common to
those with it, but isolating them, let alone duplicating
them—particularly in people not born with them—is
beyond me. Perhaps with all my old laboratories and
analytical computers I could do something, maybe
even on Lord Kreegan's satellite base, but here I am
forced to be slow and primitive, I fear."

I perked up. "Satellite base?"

"Oh, yes. Didn't you know? The Medusans built it
for him years ago. Since it's Medusan, our own little
pet Wardens won't touch it, since it already has their
cousins, who are much nicer about machines and
such. He lives there most of the time."

I doubted that very much. Although Kreegan might
go there when he needed things, he'd be far too exposed to the Confederacy on such a satellite, liable
to get blown out of the sky at any time. If I were
Kreegan, I decided, I'd almost never go there. Rather
I'd let underlings take the risk and just use it as my
chief communications and command center with the
other Warden worlds and Outside.

There was nothing more to be gained from that
tack, but I wondered if I could draw him out a little in
his project. "Interesting what you say about common
chemical factors," I said casually. "I had come to the
conclusion that emotion triggered my surge of power
and that the chemicals released into my body when I
was really mad were the catalyst."

"Very astute," he responded, beaming a little.
Clearly he enjoyed his subject. "Yes, emotion is the
key, as you will find out. But each individual's threshold level for release of those chemicals is very different, nor are the amounts the same—yet the Warden
organism is very demanding of its precise catalyst.
Chemical triggering *and* will is the key. Your anger
gave you the *power* to kill; your will to kill him directed and released it. I have often suspected that
the initial trigger is what we've always called the
'killer instinct,' for want of a better psychological

term. Everybody on Lilith really has the latent power, but not everyone the force of will to use it. That's why pawns remain pawns, I suspect."

"You said you were trying to duplicate the catalysts in those who didn't have it, or didn't have it in sufficient quantities," I prompted. "How?"

He shrugged and got up, obviously pleased with my interest. "Come on, I'll show you."

We walked out and down the hall a short way, then entered a larger chamber. I stopped, a little stunned at the sight. There were a dozen slabs, equally spaced, with bedding on top of each. On each slab there appeared to be a sleeping or comatose young girl. I looked hard and spotted Ti's distinctive form far off on the slab opposite us, but while my heart felt a twinge I clamped down hard on myself so as not to betray anything I didn't have to. Not yet, not yet, I told myself.

"Are they—still alive?" I asked, hesitant, a little fearful of his answers.

He nodded. "Oh, yes, very much so. These are pawn girls who've shown flashes of strong power, usually right around puberty, but have proved incapable of repeating it, or at least of doing anything by force of will. Between their first and twelfth menstrual periods girls undergo physiochemical changes far more radical than do boys at the same stage in their lives. Since a lot of these chemical changes trigger Warden phenomena, we tend to monitor all the young girls in the Keep at that stage. In these girls it was exceptionally strong, as you might guess from their highly overdeveloped bodies."

"I thought *you* did that," I blurted, then tried to cover. "I knew one of these girls. That's why I'm so interested." At least that much was the truth.

He appeared to be a little surprised, but accepted the statement without further thought. "Oh, no. The condition's a by-product. I believe that during this critical change in the body, the Warden organism gets confused, misfires, or receives the wrong instructions —or misinterprets the chemical stimuli it does receive. Not all girls experience this, by any means. One in a hundred, at best, and out of these, one in another hundred show strong power and bodily misdevelopment. Those are the ones we test and measure and keep a close watch on, although the very unpredictability of the power during that stage limits me. I could be killed or maimed during such an involuntary exercise of the power, and though I'm willing to risk it, Sir Tiel is not. Therefore we leave them in pawn villages until the danger is past. Which one did you know, by the way?"

I pointed to Ti. "That one, over there."

"Oh, of course. She's the newest, so it's most likely. I'm still doing a preliminary analysis on her, so I can't say much as yet, but she had the most potential of any I've seen. All sorts of phenomena around her, including the most severe. Among other things, she crippled half a dozen people around her, including her mother."

I shook my head in wonder. Little Ti a crippler? It didn't seem possible, I told myself. Still, it made me slightly uneasy, too. I'd slept with her a great deal in the past few months, and if she'd still had any of that wild power I could have been harmed, too.

"What are you doing with them now?" I wanted to know.

"Testing and measurement, as I said," Pohn replied. "All Masters and above have the power to see within others. Rank is mostly a matter of fine-tuning your reception, you might say, in our little society. A Supervisor senses, and therefore controls, only the total organism. You killed Kronlon, it's true, but you couldn't discriminate enough to affect just, say, his arm. I can isolate even more than that, much more. What I used to do with microscopes and microsurgery techniques I can now do without any mechanical aid. By concentration and study I can actually follow a single white blood cell completely through the circulatory system—and divert it, slow it, alter it, even destroy it. You can sense the Warden organism in everything, can't you?"

I nodded.

"Well, imagine being able to isolate individual cells

in any organism. That's what a Master can do. Naturally, without my medical training they'd have no idea what they were doing, so my knowledge gives me the edge here. Masters have different skills based on knowing what they are looking for and what they want to accomplish. All the power of a Marek Kreegan will do you no good at all if you don't have the knowledge and the fine touch, the skill or art, to make full use of it. That's why you see the power used so often for purely destructive ends. To destroy something is easy and requires far less knowledge or skill."

I could see his point, and thought that many doctors back on the civilized worlds would envy his power as much as he envied their technology. To be able to look into the human body, to focus on any part of it one wanted, to study it at will in the most exacting and intimate ways possible—none but sophisticated medical computers Outside could accomplish anything like it, and the doctors and technicians controlling them had to trust them, never knowing exactly what it was the computers saw as they probed and analyzed.

Pohn, however, knew.

"They're so still," I noted. "Drugged?"

He shook his head. "Oh my, no! That would simply complicate things. No, I simply applied a block to certain areas of the brain, one I can remove at will. They go into deep coma and I can then study them, probe, do whatever I want or need to do. Of the batch, I'm looking for ones with key enzymes in sufficient quantities perhaps to trigger the power. Those I'll work with until I feel I can trigger them at will; then I'll start trying to educate and train them as best we can. Kria there, for example, can now dissolve solid rock at my command." He pointed at one girl near the door.

I frowned. I had a bad, uneasy feeling about all this and about Pohn in general. Why was a doctor like this on Lilith at all? I asked myself. Did he perhaps have an unhealthy fondness for little girls? Or did he perhaps experiment capriciously on such people back Outside? I knew him now, although I'd never met him or heard of him before. There have always been people like Dr. Pohn in human history, the monsters whose thirst for experimentation caused a total disregard for any concept of morality. Shades of the old story about the man who'd created a bloodthirsty monster, leaving the question of who truly was the monster—the thing, or the man who created it?

These young girls—reduced to zombies, biological specimens, perhaps playthings for this man's sport. I thought of Ti in his hands and didn't like what I was thinking at all. Still, I said nothing of my feelings. Instead I asked, "I assume you're trying breeding experiments, too?"

He nodded. "Oh, yes. Based on the idea that the proper chemical in the proper amount is an inherited and inheritable characteristic. Frankly, I doubt it is more than one in many factors, but Sir Tiel is obsessed with the idea. I'm afraid that his level of biological sophistication is about on a par with the belief of spontaneous generation, but what can I do? I work for the man, and he's a skillful and able administrator. I humor him; he indulges me. What's the harm?"

What's the harm? I thought sourly. What, indeed? As long as you didn't regard any of these girls as more than lumps of flesh, no higher or lower than the great insects raised and bred in the Keep. *That* was the barbarity at the core of this civilization, I told myself. Only a select few were people.

Precisely the underlying philosophy you'd expect on a world run by the most brilliant criminal masterminds humanity had spawned. Men like Dr. Pohn, sociopathic and probably psychopathic—and men like Cal Tremon, pirate and mass murderer, I reminded myself.

"We really have to ring for Artur now," Pohn said, turning and leaving the chamber. I followed him. "I'm afraid I've taken much too long with you, and it doesn't pay to get him too angry."

"This Artur—what did he do? Outside, I mean?"

"To get here?" the doctor chuckled. "Oh, I don't know the details. He was somebody very big in the Confederacy military hierarchy, I think. A general, maybe, or an admiral. Ignited the atmosphere of

some planet years ago, as I remember. Killed a few
billion people. Something like that. Always said he
was scapegoated for doing somebody else's dirty work.
That's all I know. A nasty man, though."

I had to agree. *Killed a few billion people* ...

Given enough time I'd remember who he was, I
was sure of that. I'd also remember that the comment
on the death toll meant as little to Dr. Pohn as if the
death toll had been in cockroaches.

Chapter Eleven

Choosing a Different Road

Master Artur was prompt and didn't seem the least
put-out. He was just as cold and mean as always, with
no trace of anything more or less. I began to wonder if
the man were human.

For the next hour or so we went on a tour of the
Castle, armed with a nicely drawn map that Artur
handed to me. The place was very logically laid out
more or less in a D shape, with corridors fanning out
in all directions to main function halls and rooms,
each of which were also connected in the rear semicircle by service passages. Along each corridor were
living quarters, storage, and other necessities, including group bathrooms. The corridors were arranged
somewhat on a caste basis, with the bulk of them devoted to the Supervisor class that did the real work of
the place, then the two on either side of the central
passage for Master rank, and the center of course
leading to Sir Tiel's luxurious quarters and those of his
immediate family.

Not shown on the map, I noticed, were the inevi-
table secret passages between rooms and those perhaps
above and below as well, such as the one from which
they spied on me. Their absence didn't surprise me,

but I decided that I really wanted to know more about them.

Outside the Castle Artur's pride and joy was quartered in a large compound against the side of the hills. It was almost a stockade, made of great logs with catwalks and guard towers that reminded me of some primitive fortress. Artur had been totally cold, dry, and formal during our tour and seemed distant from everything and everybody, but now he seemed to warm and those chilly eyes lit up.

"Not a part of the regular tour," he told me, "but I have to go down and check them out anyway, so you might as well come along."

"Them" turned out to be enclosed herds of great insects the likes of which I had not really seen before on Lilith or anywhere else. Trained Supervisor-grade personnel scurried about when Artur approached, so by the time we entered the huge compound they were all set and waiting for him. Lines of them, rows and rows of them, in tight quarters but nonetheless mighty impressive.

They sat there in formation, huge *wuks,* as they were called, their bodies a bright green with a whitish underbelly; they were fully three or four meters long on six thick, powerful bent legs, their heads dominated by great luminous ovoid eyes flanking a curled, whiplike proboscis that concealed a nasty, beaklike mouth. Their skins were perfectly smooth, but I got the impression of a strong skeleton just beneath that made them far less fragile than they looked.

Each had a saddle tied to it between the first and second pair of legs; it was an elaborate seat with a hard back and an X-shaped restraint to cover their riders and hold them in. The riders, in black pants and boots, were both male and female, but all looked tough, hard, and well-disciplined. There was an array of what I could only guess were weapons, from pikes and staffs to what might very well have been blowguns. They were situated so that the restrained rider could get at them easily and quickly.

"I am impressed," I told Artur (and I wasn't kidding). "But this looks like an army to me—mounted cavalry. I wouldn't think you'd need an army here."

Artur chuckled. "Oh, yes, indeed we do," he responded. "You see, basically in order to move up in this society you have to kill somebody—be stronger than they were. Now, *you* tell *me*—if you were Sir Tiel, would you keep going day after day in challenges against everybody who thinks he can knock you off? Of course not. And neither do any of the other knights. And what do you get for it? A lot of bowing and scraping, of course, but mostly a shitload of administrative headaches. There are probably hundreds of masters stronger than most of the knights, maybe even stronger than the Duke himself, but they just don't want the job. A lot do, though. So I'm charged with seeing that it's a bit more difficult to challenge the Knight of the Keep—a policeman, you might say. And if one knight wants something another knight has, well, they can challenge knight to knight —but they'd probably end up either dead or in a draw, so there's no profit in it. So we fight a little. Anybody who wants anything from *this* Keep has to either bargain for it in a nice way or fight for it—and that's where these troops come in."

I nodded, my view of Lilith changing a bit once more. At first I couldn't see why they'd have fighting on a local scale, but then I realized that it was the safety valve, you might say. These squabbles tended to keep the most dangerous of people on Lilith—the psychopaths, war-lovers, violence-prone troublemakers, that sort—occupied. If they liked to beat one another's brains in, give them a forum for doing so, an outlet for their violence that didn't mess up the nice, neat system. I could see an astute administrator, particularly one with a lot of troublesome, violence-prone people, actually starting a war with a neighbor now and again just to relieve the tension—and perhaps the boredom.

"The *wuks*," Artur was saying, "use those big hind legs of theirs to leap high into the air if they want to, with the soldier aboard. That's why the people are strapped in, but have their arms free. They can jump behind static ground lines with ease, making fixed fortifications useless. Up on the hill, there—you can see all those holes, almost like a honeycomb—are my *besils,* swift flyers that are, so to speak, my air force. Combine them with ground troops and you have a force that, properly employed, is almost invincible." He said that last not in a bragging tone but with the ring of truth and conviction about it. The key phrase was "properly employed." I had no doubt that Artur was one hell of a good field general.

A neat system, I had to admit. The knights, fat and comfortable, didn't want to challenge each other. The lack of any kind of instant communication meant that the acquisition of large areas, the consolidation of Keeps under one rule, would be difficult and profitless to maintain. And any challenger to the knight would first have to get past the Castle and its defenses—no mean feat. No matter what power anybody had, an arrow or spear would still kill him if it landed properly —would kill even Marek Kreegan himself.

I could just see knights sitting around at parties given by one or another of them making bets on whose army was best, whose commander was most skillful. I was willing to bet that Artur had won a lot of those wagers.

We walked back to the Castle after Artur's formal inspection. Off in the distance I could see the pawns, countless numbers of them, working in the fields and tending the herds. Only then did I think of them on an emotional level. I had been out there only a day before, yet already the social gulf separating us was an almost solid, impenetrable barrier. There seemed something wrong about that and something profound, as well, that said a lot about the ruling classes and the ruled; but I couldn't put my finger on it. Still, I was closer to them than to people like Artur and Pohn. But I was no match for the lowest, stupidest supervisor stablehand in the place.

We went to the supervisors' dining hall, and I suddenly realized how hungry I was. It had been many hours since that light breakfast, and even though I'd done little to work anything off, I was used to a lot more bulk.

"I will leave you here," Artur told me. "For the next few days, you have the run of the Castle. Relax, talk to people, learn the system. When we're ready, you'll start classes to see how your power can be developed." His furry brows narrowed a little and he looked at me hard. "Don't get too cocksure in those classes, boy. Remember, it's not just a test of power and will but an intelligence test, too. Remember where Kronlon wound up." And with that he was gone.

I was dimly aware that I had been given a kindness by this strange, aristocratic man. I pondered his words as I ate heartily the best meal I'd had in months, and I think I understood what he was saying.

They wanted you to develop what powers you had, of course, the better to fit into the system and serve the bosses. But suppose you did *too* well. If you proved out stronger than a Master, say, would your host and boss suffer you to live? Not likely. But it wouldn't do to slack, either—or you would wind up out in the muck with the pawns. Tricky indeed, this social system.

I spent the next couple of days making friends with some of the Castle staff, exploring the Castle and its many byways and learning what I could about the passages, somewhat euphemistically referred to as "service corridors," not shown on the maps. From casual friendships I learned several things I had to know, not the least of which was that the party held the night I'd arrived on the scene was in honor of Marek Kreegan himself, in on one of his surprise tours. Nobody had seen him—not even those who served at the fete could say what the Lord of Lilith looked like. I had the strong impression that not even the man who owned the place knew which of his guests was Kreegan, whose powers to cloud minds was legendary and whose passion for anonymity was absolute. Duke Kosaru was the nominal guest of honor, but they all knew that Kreegan had been there.

Was he still here? I couldn't help but wonder and looked suspiciously at all those of Master class I came in contact with who were not obviously of Zeis Keep.

I also dropped in on Medical from time to time, mostly to see what, if anything, was to happen to those girls on the slabs, particularly Ti. I could hardly understand my fixation with her; in the past I'd always been coldly detached toward sexual partners and even friends. Most were shallow individuals anyway, and those who weren't were a danger to me of one sort or another, as I might have been set after one or another of the exceptional ones at some point. That worried me, really, since I always had such a clear idea of who I was, what I wanted, and what my place in the universe was.

Cal Tremon, what was your body making me into? Was I in fact no longer immune from the emotional factors I always believed had set me apart from the rest of humanity?

Most of my attempts to see Pohn failed. He was a busy man, it seemed, and hard to catch in any one spot. A doctor on a world where nobody got sick and where almost all injuries healed themselves perfectly or regenerated what was missing had a lot of time for research, and I knew some of the directions that research was taking. I *did* learn from his assistants that he was responsbile for the supercreatures of Artur's force, selective breeding and genetic manipulation by sheer force of will alone accomplishing wonders. Anybody that godlike could hardly resist doing the same to people.

I *did* catch him in one afternoon, though, and he was happy to see me. Apparently I was one of the few who seemed truly interested in his work, but I realized I was treading on eggshells around him. In his own way he was at least as dangerous as Artur, if only because his powers were more far-reaching and far more subtle.

Finally, though, we were again in that eerie, funereal room with the twelve comatose girls. I saw that Ti was still among them.

"How do they eat?" I asked him. "How do you keep them from developing circulatory problems, all the troubles inherent in not moving? For that matter, how do they go to the bathroom?"

He chuckled. "It's a matter of routine," he explained. "I and my assistants handle each of them at four-hour intervals. It's quite simple. Watch." With that he went over to the nearest unconscious girl, made a cursory examination of her, then stepped back a little.

"Kira, sit up," he coaxed more than ordered. The girl, still dead to the world, eyes closed and breathing regularly, sat up. It was a ghoulish sight, as if a corpse had suddenly reanimated itself without ever really coming to life.

"Open your eyes, Kira," he instructed, still using a gentle tone, and she did; but it was clear there was no thought behind the large, pretty brown eyes revealed there.

"Get out of bed and stand next to it, Kira," Pohn instructed, and again, with a smooth, fluid motion and no wasted moves, she did as she was told. I, who had killed without thinking about it more than once and had seen a lot of horrors in my life, shivered slightly.

"She's like a machine, an android," I said.

Pohn nodded. "Yes, yes, that's pretty much it," he agreed. "But an android is as complex as the human body. Here, with techniques like these, I will one day learn the secret of the Warden organism. With subjects like these I have already gone further than I dared hope when I started."

"Are they—aware—of what is happening?" I asked him.

"Oh, no, no, no," he assured me. "That would be far too cruel. With a lot of experimentation I have determined the location of what I might call the key neural connectors, although that's a layman's simplification. Their thinking part remains as if in the deepest sleep, while the rest, their physical part, can be awakened and stimulated—I call it external motivation—to do things their conscious minds could not. Here, I'll show you. Kira, follow me one step behind me, stopping when I stop and walking when I walk."

The girl followed him out the door like a shadow, and I followed them. We wound up in a small lab whose walls were the solid natural bedrock of the mountain itself, rough and unfinished. He positioned her at least three meters from one of these blank, rocky walls.

"During that key puberty period, Kira was able to influence the growth of plants—they grew almost as you watched—and she actually made small earthquakes in her local vicinity. Then the power passed, as it does in all but a few, and I wound up with her here. Working with her, I've been able to discover a large number of chemical stimuli to certain areas of the brain. She supplies the power and the stimuli, I supply the willpower." He looked around the barren room. "Do you sense the Warden organism here?"

It had become almost second nature to sense that odd feeling of life all around, even in the most passive and inanimate of things. I felt it, of course, in every molecule of the rock that framed the room, and nodded to him.

"Good. Now watch. Kira, about two meters up on the far wall I want you to hollow out a fifty-centimeter cube from the rock with your mind." He stood back, and for some reason I shrank back as far as I could.

I was aware that Pohn was concentrating on her, more than likely triggering those stimuli, those enzymes or whatever that built up the power.

"*Now,* Kira," he breathed.

What happened was almost anticlimactic. No crackle of lightning, no rumblings or anything like that. It was just that . . . well . . .

I heard a click and then a sound like falling plaster or dirt dislodged over the side of a precipice. Just a little sound—but there was now a cube of roughly fifty centimeters cut into the wall, with a heap of fine powder inside.

Dr. Pohn went over and brushed the powder out and gestured for me to approach. I was a little nervous about getting in the way of that kind of power, but I did examine the hollow the girl had created at Pohn's direction. It was perfectly smooth, very regular, with no sign of how it had been formed.

"Just proof that the potential is in all of us," he told me. "More, I think, in women than in men for some reason. At least the women seem stronger in their powers, although more erratic. I have girls in there who could possibly reduce this castle to dust if properly stimulated and motivated."

"It would seem to me that the Boss and his superiors might find you something of a threat, Doctor," I noted.

He laughed and shook his head from side to side. "Oh, no. I'm quite strong, quite powerful, but I have no taste for knighthood. It would end my work, really. I'm no risk because they all know of my lack of ambition with regard to their jobs. In fact, they encourage my work because it might help them. Master Artur, for example, is quite interested in one of the girls, who, we think, might well be able to freeze an attacking army, perhaps even dissolve it."

We walked back to the "morgue" as we talked, the zombielike Kira following obediently.

"Which one?" I asked, feeling a little queasy.

"That one," he replied, pointing, as I suspected, directly at Ti.

I was becoming pretty good at locating the secret passages. Oh, I'll admit I didn't try the ones they'd guard and booby-trap, the ones leading to Sir Tiel's quarters, but the rest were more than handy. You could almost live inside the small passages and corridors in the walls, although you'd have trouble avoiding the others who used them regularly—some on business (such as spying) and some just for fun, such as voyeurism. Everybody knew about them, of course, but few really thought much about them.

My lessons started about a week after I arrived at the Castle, and they were what I was most interested in. My tutor was Vola Tighe, sister of the elderly matron who'd admitted me in the first place. Unlike her sister, though, Vola was far more serious and businesslike and seemed to have a better idea of herself and her duties. Still, outwardly they might have been twins and may well have been.

"The key is chemical stimuli, as you know," she told me. "The *trick* is to be enough in control of yourself that you can reach inside your own head and trigger exactly what you need when you want it, then direct the result by force of will. Everyone on Lilith has this potential, but it is psychology that makes the difference. Not everyone on Lilith—not most, thank heavens—possesses the concentration, willpower, sheer intelligence to learn and execute the techniques properly."

"Dr. Pohn thinks otherwise," I pointed out. "He thinks we're born with different levels of stimuli and most of us can only do so much."

"That pervert," she responded in disgust. "He was a quack even back on the frontier. He's just a sadist with a fondness for poor little girls, and don't you forget it. The Boss indulges him—partly because he fears him, I think, but mostly because Pohn feeds him the scientific nonsense to back up what Sir Tiel wants to hear. I think it's simply *disgusting* what he does up there to those poor little girls; it's very much like what he got caught doing that caused him to be sent here in the first place. But as long as he restricts himself to pawns, he's safe."

As long as he restricts himself to pawns . . . I thought back at my own condemnation of the villagers, my almost identical feelings, and really couldn't see what was wrong with the logic. And yet somewhere there *had* to be a flaw, for the wrongness of this casual attitude toward the majority of Lilith's population nagged at me. On the civilized worlds it was different, I told myself. There the majority was *Homo superior,* perfect in mind and body, sharing equally in the work and in the good life, the utopian dream realized. There the inferiors were cast out to the frontier, or ferreted out and eliminated by ones like me and killed or . . . .

Or sent to the Warden Diamond.

If Vola was right and Pohn wrong, though, I told myself, it meant that the potential to turn this class-infested tyranny into a true paradise was possible, and perhaps the result most to be wished. The parallels with human history generally seemed to apply here. Those with the power had always enslaved the masses and gathered the wealth for their own ends until finally the masses rose up against the unfairness and the revolution came, casting the tyrants out. With human civilization, the enormous explosion of technology had put most manual labor into the history books and a master computer in everyone's pocket. Control of technology had been the key to human advances; control of the Warden power here would be the equivalent. If everyone on Lilith could be taught the power, then the Dr. Pohns of this world would quickly be eradicated. I realized then that Vola didn't understand this extension of her own logic, didn't follow the implications to their ultimate conclusions, but I knew now what sort of cause I might devote my life to after . . . what?

After I became Lord of Lilith.

I turned back to my lessons.

Most of the preliminaries were basic stuff, a lot of esoteric biology, a lot of Warden history, that sort of thing. Most of it I knew, and some of the mental conditioning exercises were pretty similar to those I underwent in training as an agent. It was absurdly easy —and obviously only preparatory to the real thing. What I lacked for the first few days was the key, the catalyst. I could already regulate a lot of my autonomic functions—heartbeat, respiration—and could deaden pain centers, that sort of thing. It took a little adjustment with a new body, but once you knew how, it was easy to reassume control. But these people weren't mental marvels or miracle workers; there was an edge they had and I needed it.

I had made such progress, though, that by the fourth day Vola decided I was ready. She entered my study cell with a small gourd brazier and ignited a fire under it. From a small skin pouch on her hip, she poured a transparent golden liquid into the gourd and allowed it to boil. The vapors alone were pretty odd and made me feel somewhat light-headed.

Satisfied that it was right, she turned to me. "This is a drug," she explained needlessly. "It is distilled from a somewhat poisonous plant, the *hudah,* found in the wild. The early science team that was stranded here started experimenting with all the wildlife, for they realized they had to understand their environment in order to live in it. This particular mixture provides the best catalyst they found for the Warden organism, causing a permanent change in you over a period of time—several dozen administrations, at least. The carefully measured dosage, given at exacting intervals, changes a key element within your cellular structure, giving a message, as it were, to the Warden organisms inside to direct a slightly different enzyme balance. Drink it down, completely if you can; if it is too hot for you, let it cool slightly. The heat simply aids absorption into your bloodstream."

I nodded and told her I understood. Inwardly I was elated. *This* was the edge, the key to real power. I drank the steaming liquid eagerly, burning my tongue slightly as I did so, but I didn't mind. It tasted bitter and nasty, but I'd expected it to be even worse. The potion made sense, in a way. It was a natural product of Lilith, it contained Warden organisms in its own molecules, and it was the natural complement to what I'd been told about how this all worked.

The only question I had, one not likely to find an easy answer, was how the hell anybody had ever come up with it. You could ask that about most great discoveries, though, I admit. Accident, probably.

The stuff burned inside me, but I felt no immediate effects. I looked at Vola. "If this is truly a chemical key, then why won't it work for everybody? Why wouldn't it work for the pawns?"

She smiled a little patronizingly. "It has only slight, random, and usually destructive effects on pawns. We have found that you have to have reached a state of power without its aid before it will work. Your action with the unfortunate supervisor prepared the way, made your brain willing to accept what is

now being done. You see, this is the next test. Anyone
not of the power will die from the poison."

I coughed a little and looked at her in surprise.
"Now is a fine time to tell me that!"

"Sit back and relax," she instructed, an undertone
of amusement in her voice. "Let it take control."

I *could* feel the potion start to work now, causing an
odd, slightly hallucinogenic effect. The dimensions of
the room seemed to be wrong, for one thing, and
Vola herself, even the little brazier she was now putting away, seemed slightly fuzzy, distorted. I felt
slightly flushed, as if I had a mild fever, and I realized
I was sweating heavily.

Vola came over, put her hand on my face, turning
it slightly, then examined my eyes. She nodded to herself, then stepped back. "Now," she said, her voice
sounding hollow and like an echo in my ears, "let's
see how strong you really are."

The distorting effect seemed to pass rather quickly,
to be replaced with a different sense that might be
equally false. Suddenly everything seemed sharper,
more detailed and focused, than I could ever remember in my life. I had been slightly sighted, it appeared,
and now I could fully see.

I saw more than room and its human and inanimate contents; I also saw the Warden organism. Saw
it and heard it, sort of, but in a way I'd never known
before. For the first time I realized how Dr. Pohn
could literally see into cells, or the physicist into the
very molecules. The whole universe seemed open to
me, big and small, depending on the focus of my will,
and I could see any part of it no matter how tiny. It
was a heady, godlike feeling like nothing any human
off Lilith could possibly imagine. And I kept thinking,
*this is no drug-induced hallucination, no distortion of
the senses—this is for real!*

More important than sensing the Warden organism
in other things, I was equally if not more aware of
it within myself. The incredibly minute living things
were within me, were one with me, part of me. I
reached out and touched them and felt them return
that mental touch, felt a sense of pleasure and excite-

ment within those tiny creatures at the recognition of their existence. And yet the Wardens within me were also part of a larger organism, the organism that was everything on this crazy planet, all linked, all one, in communication as the cells of the body are in communication with their parts and with the cells around them.

"Now you see how it feels," I heard Vola's voice as if from some distant place. "Now you know the truth of the power. Now you can use it, shape it, bend it to your will and your direction."

I turned and looked at her as if seeing her for the first time. Kronlon had acquired a shine, an intangible brightness you more felt than saw, when he'd mustered his limited powers against me. Vola, too, shone, but her light was so much more intense than Kronlon's that it made him seem less than a pawn, less than a tree or blade of grass. It was not a physical shining; another observer would have seen nothing. It was instead an inner burning sensed by the tiny microorganisms within my very cells and related to me.

She pointed, a radiant, supernatural being, at a small wicker-type chair in a corner of the cell, and I followed her arm to focus upon it.

"Look not at the chair," she instructed, "but *within* it. Make contact with the host within."

Doing so was absurdly easy, requiring no thought at all. I just looked and lo! I *knew* that chair, was one with that chair, saw how it was made and how its very molecules were bound together.

"Order the chair to decompose, but do not kill that which is within," Vola ordered. "Release it to become again what it was."

I frowned for a moment, trying to understand exactly what she was saying. Then suddenly, I saw the whole pattern in her meaning. The chair was alive, bound together as an organism by someone's commands, the Warden organism there going against its nature to hold itself in that pattern and remain a chair. The geometry of the pattern was clear to me, and it was hardly a gesture to release it, to snap the pattern and allow the organism within to redirect the cells of the chair—somehow still living, although long separated from its parent plants—to their normal state.

The chair decomposed rapidly, but did not come apart. As old patterns were dissolved, new patterns were woven, patterns that were instinctive to the tiny things within it. The visible effect was as if the chair had dissolved into dust, then swirled around, the tiny dust particles coming together in a new series of shapes that were somehow *right*.

Where the chair had stood were now the stalks of seven plants, the parent plants from which the reeds that had made up the chair had been cut. They were living plants, and they were drawing from the stone floor beneath them to gain what was necessary to sustain themselves.

"Now," Vola breathed, sounding slightly impressed, "put the chair back together again."

That stopped me cold. Hell, that pattern was so complex it was almost unbelievable. I could undo it, of course, but to put it back—that was something else again.

Damned killjoy, I thought sourly. Until now it was so much fun to be a god.

"The next lesson," she told me. "Power without knowledge or skill is always destructive. You can unmake with ease, but it takes a lot of study to build instead of destroy."

"But how?" I cried in frustration. "How can I know how to build, to create?"

She laughed. "Could you have physically made that chair?" she asked me. "Could you have taken an axe, cut the right stalks to the right lengths, then bound them together physically to make such a thing?"

I thought about it. Could I? "No," I had to respond. "I'm not a carpenter."

"And that is the way of Lilith, as elsewhere," she told me. "To use the power well in a specialized area is important but requires memorizing the proper patterns and then some practice. But we have an advantage here that those who do not have the power lack," she went on, and I was aware she went to the door, stepped out, then came back in with an identical chair, placing it near the plant stalks in the corner. She stepped back.

"Look at the chair," she ordered. "Be one with it. Know its pattern."

I did, and it was far easier than last time now that I knew just what to look for.

"Now, using the chair as a model, put the other chair back together," she instructed.

I frowned. Having just been pulled down to earth from godhood, I was now being ordered to elevate myself again.

"Is that possible?" I managed.

"It is if you are powerful enough," she responded. "Supervisors can destroy and, to a limited extent, stabilize things they make. You have already shown yourself a Supervisor. But the supervisor, like the pawn, must build or physically make everything himself. A Master may do more. A Master may take the very elements that make something up and rearrange them to suit himself. Are you a Master, Cal Tremon? Can you be a Master?"

She was pushing, I realized, and I hesitated within myself before going further. We were beyond this lesson, I suspected, beyond whatever we were supposed to prove. Had I in fact done what Artur cautioned against—done what I was supposed to do too effortlessly, too well? Should I make this attempt she demanded of me?

The hell with it, I told myself. Let's see just what I'm made of, whether the computer that selected me as the best person for the job knew its stuff. If I had the potential to be a Master, and I'd better, I wanted to know it. I'd spent too long marking time in the mud and the muck and I was impatient.

I stared at the chair again, saw its pattern, how it was bound up and tied together. Now I looked at the strange tubular plants growing where the other chair had been, and I again linked with the Warden organism within them while trying not to lose the contact and, well, *communion,* with the chair. It was a tricky juggling act, since the molecular structure was the same for both and it was hard not to confuse them.

I ordered the Wardens in the plants to disunite once again, to break down as they had before, untying their current plant pattern. Keeping a mostly mental eye on them, I concentrated hard on the existing chair, the pattern, the way it was bound up and tied together.

There were a lot of false starts, a lot of confusion; at one point I almost had the chair dissolving instead of the plants recombining. I don't know how long it took, but finally I succeeded. Two chairs stood there side by side, looking like twins from the same mass-produced, computer-controlled factory. I was sweating like mad and my head throbbed, but I had done it. Totally exhausted, I sank to the floor and gasped for breath. Vola, however, was more than pleased.

"I didn't think I could do it," I admitted, breathing as hard as if I had been lifting heavy stones.

"You are strong indeed, Cal Tremon," she responded. "Very strong. Many of my past students have risen to be Masters, but only four have ever accomplished that exercise on one dosage. Most never are able to do it, and they remain supervisors. Many, like your Kronlon, could not even decompose the chair without killing the organisms within. Others, the bulk of them, manage that much—and no more. A *very* few can do the reassembly, but only four before —now five—have done it on the first try. It will become easier now each time you do it, although the pattern for such a chair is simple compared to most other things."

"The other four," I pressed, feeling completely washed out. "Anybody I know?"

She shrugged. "My nephew, Boss Tiel, for one," she replied. "Also Dr. Pohn and Master Artur. And Marek Kreegan."

My head came up. "What? You taught *him?*"

She nodded. "Long ago, of course. I was very young then, no more than sixteen or seventeen, but I was here, as I have always been. I am one of the rare ones, Tremon—a native of considerable power."

That was interesting, but the information about Kreegan was more so. This explained why he returned here off and on and why he might permit a party in his honor here, of all places. Decades ago Kreegan, too, had been landed right here in Zeis Keep, had worked in those same fields, had been brought to the Castle—if there was a Castle in those days—and had been trained by a very young Vola. There was too much going on here for it to be chance. The Confederacy had arranged this, of course. Picked the man who most matched Kreegan's old agent profile and sent him to the same places under the same conditions. I could see their thinking clearly now, and I had to admit there was nothing wrong with it.

"I'll bet you made the chair the first time," I said. She grinned and winked at me.

"Tell me about Kreegan," I pressed. "What's he like?"

She stood up and stood back a moment, studying me. "A lot like you, Cal Tremon. An awful lot like you." But she would say no more, leaving me to recover from my increasingly nasty headache as the effects of the drug wore off. Power was not without its price.

Chapter Twelve

Too Dangerous to Have Around

I slept fitfully, wrestling with my headache, and awoke several times to the stillness around me. Several times I thought someone had come into the room, and once I had a strong feeling that at least one individual was actually in the room standing next to the bed, looking down at me in deep thought. A mysterious figure, a wraith, yet huge, looming, dark, indistinct, powerful—the stuff of which children's nightmares are made, yet so compelling you hesitate to open your eyes and see if anybody's really there.

I cursed myself for this reaction, for giving in to

primal fears I never even knew I had, but that terrible feeling remained. Finally I shamed myself into a peek, but the room was dark and apparently empty.

I was just about to turn over and try and get back to sleep when my ears picked up a slight sound near the door. I froze, half in caution and half in—I was ashamed to admit to myself—fear of that nameless childish boogeyman.

"Tremon!" I heard a soft, female whisper.

Suddenly wide awake, I sat up cautiously. Fear had given way to puzzled curiosity now that another presence was tangible.

"Here!" I whispered.

A figure approached easily, not at all bothered by the darkness, and crouched down beside me. Although I could see only a slight form in the near-total darkness, I knew it was Vola.

"What's the matter?" I whispered.

"Tremon, you have to get out of here," she told me. "They're going to kill you before morning. There has just been a meeting about you with all the big shots present."

I remembered Artur's warning. So I *had* gone too far for prudence despite all the logic at my command.

"Now, listen carefully," she continued. "I'm not going to let them do it. Not even if what they say is true. I've seen your kind of potential too rarely here, and I won't see it nipped in the bud."

I frowned and sat on the side of the bed. "What did they say?"

"That you aren't Cal Tremon," she whispered. "That you're some sort of assassin sent here by the Confederacy to kill Lord Kreegan."

"What!" I exclaimed, perhaps a bit too loudly. All traces of fatigue and headache vanished as the adrenaline started flowing.

"Shhh . . . I don't know how much time we have—maybe none," she cautioned. "Still, I like you enough to give you a fighting chance." She hesitated a moment. "Is it true?"

I owed her an answer, but this wasn't the time for honor. "I don't know what they're talking about," I replied as sincerely as I could. "Hell, my prints, genetic coding—everything is on file. You ought to know I couldn't be anybody *but* me, and believe me, the *last* thing Cal Tremon could be is a Confederacy stooge."

"Maybe," she responded uncertainly. "But even in-system the Cerbrians swap bodies all the time, so I wouldn't depend too much on that defense. Look, it doesn't matter to me, I—what was that?"

We both remained perfectly still, not even breathing. Whatever she'd heard, though, I couldn't make out, and we both relaxed, although only slightly.

"Look, you have to go now," she said urgently.

"Go? Where?"

"I don't know," she responded truthfully. "Away. Away from Zeis Keep entirely. Into the wild, I suppose. If you survive the wild and bide your time, make your way south to Moab Keep, find the Masters there, who are a sort of religious order descended from the original scientists who were stuck here. There and the wild are the only places you'll be safe, and only at Moab can you complete your training. It won't be easy. You'll probably die anyway, or be caught by Artur and his agents, but at least you've got a chance. Stay here and you're dead by sunup, I promise you."

"I'll go now," I told her.

"Do you know how to get out at night?" she asked.

"I know," I told her. "I make it a point to locate all the exits as soon as I'm in a place."

"You'll have to avoid the other organized Keeps," she cautioned me. "The knights will all have the word in a few days, all over the planet. Now go. Fast and far!"

I grabbed her and hugged her. "Vola, fine lady, I won't forget this."

She laughed softly. "I really think you might make it," she said with a mixture of sincerity and wonder. "I really think you might. I have to admit I sort of hope you do."

I left her and eased out into the hallway, which was dimly lit by two lanterns far down on either side. I knew the way out, but I wasn't about to take it right away. Instead, I waited in a darkened recess until I saw Vola leave and go the other way. Maybe she *was* doing me the biggest favor of my Lilith existence, but I never trusted anyone completely.

Once she'd gone, I sneaked back into the room and used the bedding and pillows to make a rough form in the bed. Then I went out and down to one of the small holes that accessed the service corridors and crept back toward the room on the level above it. I located the peephole with some difficulty in the pitch darkness only by knowing where it had to be and by counting the number of such holes from my entry back to the room. I wanted to see what would happen next. Zeis Keep was a large area; I could hardly clear it before the alarm went out anyway, so I didn't intend to try, not right away. First I would see if anyone *did* come in the night to do me in—and if so, who. If not, I was fully prepared to return to the room in midmorning and face down Vola.

The fact that they'd somehow gotten word I was an agent was important enough.

There probably weren't three or four people in the whole Confederacy who would have known, and everyone but my counterpart hovering up there somewhere would have been mindwiped of the knowledge. Then I remembered the penetration of Military System Command's core computers and realized that somewhere in there the information could be pieced together. What they had done once they could very well have done again. For all I knew, the Confederacy was currently at war with those mysterious aliens.

But the fact that they'd pieced together some facts and come to the correct conclusion about my status didn't mean they were totally convinced of it. This could merely be a test to see if I really would jump. At this point I was determined to play by my own rules.

Suddenly I heard noises in the corridor. Two, maybe more, people walking with firm, confident steps toward me. I heard them now below, just outside the door to my room, then saw the door open cautiously.

There were three of them, I decided, two of whom stepped into the room while the third remained outside. One was Artur—he was hard to miss. The other was a rather ordinary man of middle years who was obviously from the civilized worlds. He, too, was dressed as a Master and held a small lantern which lit the room with an eerie glow.

"He's gone!" the stranger whispered unbelievingly.

"What?" Artur thundered; then he stalked over to the bed and violently ripped the fluffed-up bedding away. He spun around angrily, and I had never seen as nasty a look as he radiated then. "Someone tipped him off. I'll know who and I'll make him pay, by God!"

"You will do nothing of the kind," said the third man, out of sight outside the door. His voice had an odd quality, somewhat diffuse and unfocused, almost mechanical; it hardly sounded human at all. "He is a fully trained and capable agent. One of their best, we must assume, perhaps *the* best of the current crop. I think he realized he overplayed his hand this afternoon. We will have to find him, Artur. I charge you with that task. You find him while he's still weak and vulnerable and untrained, or he'll fry you with a glance and eat you for breakfast. Right now he is a minor nuisance, but potentially he is the most dangerous man on this planet, possibly as dangerous or more so than I. You find him and kill him, Artur—or one day he will seek out and kill us all."

Artur bowed subserviently, his face impassive to that threat, which did a lot for my ego and hopes. And then the dark Master uttered words that chilled me beyond belief.

"Yes, My Lord Kreegan."

I cursed inwardly that I had no way of getting a look at the Lord of Lilith himself without his also getting a look at me.

Artur gestured to the other man. "Come on, let's roll out the troops. We have work to do. He's got to cross a lot of open area within the Keep to get to the wild, and he'll be moving fast to beat the sun. We may catch him yet."

With that, both men left and I heard their boots against the stone and tile floor clicking swiftly away. Still I did not move, nor did I intend to do so for quite some time. Artur was right, of course—there was almost no way at all I could cover the distance from the Castle to the wild in the remaining darkness, and to be caught in daylight with all the pawns out would be to be absolutely trapped. No, I intended to stay right where I was for the next hour or two, then to exist by day inside the corridors of the Castle itself. I would flee, yes, but as prepared as I could and on my own terms and schedule, not theirs.

I spent most of the day hidden from everyone I could, and this proved easier than most people would think. The Castle would be the last place in which they would look for me, the last place they expected me to be. Trained cops and agents might have thought of it, but these were mostly petty crooks, naive natives, and a couple of tough old ex-military birds like Artur. Several times I ran into people, but I just looked like I belonged and nobody really noticed. All I was really concerned about was minimizing my visibility and not running into anybody who knew me. I even managed to liberate a meal or two from the ones packaged for on-duty personnel, so I was hardly uncomfortable.

Still, I didn't want to make the mistake of vastly underestimating my opponents, either. If Kreegan was still around, and I had no reason to believe he was not, he would at least block the exits as an afterthought. That wouldn't entail much—just posting a couple of supervisors at every exit, particularly those from the service corridors. Getting out would be no picnic, and I really couldn't afford a week within the walls. Each hour increased the risk of discovery and pushed my luck.

I checked all the possibilities, made my decisions, and was all set for the onset of darkness. Farewell, Zeis Keep, may you rot in the muck. I'd never see *this* place again, that was for sure.

That thought suddenly brought me up short. Ti.

She was still here, up there with that butchering sadist and his experiments.

I didn't know exactly why, but late in the afternoon, I made my way back to Medical. From experience I knew that just about everybody in Dr. Pohn's little shop of horrors knocked off work early. There really wasn't much reason not to go there, and the only real danger I faced was running into Pohn himself. Now that I knew the potential of a Master I had no desire to meet up with Pohn in an adversary role. I'd timed my arrival pretty much for supper, in the hopes that my route would be clear, and I was lucky. There appeared to be nobody in the Medical area.

I stole quickly into the area that I would always think of as the morgue and saw the twelve silent sleepers there. Hurrying over to Ti's tiny, still form, I looked down at her, trying to think clearly. Up until this point I'd thought of this as more of a goodbye visit than anything else. But now, looking down at her, I knew that I couldn't leave her here to Pohn's tender mercies.

I looked around at the others in the gathering gloom. No lights needed here, but the darkness made the place look even more like a repository for the dead. And they *were* dead, I thought sadly. The walking dead. What ancient superstition could conjure up only as a nightmare, the twisted sciences of Lilith had made a reality. I wanted to take them *all* with me, and would have if I could. Surely what one madman had done others not so mad could undo—but there was no way.

Without even thinking about it, I picked Ti up from the slab and carried her back to my service corridor hideaway. She seemed to weigh almost nothing; except for her shallow and almost imperceptible breathing, she was like a doll, a mannequin rather than a person. Picking her up again, I made my way toward my planned escape route, figuring I'd reach it at just about the point of total darkness. I had almost reached the point below the Castle's left wall when it occurred to me that I had done something monumentally stupid in carrying Ti off. If anyone came back to that lab and saw her missing, they'd realize I was still on the grounds.

Still, leaving her here now would be cold-blooded murder. Moreover, it wouldn't gain me anything, since she'd still be missed upstairs. No, stupid or not, the deed was done and I was committed now.

Although leaving Ti would have weighed on my conscience, what I was about to do didn't bother me in the slightest. Somewhere there are classifications of crimes against others such as murder, and this came under the heading of "necessary."

Just outside the small tunnel I was in was the Keep itself, the outside world—and two young paramilitary supervisors from Artur's force. If either of them so much as knew where I was, they could inflict pain and stop me dead, at least long enough to raise an alarm. I had now to get by without any of that happening, and that meant killing the guards. I wished for the power that had allowed me to fry Kronlon, to reconstruct a chair from basic cells, but that was denied me now. I was faced with the problem of eliminating two threats who didn't even have to touch me to get me—yet I had to get both of them.

I had the benefit of surprise, of course. They weren't telepaths, nor did they have any special powers that would betray me any more than if they were two normal humans. And the knowledge of their power and my lack of it made them supremely confident.

I had several different plans for drawing them near enough to get, but it suddenly occurred to me that I had the almost perfect diversion in Ti—if in fact I could control her actions as simply as Pohn had. I certainly intended to find out. I put her down on the cold stone, confident that I was far enough away from the exit not to be overheard.

"Ti, open your eyes," I commanded in a hushed tone.

Her eyelids flickered slightly, then opened. I breathed a sigh of relief in the discovery that this wasn't going to be as difficult as I thought, although tricky.

"Ti, stand up and face me."

She did as instructed, and I began to feel a little better. Still, I didn't know how many instructions in sequence she could carry out.

"Ti, softly say hello."

"Hello," she responded dully, without a trace of life in her tone. Its very woodenness made me shiver slightly.

Well, now was the time to see how complex the instructions could be.

"Ti, I want you to walk two steps forward, stop, turn around, raise your right hand, and say 'come here,' " I instructed. Those were enough separate instructions to tell me what I wanted to know.

She paused a moment after I gave the orders, then walked two steps forward, turned around, and did everything perfectly. I got a sort of erotic thrill from seeing her do it. The ultimate adolescent male fantasy, I reflected—except that it bordered on necrophilia.

The only other thing left to check was whether this was similar to a case of hypnotism and if the effect could be delayed.

I gave her a couple of minor instructions, then told her not to carry them out unless I said the word "escape." Then I said the word and she did them, after which I tried a couple of other random instructions, then said "escape" once again. She immediately carried out my original commands, so I was satisfied.

I had deliberately picked this exit because a fairly large rock stood right near the entrance. Now, I felt, I had the best way of using all the elements, and I began to think that perhaps bringing Ti along hadn't been such a bad idea after all.

"Listen carefully, Ti," I said. "Forget all previous instructions. When you hear me say the word 'trap' you will do the following. . . ."

It was dark outside the mouth of the cave into which the service corridor dumped. The two guards, a young man and an older woman, each wearing the black cape, pants, and boots of soldiers in Artur's force, sat around looking very bored. They had been there quite a while and had exhausted most of what small talk they could muster, yet they couldn't do much else but stand guard for fear that someone would get by them or, worse, that Master Artur would make a surprise inspection and find them doing something other than their military duty.

Still, each sat with the relaxed air of someone who is certain that the quarry is long gone and nothing whatever is going to happen. It was, then, with considerable surprise that they heard someone emerge from the small tunnel mouth. They both jumped to their feet, whirled, and advanced with tense curiosity.

"It's—it's a girl," the female guard said in wonder. Her companion nodded and called out, "Who are you? What are you doing here?" His voice possessed the confidence of authority; he was secure that he had the power to meet challenges.

The tiny figure, several meters away, seemed to start, then silently slipped behind the large rock near the cave opening, vanishing from view.

"What kind of children's trick is this?" the man muttered, irritated.

The other was not so easily lulled. "Take it easy. It could be a trap of some kind. Remember, somebody tipped him off to run. Let's just give her a jolt."

"Aw, you're too nervous," the man griped, but he was still unsure enough not to advance.

"There. That should have fixed her," the woman said confidently.

"I don't hear any groaning," the man responded, becoming a little nervous himself now. "Did you get her?"

"I'm sure I did," she assured him. "Come on. Somebody that little probably passed out."

They advanced cautiously, turned behind the rock, and saw the girl, apparently unconscious, stiff and flat against the rock.

"Jeez, Marl, what'd you *do* to her?" the man asked, concerned. "She looks like she's dead."

They both approached the still form against the rock, no longer cautious. When their heads were but inches apart I leaped with a yell from the other side of the rock, and before either could recover from the freeze surprise brings, I brought their two heads together as hard as I could, knocking them down with my spring as I did so.

I hadn't done that sort of thing that way since practicing with androids in training, but by God, it worked. Timing was the key, I told myself, feeling satisfied. Timing and a little knowledge of the weaknesses in human psyches.

The man was dead, I saw. The woman seemed to be still alive, but was bleeding from the scalp. Quickly and quietly I snapped her neck and then dragged both of them into the cave and hid them as securely as I could. I wanted no alarms now, and the uncertainty over their disappearance, when it was discovered, would still raise alarms in the wrong places.

Artur, after all, was charged with Castle security and would not be sure whether the two had been surprised by someone coming out or by someone going *in*. I counted on that, and on the general feeling these people would have that someone with the voluntary powers of a mere pawn could have neutralized and physically killed two trained supervisors.

I wondered idly why the hell I hadn't done *that* to Kronlon long ago. This damned world had sapped my self-confidence; I was only now feeling like myself again.

Picking up Ti for speed's sake, I made my way out of the Castle and down into the valley below.

Now for the first time the map Intelligence had arranged to be imprinted in my head came in handy. Wild areas, not under any knight or other administrative control—jungle and forest and mountains and swamp—lay as buffers between the keeps.

The Keep itself was easy to navigate in the darkness. The villagers were mostly bedding down for the night or relaxing after eating, so no one would be in the fields except for herdsmen, who could easily be bypassed.

Zeis was a bowllike valley on three sides and ran up against a swampy and somewhat unhealthy lake on the fourth. The lake was definitely out—I had no desire to navigate through unknown water in daylight, let alone in darkness. Who knew what quagmires and hostile creatures were about? That meant going over or through the mountains, which was almost as bad. Naked, without tools, and carrying Ti along, I would be restricted to well-worn trails that were probably staked out by Artur's boys.

The map in my head told me I had at least a six-hundred-meter climb ahead of me, at which point I'd have to descend almost that far to make a forest on the other side. Unfortunately, though the map included both physical and political information, it was no road map. I would have to ferret out the trails myself, and I couldn't be too choosy about the ones I found, either.

It was easy to find the trails, although none looked particularly well-worn. The network of pathways in the Keep all led to them in the end, of course. A number of times I'd had to flatten when great flying *besils* with mounted riders flew past. Their buzzing sounded like a great series of motors in operation, but they were too large and cumbersome to be more than a deterrent patrol. To spot anybody while atop those creatures would take a lot of luck indeed. But if someone on the ground sounded an alarm, they'd be on me in a moment, and then I'd be totally defenseless.

If the trail I finally made was typical, at least I knew I wouldn't have problems mountain climbing. Obviously designed for cart traffic, it was wide, with a great many broad switchbacks. Those switchbacks, though, would make anyone on the path plainly obvious to guards further up, and I worried a little about this. After all, this wasn't like escaping from some armed force; these adversaries merely had to see you to knock you off the path with a strong glance.

All I could do was start up the trail as rapidly and cautiously as possible and then trust to a little luck and the fact that the hunt would still be a day stale at this point. By this point I had Ti clinging to me piggyback and was certain that her grip would never falter.

I was about a quarter of the way up and feeling

pretty confident when I heard voices below. I froze, listening, but they were still far below me and, from what I could determine, on foot. The sounds of voices carried along here but with little definition, so I really couldn't tell who they were—as if I needed to know who'd be walking a trail like this in the dark so late in the evening.

After deciding that my best course was simply to keep ahead of them, I resumed my climb. A few minutes later I realized I was also hearing other voices from the trail. These sounded like the voices of two women, whereas those below me had both definitely been male—of that I was certain. I now realized that Artur had done the most obvious thing under the conditions Lilith and the geography of the Keep imposed on him. At intervals, probably somewhat at random, one team would start down the trail. A little later, another would start up, and they would cross somewhere in between. On a trail like this anybody else would be caught in between.

I tried to judge how far away from me the pair coming down were. It was almost impossible. So I had to take the chance that perhaps they were far enough up to allow me to make the edge of the accumulating fog that always shrouded the sky of Zeis Keep because of the inversion caused by the mountain ring. The fog had been thickening and lowering as the night wore on. I hurried to reach the almost tangible blanket of gray I could see perhaps two turns of the trail ahead of me, the blanket that currently masked me from the descenders' view as they were masked from mine.

Without Ti I would have been more agile, but she had become something of a crusade, an obligation to me now. I was determined that she would at least awaken and be whole once again. She no longer weighed nothing. I was becoming tired, and forty-two kilos was beginning to have a real effect on my back and neck muscles.

I had only one more switchback to go until I reached the edge of the cloud cover, but I was to be denied it, I now realized. The sound of the women's voices was coming in quite clear and I could see an eerie, disembodied glow from a yellow lantern one of them was obviously carrying. I looked around for a place to hide, but the trail had been cut into sheer bedrock, the only thing at its outer edge except air and a long, long hard fall was a small sculpted rim that obviously served to keep wheeled carts from slipping over.

I had no time and no choice: the rim would have to do. I was about to see just how strong and able this Cal Tremon body was, I thought sourly.

I worried about the men below me, but they were the least of my problems, I realized. It was pretty damned dark up here, and their light would not carry far.

As carefully as I could, I eased myself and my burden over the side and held on to the trail rim with both hands, otherwise dangling free. The drag from Ti on my back became so great I almost cried out, but I hadn't gone through all that training for nothing, nor had a week or so of soft living undone months of hard toil. I managed to keep myself hanging there; how long until I lost my grip and dropped off, I couldn't tell.

Again I counted on normal human behavior to help me—and I needed all the help I could get. These people had been walking the trail, up and down, down and up, for all their shift, and they were likely to be more bored than totally vigilant, like the two guards at the Castle had been.

They came out of the clouds, walking slowly down the trail. One of them idly picked up a pebble and tossed it over the side, barely missing me only one level and one switchback below them.

"Well, we finally got outta that stinkin' mist," one of the women noted with relief.

"Yeah, let the guys get soaked," the other one cracked. "Maybe if we take it slow enough it'll be dawn and we'll be relieved before we havta go up again."

"You said it," the first one agreed. "I've had it with

this mountain business. Me for a hot meal, bath, and bed, and I don't care in what order."

They were very close now, around the turn and coming back toward my precarious and increasingly agonizing perch. All I could think of was *Don't stop! Just don't stop!* But there is a law governing such things and stop they did, not more than three or four meters from where my aching, raw hands were visible if they cared to look.

"Hey! Look! I see 'em coming!" one noted, pointing —I could see the arm and finger outstretched, far too close for comfort.

"Wanna wait here for 'em?"

No, no, you don't want to do that! I thought and prayed so loud that if there had been any such thing as ESP receptivity here they would certainly have heard me.

"You mean stall?" the other responded, thinking it over. "Naah. Why bother? Let's get this over with."

As they both turned and left the ledge, I chanced a glance downward to see where the approaching men were. Too close, I decided. Their lantern was already lighting the way only a couple of levels below me, and the women's own light would expose me when they made the turn. I would have to time my move pretty well and do it silently. I judged the light from their lantern that was thrown forward against the curve of the switchback to be about twenty or so meters further on and watched it grow brighter and brighter.

I almost blew it, for they actually came in view just as I hoisted myself and my heavy burden up and over onto the roadway, flattening there and freezing as still as Ti.

"You hear something?" one of them asked the other.

"Yeah," the other replied suspiciously. "Sounded just ahead. Let's take it slow and easy."

Not too slow, I wished, nor too cautious. I had to get up and start moving before the men got too close —and never had I felt less like moving. My neck and back ached, and my arms felt as if they were disjointed and incapable of anything. I summoned what reserve strength I had and tried some mental exercises to sponge away as much of the discomfort and ache as possible. Controlling my pain centers was no trick, but it was a false control, of course. My muscles and joints were in such pain because they had been pushed to the edge of endurance, and no longer feeling the warnings of the body didn't lessen that fact. I wondered how much further it was to the top, and whether I was up to it. I didn't even want to think about meeting yet another patrol on its way down or at the top. Judging by the light and sound, I made my way up toward the still-inviting fog, and made it.

The going was a lot slower now, since I couldn't see three meters in front of me, and the air became suddenly very wet and sticky. Still, I welcomed the gray cloak as a friend and ally, the first and only one I had ever had on this insane world.

I wasn't worried about the men approaching from below. Being human and bored, they would stop and exchange small talk with the women coming down; that would buy me a few precious minutes to add to the distance. Their lantern would be little help once they made the dew line, so they'd be going as slowly as I. If I ran into no one else and if I could just make it over the top before the sun came up, I felt I might just get away.

The sky was certainly getting light by the time I reached the summit, but by then I really didn't care any more. From this point on I'd be descending toward the wild—too early for any commercial traffic, I hoped—and into whatever brush there might be. I was out on my feet, every step a horrible experience, but I drove myself, knowing that I had to make it down, had to make it to cover, before the day really began. I hoped there would be only light patrols on this side of the range—if any at all. Not that they wouldn't be looking for me here, but with limited manpower Artur would concentrate mainly on keeping me bottled up. Only when they discovered the dead guards would their search become frantic, and only after that would they begin to widen it into places they did not control.

At least I hoped so.

I was soaked through by the time I made it to the lower edge of the dew line, had been for a couple of hours. For the first time since being on Lilith, the combination of wetness, a light wind, and the slight elevation threw a genuine chill into me. It was getting really light now; the sun, I was sure, was going to peek through any minute now and perhaps burn off some of this cloud cover.

Now, out of the thick mountain-bred fog, I could see ahead of me my first real view on Lilith of a place other than Zeis Keep. There were rolling, thickly forested hills, it appeared, the trees and hilltops peeking out a dark blue-green from trapped pockets of thick ground fog. The place had an eerie stillness about it, and I felt certain that I would at least make it to the shelter of those trees.

I could no longer carry Ti, and ordered her to let go of my back and walk beside me. Though she could keep up by running if she had to, I took it slowly and carefully nonetheless. The stone path was slick and wet, and I wanted no accidents for either of us, not now—not when I had accomplished my immediate goal.

The sun was well up and warming the place into a steam bath before I finally decided I couldn't take any more and picked a spot not far from the road that seemed well concealed from prying eyes and barren of any obvious threat from natural causes. I sensitized Ti with a series of commands so that she would remain listening and would wake me if she heard anyone or anything approaching, then settled down under tree and bush cover on the grass and rock-strewn forest floor and let myself relax for the first time. No matter how rotten I felt, I *did* feel a strong sense of accomplishment.

I'd escaped! I'd made it! I was, for the first time in this body, once more a free man, a free agent! It felt really good.

Deep down, though, that nagging little voice I always carried with me sang a different tune. *All right, superhuman,* it mocked. *So now you're naked and unarmed in a strange and hostile world whose inhabitants are all raised against you, saddled with a robot-like girl, and you've got no place to go and no help to do anything else. All right,* Homo superior—*now what do you do?*

There was only one response to that. I fell into the deepest of sleeps.

Chapter Thirteen

Some Interested Parties

How long I slept there I have no idea, but it was late in the day when I awoke, feeling none too good. My body still ached, at least those parts that weren't already numb, and the uneven, rocky ground hadn't helped matters much. Still, I felt now as if I could do all right as long as I didn't have to climb any more mountains or carry Ti.

I realized that at least we wouldn't starve. Warden had described Lilith as something like Paradise, and in that he hadn't been far wrong. All the cultivated food of the Keeps came originally from plants that grew in the wild, and though the naturally grown stuff wouldn't taste as good or be as perfect there should be enough to sustain us.

But sustain us for what? The trouble with breaking out of a prison is that all of your energies are directed toward the breakout. What you're going to do once outside is vague and nebulous and never very practical. Such was the case here. Moab was roughly 4,800 kilometers south-southeast of where I was—a nice hike under any circumstances, and when the powers that be were hunting for you, it might as well be on another planet.

And they *were* hunting. Just sitting there in the few minutes after waking up I could see, far off, huge black leathery shapes, two great wings supporting a giant, wormlike body whose head was a mass of tendrils, combing along the sides of the road. *Besils* from Artur's force, without a doubt. I sat there and admired the way the riders could control the beasts, so that they didn't seem to fly in any normal fashion at all but rather to swim and flow, snakelike, through the air.

I had to make plans, both immediate and long-range, whether I wanted to or not. I certainly couldn't stay where I was; for one thing, we needed to find food, and for another, it was too close to the road directly to Zeis for me to remain long. The more distance I could put between Artur and me the better.

Nor would the trip be as comfortable as it would by necessity be leisurely. I was already becoming aware that chairs and castles weren't the only things held in Warden patterns—the entire Keep was under such a pattern. Lilith was a world where plants and insects thrived, but there'd been no mammalian or reptilian development. The microbes were unimportant; aside from the Warden organism itself, all the microscopic beasties were far too alien to affect human beings. But the insects swarmed and bred and swarmed some more in millions of shapes and sizes. In Zeis Keep, the minor insects and pests were in some way locked out, absent. Now I found myself in a world where millions of things, many quite small, flew and crawled and creeped and hopped. I already had several small itchy bites from something or other, and a close examination of Ti showed more of the same.

True, though I had only a few hundred meters' walk into the brush to find familiar, edible melons and berries, only a few were usable. The natural food chain here was oriented toward the insects, not people; and insects infested whatever was ripe for the picking. Nonetheless, I found enough to feel reasonable again and scooped and broke up enough to hand-feed to Ti. Water was less of a problem, since there were small pools and rivulets everywhere. Some of it looked pretty scummy, but I didn't hesitate simply because I knew that my little Wardens—and Ti's— would protect us from the worst.

Only after these necessities were taken care of did I allow myself to think beyond to what I was actually going to do next. I simply couldn't manage to reach Moab Keep, help Ti, and stay out of Artur's clutches all on my own. I needed help—friends, people who could do more than I. But whom did I know on Lilith that wasn't either out to get me or locked inside Zeis Keep? The answer was obvious but unnerving.

I was somehow going to have to find Father Bronz and talk him into helping me. If the old priest wouldn't do it for me, I reasoned, he might do it for Ti, whom, I recalled, he had said he knew and for whom he had expressed some affection. Bronz it was —but where? I tried to remember. It had been a couple of weeks since I'd seen him, but he *had* mentioned where he was going next. South, he'd said— and that was good, because that meant along this road. Shemlon Keep, I thought he'd said, making his rounds.

The map in my head clicked into play once more, and I easily located Shemlon, about twenty kilometers down this road, or off it.

Near dusk we started walking, not on the road but parallel to it, choosing whatever cover we could find from random patrols and routine courier and other service. The road was lightly traveled, but during the late afternoon a few carts passed and even a few individuals, almost all masters, heading one way or the other. I had no illusions that word of me would not have reached Shemlon long before now; the aerial *besils* would have been active.

A long and dangerous trip, yes, but it didn't bother me very much. At least now I had some place to go and some reason for going there.

It took several days of lying low and several nights of slow walking to reach the border of Shemlon Keep.

During that time we had occasional problems finding edible food, but in the main Lilith proved bountiful. I wouldn't like to have had to feed a mob, but for just two of us it proved fairly easy going.

Shemlon was definitely quite different than Zeis. For one thing, the hills seemed to vanish into a nearly flat plain, much of which appeared to be thinly covered with water. A more careful examination showed that they were growing *rasti*, a reddish, ricelike grain that was something of a Zeis staple. Now I knew where it came from.

. There was but one village, it appeared, a large complex of hollow *bunti* huts arranged in a huge circle around the main building—a large mansion that appeared to be painted adobe. The mansion was about as primitive as Tiel's castle had been—eighty or a hundred rooms at least, in an odd geometrical assemblage of yellow-brown cubicles that looked as if it shouldn't stay up. Shemlon was obviously much smaller in terms of personnel than Zeis, although it might have been as large in area. It could have been the economics of the operation or it could mean that the knight here was simply lower in rank, perhaps slightly less powerful, than Tiel.

The layout worried me, though, since I'd spent a lot of time getting here and it had been some time since Bronz had been at Zeis. He had probably already been here and left. With but a single large village, I could hardly pass myself off as a pawn among them. I had to resort to extreme measures. My survival was at stake. So I bided my time for a day, checking out the layout and seeing who worked where, then selected a spot and finally a single individual working off by himself. He seemed to be repairing a gate on some sort of channel that fed river water to the paddies.

Leaving Ti well hidden at the edge of the bush, I stepped out near dusk, a time when most of the field hands had already returned to their village and the repairman was getting ready to depart himself. I stepped out plain as could be and walked boldly toward him. His nakedness showed him to be a pawn, albeit a skilled worker of some sort, and my casual manner and rough appearance did nothing to arouse alarm.

I walked up to him with a wave and a nod. "Hi," I said, really friendly. "I'm new here, and I think some people played me for a sucker, sending me over into the mud. When I got back there was nobody left in the field."

The man looked up, a rough old face with a beard flecked with gray, and chuckled. "Yeah, I know how it is. You wait up a moment and I'll take you in."

I nodded appreciatively. It had all gone so easily that I really hated myself for what I would have to do. This was an ugly business and an ugly world.

We exchanged a little small talk, and then I got to the point. "You know, I was a Catholic back Outside. Somebody told me there was a traveling priest around. Was that just more kidding?"

"Aw, no, he's for real," the old man replied. "Was through here not far back. Too bad you missed him. He probably won't be back until after the harvest, several months from now."

I looked surprised. "Where would he go?"

"Other Keeps," the old man replied matter-of-factly. "He's probably just getting to Mola Keep, way off to the west there, right 'bout now. He's a good man, though I don't take much stock in his beliefs."

"How long ago was he here?" I pressed. "I mean, when did he leave?"

"Day before yesterday—say, what's that to you?"

I sighed. "Because I'm Cal Tremon," I told him, and while he was still looking surprised, I killed him —as quickly and painlessly as I could. Killed him and carried his limp and lifeless body back to the bush so that, perhaps, he wouldn't be missed for a while.

The map in my head clicked again and I saw where Mola was—another thirty kilometers, by a side road. Not a long ride, no more than two days by *ak*-cart, the method Bronz likely used, but another long, wet, itchy, hungry walk all the same.

I felt bad about killing the old man. Certain people wouldn't bother me in the least—the upper classes here in particular, ones like Artur and Pohn and Tiel and Marek Kreegan. I felt no remorse for Kronlon, yet I mourned the old man, so casual and friendly, so totally innocent in all this. Mourned him, yet accepted the necessity of doing what I had done. I could hardly have walked back to the village with him, and any other behavior would have had him telling stories about me, stories that would be all too plain if he were pressed by a supervisor.

Still, I couldn't forget the look in his eyes when I'd said my name, a look that would haunt me for a long time. A look that said he hadn't the slightest idea who or what a Cal Tremon was.

Another two days of cautious walking. Another two days of insect bites, rotten fruit, stale water, thunderstorms I couldn't hide from, mud I couldn't avoid, bruises, and sore feet. The only good point about leaving Zeis Keep was that now I could really see the sky, which was a deep blue streaked with hints of red and violet, filled with but not totally blotted out by brownish clouds. By night you could sometimes see stars, a sight both reassuring and sad as well. Stars I could never again reach. Stars forever closed to me.

I was still three or four kilometers from Mola Keep when I spotted a small camp just off the road. This was highly unusual. I was curious to see what this was all about, curious and suspicious as well. Were they perhaps throwing up roadblocks now?

There was a small campfire, out now and glowing slightly, and a fairly fancy-looking bedroll. I looked at the *ak,* the huge rounded creature with the tiny head you could barely see almost dwarfing the cart it normally pulled. Though it was still, it looked alive and in good shape, as did the cart. Not a breakdown, then, I told myself—but one person alone, asleep out here in the wild. One person of some rank—a Master, probably.

Leaving Ti again in the protection of the bush, I crept as close as I dared, wanting to check out who or what this person might be. Definitely a man, snoring fit to wake the dead. I felt hope rise within me. It couldn't be, I told myself. He'd be too far ahead, and in any event wouldn't have any reason not to make Mola—but sure enough, there he was.

I had found Father Bronz.

In my excitement I made a rustling noise that, considering the level of snoring, shouldn't even have been heard. Suddenly his eyes opened. Lying still, he cocked his head, a slightly puzzled expression on his face.

"Father Bronz," I called to him in a loud whisper. "It's me—Cal Tremon!"

The priest chuckled, sat up, yawned and stretched, then rubbed his eyes and looked around. I stepped cautiously out into the open. I had no real reason to trust the man, but all things considered, I had no choice *but* to place myself in his hands.

"Tremon!" he croaked, still sounding half asleep. "About time you got here. I'd about given you up."

Chapter Fourteen

Savages and Amazons

I just stood there dumbstruck, staring at him. Finally I managed, "You were *expecting* me?"

He looked around. "'Why else would I stay in such a wondrous natural hotel?" he grumbled sarcastically. "Come on over and sit. I'll put on some tea."

I walked toward him, then stopped. "I've forgotten Ti!" I exclaimed, mostly to myself.

"I have tea here," he responded, sounding confused.

"No, no. Ti. The girl."

He laughed. "Well, well! So you *did* take her! There was some question as to what happened."

I decided to fetch her before getting the details. At least I was no longer alone, and I hadn't been incinerated or otherwise molested, so whatever game Bronz was playing was in my favor.

I carried her back to Bronz's camp and he rose and walked over to her immediately, doing a fairly good imitation of Dr. Pohn but with far more compassion and concern. "That bastard," he muttered. "May he rot in hell forever." He closed his eyes and placed his hand on her forehead.

"Can you do anything for her?" I asked, genuinely concerned. "She's nothing more than a living robot right now."

He sighed and thought for a moment. "If I were a doctor, yes, I *could.* If I knew my biology a little better, maybe. I can see where he's meddled, all right, but I don't dare risk doing anything myself. I might cause permanent brain damage or even kill her. No, we'll have to find help for her, that's all."

"Not at a Keep," I responded hesitatingly. "All they'd do is give her back to Dr. Pohn."

"No, not at a Keep," he agreed, thinking. "Not you, either. We have to get you someplace safe where you can get some help and Ti can get some expert care, though. I did anticipate the problems we'd have finding friends and allies and a hideout, although I didn't realize I'd have this kind of difficulty." He sighed again and went back over to the rekindled small fire, taking the gourd of water from the flame and adding some ground leaves from a pouch on his belt—one of several, I noted.

"Come on over and sit down," he invited. "It'll be ready in a few minutes and we have some time to kill anyway."

I did as instructed, already feeling a little better. I wanted to know a little more about Father Bronz, though.

"You said that you anticipated our needing a hideout, that you were waiting for me," I noted. "Maybe you better explain a little."

He chuckled. "Son, I was late getting out of Zeis. They had all the bigwigs coming for a party and it was decided that I should attend. Besides, the Duke and I are old friends—I occasionally do him some favors."

"I remember the night," I told him. "It was the night I killed Kronlon and graduated, you might say. I thought you were long gone, though."

"I'd intended to be," he responded, pouring tea into two smaller, nicely carved gourd cups. "Politics is everything around here, though. Well, that got me a couple of days late into Shemlon, and I was still there when couriers from Zeis arrived with the news that you had been condemned to death but had escaped and were now a wanted fugitive. You are really hot, as they say, my son. Any pawn that even *helps* them get you won't ever have to work or feel a supervisor's wrath again."

I nodded. Just what I expected, but it eased my conscience a little about killing the old man.

"Anyway," Bronz continued, "it didn't take much in the way of brains to figure that you'd need a friend and I was the only friend outside the Keep you had. So I was very noisy in spreading word around where I was going next. I didn't want you to try finding me in Shemlon, considering how much of a single entity the whole village setup is, so I traveled down the road about halfway to Mola, then camped here some time yesterday. I was willing to wait until somebody asked questions or until you showed up, whichever came first. But I *do* have to put in at Mola, if only for appearance's sake, you know."

"You figured out my movements so easily," I pointed out, "I wonder why Artur hasn't?"

"Oh, I'm sure the thought crossed his mind," Bronz replied cheerily. "I've been getting a careful inspection from some of those flyers, and a fellow by here earlier gave me your description and told me how to report you. I wouldn't worry, though. I'm one of *them*, son! To them I'm an old friend of the Duke's, a familiar old face. It might occur to them that you'd seek me out, but it would *never* occur to them that I wouldn't immediately fry your gizzard or turn you in."

I sipped the tea. "But you're not?"

"Of course not," he replied, sounding a bit miffed.

"Would I have gone to all this trouble if I were? No, my son, in this bastion of the most primitive age of man on old Earth I'm reviving a two-thousand-year-old church custom for you! It's called sanctuary. Back in ancient times, on our ancestral planet, the church was a power unto itself, a political power with a lot of force and clout, yet separate from the temporal powers because we owed our allegiance not to kings but to God. Political criminals in particular, but really anybody who was being chased, could run into a church or cathedral and claim sanctuary, and the church would protect that person from temporal retribution. Well, you're asking for sanctuary, and how can I, as a Christian, turn you down? I've had it up to here with this godless tyranny anyway. And besides," he added with a wink and a smile, "I've been bored to tears for ten years."

I laughed and finished my tea, whereupon he poured me more.

"Now, then," he said, settling back once more, "just what do you want to do?"

"I want to restore Ti, of course," I responded, "but beyond that, I want to complete my treatments and training. They said I was at least Master class, and I want to reach that level badly. I want the opportunity to go as far as I can with the Warden power."

He nodded. "That's reasonable. And the fact that you put Ti first—that in fact you vastly complicated your escape to get her out—is a real mark in your favor. But suppose I can get you to Moab Keep, to that crazy group down there, and you get all the power you can. Suppose you become a Master plus —Knight level, maybe. Then what?"

"Well . . ." I thought about his question, which was a fair one. Just what *did* I want to do? "I think, one day, if I have the power, I'd like to go back to Zeis Keep and take it for my own. Then—well, we'll see."

He chuckled. "So you have designs on a knighthood, huh? Well, maybe you'll make it, Cal. Maybe you will . . . Still, first things first. We have to get you to help, we have to get Ti to help, and then somehow we have to get you down to Moab."

I nodded, looking serious and feeling worse. It was all well and good to spout dreams, but the reality was a naked and mud-caked man sipping tea beside a small fire.

"I'll have to put in my appearance ahead, as I mentioned," Father Bronz said. "I've got a little extra here and you should be fairly comfortable for a couple of days. I figure if you can avoid all the traps and patrols to get this far, you certainly can just lie low."

"And then what?" I pressed, not liking to be so out of control of things and feeling a little helpless.

He grinned. "Once I reach the Keep I can pull a favor or two, send a little message to certain parties. I'll work out a rendezvous and we can take it from there."

"Certain parties? I thought this bound-up world wouldn't stand a resistance."

"Oh, they're not anything of the kind," he replied. "No, indeed. They're savages."

Chapter Fifteen

A Dialogue

Two days, longer and worse on the nerves than any since I'd started this trip, I spent doing absolutely nothing near where I'd originally discovered Father Bronz. I certainly trusted the odd priest far more than I had at the beginning. Not only did I have little choice in the matter, but if I hadn't seen Artur's grim face by this point, then Bronz wouldn't be the one to turn me in. Now the anxiety was mostly that something would happen to him before he could aid me.

I needn't have worried, though. Bronz held a position on Lilith that, though perhaps not unique, was enviable in the extreme. He went where he wanted and did what he wanted without being answerable to anyone, not even to his church superiors. As a well-known face among the keeps, he was always welcomed and never threatened. As a friend of the Duke and most of the more powerful knights in the east-central region of Lilith's single enormous continent, he was unlikely to be touched even by the most powerful psychopaths, since they, too, respected those more powerful than themselves. The price of all this, though, was that, though a Master himself, Bronz was simply not a threat to anybody else's position. As a priest, he seemed sincerely to care for the down-trodden, seeing his role in life as one of the very rare bridges between the elites in their castles and manor houses and the pawns condemned to eternal serfdom. His message of an all-powerful being who promised a heavenly life in the Hereafter to those who were good in this life appealed to the ruling classes, as a major official religion always appealed to such groups. And yet his faith, no matter how wrong or misplaced it might be, was the only rock of sanity for the pawns, their only hope. They suffered under the ultimate tyranny on Lilith: the ruling class was revolution-proof because the masses were born without the ability to use the Warden power.

Bronz returned late in the evening of the second day, looking very tired but satisfied. "All set," he told me. "We'll have to do some traveling, though. Our rendezvous is about two days' ride from here, and that's exactly how long we have in which to make it. It's pretty hairy with the patrols right now, and they won't wait. Let's get going."

"Now?" I responded, feeling a little rushed after two days of marking time. "It's almost dark, and you look all in. I don't want to lose *you*—not now."

He grinned feebly. "Yes, now. I have some straw and my bedding, so we'll be able to hide Ti and, with some difficulty, your giant frame. But you're right—I am dead tired after doing five days' ministry in two as well as the usual politicking. That's why we go now. *You* can do the driving while I get a little sleep."

I was startled. "Me? But you drive these damned things by talking to them, Warden-style! I can't do *that!*"

"Oh, Sheeba's a nice big bugger, she is," Bronz responded casually. "She doesn't need any kick in the pants, and once we get to the split down here a ways there aren't any turnoffs we need concern ourselves with for thirty kilometers or more, so she'll just plod right along."

"Why do you even need me, then?" I asked, still apprehensive.

"To stand guard, to wake me if there's any trouble, and if we are stopped by a patrol, to run like hell—but loudly."

And it was as simple as that. The huge beetlelike creature Father Bronz called Sheeba was as docile and plodding as he said and kept right to the road. The worst problem I had, other than contending with the priest's snores, was seeing every kind of terrible threat in the shadows. Twice I woke Bronz, convinced I'd seen something large shadowing us, once from the side of the road, once from the air. But after the second, his patience wore thin. "Grow up and be a big boy, Tremon. You're much too old to be scared of the dark. Listen for the bugs, boy. As long as you can hear the bugs there's nobody around."

The truth was I felt more than physically naked standing in the *ak*-cart looking at nothing except an occasional star that peeked through the ever-present clouds. But the ever-present crescendo of insect noises, a background I'd gotten so used to by this time I'd just about tuned it out of my conscious, never ceased.

Bronz awoke before dawn on his own, and we stopped for tea.

"Damned nuisance, this place," the priest muttered. "You can't take food with you, it rots in a day unless you have a couple of agriculture masters around to see it shipped safely and some others to store it properly. Me, I get along by roadside pickings and save my Warden energies for my gourds and teas."

I took the hint, and shortly before dawn was on a foraging expedition into the bush. I didn't come back with much, since I dared not risk going too far from the road, but it was enough—a few melons, a handful or two of berries. Bronz worked some of his Warden magic on them so that we were able to keep a tiny supply, but clearly his area of expertise, if he had one, lay elsewhere.

Daylight was the time of greatest risk. Although Bronz had chosen a route that took us away from the more congested Keeps and where the wild was dominant, we came upon the occasional traveler nonetheless.

Scrunching down in the cart, covering myself with straw and bedding as best I could, I had to stay there, still as possible, praying I could keep from coughing or sneezing or moving no matter how long the conversation (and some were *very* long). Most were supervisors, some with *ak*-carts of their own, who were delivering something from one Keep to another, but there was an occasional master as well. All were worrisome, since I doubted if Father Bronz would kill even to protect me. But the masters were the most irritating, since they possibly could outdo Bronz himself.

One time we even ran into an actual roadblock, the one thing we never expected, which indicated just how far afield Artur was willing to go. Fortunately, Father Bronz knew the two guards and talked us through it. Since I didn't really have a low opinion of Artur, I suspect that if those two mentioned in their report they passed Bronz without conducting an inspection there would be two fewer guards from Zeis Keep, no matter how reliable the priest was deemed to be.

It was like that all over, though, I knew. Act as if you own the place, betray no anxiety, and you can get away with the damnedest things, even in a crowd.

Most of the time, though, the road was empty, so Bronz and I could talk—and did we ever. There was little else to do, and I was anxious to learn.

"You don't much like the system on Lilith, I note," he commented once.

I gave a dry laugh. "Stratified oppression, a tiny ruling class in permanent power—mostly the best criminal minds humanity has produced. I think it stinks."

"What would you do, then?" he came back, sounding amused. "What sort of system would, say, Lord Cal Tremon impose that would supplant this one?"

"The Warden organism makes that tough," I replied carefully. "Obviously power corrupts"—Bronz gave me a hurt look—"most people," I rescued myself. "The people with the power are generally the most corrupt to begin with, since outsiders tend to have a higher degree of this power, and only the corrupt are sent here."

He smiled. "So corruption cometh to Paradise, and the snakes rule Eden, is that it? Get rid of the snakes and Eden returns?"

"You're mocking me. No, I don't believe that and you know it. But a more enlightened leadership could produce a better standard of living for the pawns without all this torture and degradation."

"Could it?" he mused. "I wonder. This is a complex planet, but I think you are being too one-dimensional on its limitations. You think of the Warden organism only in terms of the power it gives some people. You must recognize it as a *total* fact of life for *everything* on Lilith, not merely for who's got the power. The Warden organism is a peculiarity of the evolution of this world; it was not designed for human beings. It is just a freak of nature that we're able to tap into it."

"What do you mean?"

"Think of the Warden beast as a regulator, a balancer that evolved of necessity here. Exactly why it evolved is not for me to say, but my best guess would be that this world, for much of its past, went through some pretty violent changes. I don't know the nature of them, but there are reptiles, mammals, crystalline creatures of some sort—all sorts of creatures on the other Warden worlds that are not found here. Here only the insect was able to survive, it being the most adaptable and, ironically, the least likely to change. But I suspect that even the insects and the plants were threatened by whatever changes the planet underwent, so much so that there evolved a mechanism in nature to keep things stable—at equilibrium, you might say. *Why* the planet needs to be kept in that state is another question for which I don't have any answers, but it does. In some funny way the planet *needs* this ecosystem, at least to survive. That's the reason for the Warden organism."

"You talk as if the planet itself were alive."

He nodded slowly. "I have often found it more convenient to think that way. Look, when man originally set out from Earth centuries ago he expected to find very alien worlds. What did he find? Mostly worlds that were crater-strewn and dead, gas giants, frozen rock piles, and occasionally a planet that perhaps was a mess but could be terraformed. Most of the livable planets not needing a lot of work were already inhabited, some by mere plants and animals but some by other species. And yet—no matter how crazy the biology was or the ecosystem balance or the patterns of thought and behavior of nonhumans—they were all *comprehensible*. We could say, 'Oh, yes, the Alphans are tentacled protoplasmic blobs, but look at the environment they evolved in, look how we trace it thus and so, and look how the environmental conditions shaped their cultures, their ways of thinking, and so forth.' Their own cultures and ways of life might have been so crazy that we couldn't find anything in common with them, couldn't follow their reasoning at all, but taken as a whole they were all *comprehensible*. We never met a world so alien we couldn't at least understand, under the laws of physical and social science, how it got that way. Not until Lilith and her sisters."

I looked around at the foliage, at the deep blue sky, and at the remains of melon and berries. "Frankly, I can't see where you're heading," I told him. "In terms of familiarity, this world is more familiar than many I've been on."

He nodded. "Superficial familiarity, yes. These insects are all unique to Lilith, but they are recognizably insects. The plants are recognizably plants, since an atmosphere that will support us requires photosynthesis for complex plant life. But consider. The Warden Diamond is a statistical absurdity. Four worlds, *all* within the life-supporting range of a sun just right for them. Four worlds very close together—the distance between Charon and Medusa is only about 150 million kilometers, practically next door, with two goodies in between—almost as if they'd been placed there just for us. The idea is simply absurd. You know the slim ratio of solar systems to even terraformable worlds. And yet here they are, right in our way, and each with a tiny, inexplicable little additive that damned well keeps us here."

"You're giving the old argument—that the Wardens are all artificial," I pointed out. "You know there's never been any evidence of that."

"That's true," Father Bronz admitted, "but remember what I said about comprehensibility? It seems to be that, in this enormous universe of which we know so little, we are handcuffed by our rigid concepts. What we have here is something that's not comprehensible—truly alien—and so we ignore it, dismiss it, forget it. These planets do not fit our cosmology, so we dismiss them as aberrations of chance and forget about it. My feeling is that anything you find that can't be explained by your cosmology means that your cosmology's got some holes in it."

"The hand of God, perhaps?" I retorted, not meaning to make fun of his religion but unable to refute him, either.

He didn't laugh or take offense. "Since I believe that the universe was created by God and that He is everywhere and in everything and everyone, yes. I have often reflected that the Wardens might be here simply to slap down our smugness. But God is supremely logical, remember. The Wardens fit the rest of the universe somehow, of that I am convinced, even if they don't fit our perception of it. But we're off the track. I was discussing why your fine dream of returning Lilith to Paradise is impossible to realize."

I chuckled. "I didn't mind the digression. What else do we have to do, anyway?"

He shrugged. "Who knows? Discussion may be vital or it may be inconsequential. I have a feeling that you are somehow driven to command this world. You'll probably get killed in the attempt, of course, but if you survive—well, at least it's interesting to fence with you and see what you have in mind."

"Lord Tremon," I laughed. "Boy! Wouldn't *that* give the Confederacy heartburn!"

"You're no more Cal Tremon than I'm Marek Kreegan," Bronz came back casually. "We might as well stop the pretense, since nobody believes in it any more—and I never did."

I froze. "What do you mean?"

"You're on the wanted list here because Kreegan got information from his Confederacy agents that you were a plant, a spy, an assassin sent here to get him. You and I both know it's true. You're far too idealistic and ethical and all that to be somebody like Tremon, who was the sort of fellow who enjoyed making chopped hamburger out of his still-living enemies with carving knives. I knew that the first time we met, back in Zeis, just talking to you. You're too well-educated, too well-bred for Tremon—not to mention, of course, that you're too much a product of your culture. Who are you, anyway, by the way?"

I considered what he said, then thought about what it meant to me. I really didn't need to keep up the pretense any more. Kreegan knew it, Artur knew it— hell, *everybody* knew it.

"My name doesn't matter, does it?" I replied carefully. "I no longer exist as him. I'm Cal Tremon now and forever; I'm just not the Cal Tremon in the court dockets. And since this is his body, I'm more of him than I'd have believed."

He nodded. "All right, Cal it is. But you are an agent?"

"Assassin grade," I answered truthfully. "But it's not quite what you think. You and I know that, once down here and locked here forever, the only reason I'd have for killing Kreegan would be to challenge him for Lord of the Diamond. No, I'm here for something quite different."

"I find it interesting that they finally got that personality transfer process down mechanically. On Cerberus it's a product of the Warden organism, as physical shape-change adaptation is to Medusa and reality perception to Charon."

"You knew they were working on something like that?" I prodded suspiciously.

He nodded. "Sure. I told you I used to be a really influential power, didn't I? A few of the people involved in the research were Catholics who were very worried about the theological implications—the soul and all that. Frankly, though, not only I but the church as a whole dismissed the entire question as impossible. See what I mean about cosmologies not fitting facts?"

His story didn't ring altogether true, as I knew how absolute the security had been on the process, but I had to let it stand. Maybe my only ally on Lilith was holding out on me—but I was holding out on him, too.

"So you say it isn't Kreegan you're after," he went on, changing the direction of the conversation. "Then what? What is so vital that the Confederacy is willing to sacrifice one of their best just to find out about it, and what would force you to remain true to that end once you got here?"

Then I told him about the aliens, the penetration of the top levels of Military Systems Command, the whole story. It seemed the best course—and he might know something.

When I finished, he just sighed, then said, "Well, now . . . alien enemies, huh? Using the Four Lords . . . Damned clever beasts, you must admit that, to understand us so well."

I was disappointed. If anyone other than those at the very top of the hierarchy would know about the aliens, I felt certain Bronz would. "You've heard nothing about this?"

"Oh, yes, rumors," he responded. "I didn't put much stock in them, partly because of Kreegan. He's not like the others. He came here voluntarily, of his

own free will, after serving the Confederacy well and
loyally for his whole life. The revenge that would mo-
tivate the others would be lacking in him."

My heart sank. Wasted. All of it, me, wasted here.
Bronz was right—it had to be one of the other Lords.

But . . . did it?

"That might be true," I admitted, "but do *you*
know why an otherwise sane and even superior man
like Kreegan would volunteer to come to a place like
this? And could such a man be kept ignorant of things
as momentous as the aliens even if he *weren't* directly
involved at the start?"

Bronz thought it over. "Hmm . . . You're suggesting
that maybe Kreegan is the kingpin? It's possible, of
course. Suppose, for example, such a man as he became thoroughly disillusioned with his job, with his
employers, with the system he helped perpetuate?
Suppose that somewhere in his work he stumbled over
the aliens. It would explain much. It would explain,
for example, how the aliens instantly knew so much
about us, how they were able to use the Warden
worlds to their advantage. Kreegan would be ideal for
establishing, even masterminding an operation such as
you described—and it would take time. He'd have to
work his way up, like the rest of us. Maybe with a little alien help, of course, but it would still take time.
Then, once in power, they'd start to implement their
plans."

"I'd originally been thinking along similar lines," I
told him. "But it *would* mean that our aliens were supremely confident we could be counted on to overlook
them for the years it would take. And they would
have to have much patience."

Bronz shrugged. "Perhaps they do. And *did* you
find them? How much *did* they learn before one of
their fancy machines finally got caught? It seems to
me that, if your guess is right and these aliens are too
nonhuman to do much of anything themselves, and if
they knew they were well hidden or well disguised,
this was the best route."

"The only thing wrong with such a neat picture," I
said, "is in Kreegan's character itself. He's a good

deal older than I am, but he came from the same place. Our lives parallel to a remarkable degree, even to the type of work we did. I just can't see what would so disillusion him about the Confederacy that he'd want to destroy it, devote his whole life to doing so."

"Well, now, you've got a point there," Bronz came back, "but it's not the point you think you made. I can see an awful lot to be disillusioned about in the Confederacy. I think perhaps you have Kreegan a little backward. I could just as easily picture him as a totally committed idealist willing to do anything for his cause. Out of that background I can envision a man who just might commit his very soul to such a project, not for gain but in an idealistic crusade."

"I think you're crazy," I told him. "An idealist would have certainly changed the system on Lilith. At the very least pawns would be far better off, the ruling class taken down several pegs."

Father Bronz laughed and shook his head in wonder. "You poor soul. Let's look at Lilith first, in light of all I've said. The social system is *not* merely determined by individual power. It is determined by the need to have Lilith support a nonindigenous human population, something she was simply not designed to do. The Warden organism defends the planetary ecosystem—the plant and animal balance, the rocks, the swamps, the air and water—against change. It struggles to retain an equilibrium. Total balance. *We're* the aliens here, the incomprehensible ones, son. We have power, yes, but it's of a very limited nature. We cannot reshape this planet, but can only adapt to its existing conditions. The Warden beasties won't let us. Now, dump thirteen million totally wrong aliens here and see what happens."

I couldn't see where he was going and said so.

"It's so *simple*," he responded. "You're so used to technology as the answer to all ills that you don't see what we're faced with here. All of human history is the history of technology, of using that technology so that man can change his environment to suit himself. And we have. On Earth we changed the course of rivers, we bent sun and wind and whatever it took to our ends. We leveled mountains when they were inconvenient, and built them where we wanted. We created lakes, cut down whole forests, tamed the entire planet. Then we went out to the stars and did the same thing. Terraforming. Genetic engineering. Using our technology, we changed whole planets; we even changed ourselves. Man's history is warring with his environment and winning that war. But, son, on Lilith—and only on Lilith—man cannot declare war. He *must* live within the environment that was already here. On Lilith the environment won. One lonely skirmish, true, but we were whipped. Beaten. We can't fight it. We can build a castle, yes, and get insects to carry us to and fro, but we can make only minor dents, dents that would be instantly erased if they weren't being constantly maintained.

"You see, son, Lilith's the boss here, thanks to Warden's bug. We all dance to her tune or compromise with her, but she's the boss. And yet we must feed and house thirteen million people. We must support thirteen million alien interlopers on a land not meant for them and on which we can't really perform more than cosmetic changes. Somebody has to grow the food and ship it. Somebody has to raise the great insect beasts and keep them domesticated. The economy must be kept going, for if those thirteen million were suddenly left entirely to their own devices they'd go out and eat and drink their fill and denude the melon groves. They'd fight each other as savage hunters and gatherers, the most primitive of tribal structures, and all but the toughest would die.

"Don't you see, son? Nobody enjoys the kind of hard labor it takes to keep the system going—but *name me another that would work*. Without technology at our disposal, we are condemned to mass muscle power."

I was appalled. "Are you claiming that there's no other way to do it?"

"Nope. There are lots of other ways, all more cruel and worse than this one. There may well be a better way, but I don't know it. I suspect that's the way Kreegan sees it, too. I'm sure he doesn't *like* the system, since it's so much like the Confederacy—if we're right about him, that is—but unlike the Confederacy, he, like me, can't see any better way."

I couldn't believe what I was hearing. To have all one's basic beliefs challenged in an offhanded manner like this was a bit much. "What do you mean, this system is so much like the Confederacy?" I challenged. "I certainly can't see any similarities."

Father Bronz snorted contemptuously. "Then you do not see what you see. Consider the so-called civilized worlds. Most of humanity have been equalized into a stagnant sameness beyond belief. On a given planet everybody looks pretty much the same, talks pretty much the same, eats, sleeps, works, plays pretty much the same. They're pawns, all of them. They think the same. And they are taught that they are happy, content, at the pinnacle of human achievement, the good life for all, and they believe it. It's true they are coddled more, their cages are gilded, but they are pawns all the same. The only real difference between their pawns and ours is that ours know that they are pawns and understand the truth of the whole system. Your civilized worlds are so perfectly programmed to think the same that they are never even allowed to face the truth."

"It's a pretty comfortable pawnship," I pointed out, not really conceding his point but allowing his terms for argument's sake.

"Comfortable? I suppose so. Like pet canaries, maybe. Those are small birds that live in cages in people's homes, in case you don't know—not on the civilized worlds, of course, where pets are not thought of. But at any rate these birds are born in cages; they are fed there, and their cages are regularly cleaned by their owners. They know no other life. They know that somebody provides them with all they need to exist, and having no other expectations, they want for no more. In exchange, they chirp comfortably and provide companionship to lonely frontiersmen. Not only is no canary ever going to engineer a breakout of that cage, but he's not even going to imagine, let alone design and build, a better life. He can't even conceive of such a thing."

"Those are animals," I pointed out. "Like Sheeba here."

"Animals, yes," he acknowledged, "but so are the humans of the civilized worlds. Pets. Everybody has an apartment that is just so in size, just so in furnishings, just so in every way the same. They look the same and wear the same clothes, as if it mattered, and they perform jobs designed to keep the system going. Then they return to their identical cubicles, get immersed in entertainment that involves them totally in some formula story that's all about their own world, offering nothing new in thought, idea, concept. Most of their free time they spend on drugs in some happy, unproductive never-never land. Their arts, their literature, their very traditions are all inherited from history. They have none of their own. We've equalized them too much for that—equalized out love and ambition and creativity, too. Whenever equality is imposed as an absolute, it is always equalized at the least common denominator, and historically, the least common denominator of mankind has been quite low indeed."

"We still advance," I pointed out. "We still come up with new ideas, new innovations."

"Yes, that's true," Bronz admitted. "But you see, my son, that's not from the civilized worlds. The masters of those worlds, the Outside supervisors and knights and dukes and lords, know that they can't let progress die completely or they die and their power with it. So we have the frontier, and we have selective breeding of exceptional individuals. The elite, working in the castles of Outside."

"We don't have those ranks and positions and you know it," I retorted.

He gave a loud guffaw. "The *hell* you say! And what then, pray tell, are *you*? What is Marek Kreegan? What, for that matter, am I? Do you know what my *real* crime was, Tremon? I reintroduced not merely religion but the concepts of love, of spirituality, to those pawns. I gave them something new, a rediscovery of their humanity. And it threatened the system! I was—removed. As long as I was on the frontier giving aid and comfort to the miserable and the uncomfortable, why, I was fine. Let the churches be. But when I started making headway on the civilized worlds—oh, no, then I was dangerous. I had to be removed or I might accomplish the unthinkable. I might awaken those pawns from their total environmental entertainment mods and drug stupors and show them they didn't have to be trained canaries any more, they could be individual human beings—like me. Like you. Like the ruling class. And I got slapped down."

"For a man with that idea of the civilized worlds, you are mighty complacent about this one," I noted.

He shrugged. "Here it is necessary—at least until somebody comes up with something better and has the power and will to enforce it and make it work. But back home—oh, no. Man is master of his environment, but he is also the slave of the technocratic class that rules so cleverly that the slaves don't even know they're slaves. What of complacency? Aren't you guilty of the reverse, Cal? Aren't you raring to change Lilith, but totally complacent about the civilized worlds? Son, the time for carrying out the orders of your superior are over. You're calling your own tune now. You can think what you like. It provides a fascinating contrast, does it not? Here on Lilith man is enslaved in body yet free to think, to love, to dance, to tell stories, whatever. The *mind* is free, although the body's in chains—just like much of human history. Back where we come from it's not the body they own—hell, they *made* it—it's the mind. Nobody's enslaving your mind any more, boy. Use it to solve your own, not their, problems."

I recoiled from the dialogue. I didn't like to think about what Bronz was saying, for if I lost my belief in my own culture and the rightness of it, I had nothing else, nothing left. Worse, if what he said was true, then what had my whole life been? Tracking down those who didn't fit, ferreting out those who would challenge, subvert, or topple the system on which the civilized worlds were based.

If what he said was true, then in the context of the civilized worlds, I was . . .

Kronlon.

Could it be true? I asked myself unbelievingly. If so, did Marek Kreegan go out one day to find the enemy and come face to face with himself?

What had Marek Kreegan been like, Vola?

A lot like you, Cal Tremon. An awful lot like you . . .

Chapter Sixteen

Sumiko O'Higgins and the Seven Covens

A few hours after darkness on the second night we made the rendezvous point. Until now I'd left myself entirely in Father Bronz's hands, but now I wanted information.

"Who are these—savages?" I asked. "And what can they do for us?"

"Cal, the savages in these parts—in fact, in most parts I've seen—aren't savage, except to members of a Keep," he told me. "They are the misfits. People with the power but untrained, people with no power but determined never to work the fields their whole lives, renegades, political outcasts like yourself, and of course their children. I picked this group because of its relative power. They are strong and highly skilled, if somewhat anarchistic."

"I thought you said that wouldn't work here," I taunted, feeling good that I'd scored at least once.

"Oh, it doesn't," he responded airily. "Not on a large scale, anyway. Not even on a small one, really, but people can be made to *think* they're in an anarchy if that's what they want. On a *very* small scale they can be truly savages, of course—but they meet the fate of all true savages. They die young and usually violently. No, these folks have an organization and powerful people, but they are, ah, a bit unorthodox."

Father Bronz crossed himself when he said that last, and it was such an interesting reaction I had to press it. I'd seen him do that only a very few times, such as just before and just after the roadblock.

"These people are dangerous, then?"

He nodded. "Very. You might say that we—that is, they and I—are in the same business. Competitors."

"Another church?"

He chuckled. "In a sense, yes. They are the opposition, my lad, and you don't know how it galls me to have to use them, let alone trust them. They are witches, you see, and worship Satan."

I had to laugh. *"Witches?* Oh, come on, now."

"Witches," he acknowledged gravely. "I don't know why that should surprise you. Let's just say you were of a magical or romantic bent. Take a look at Lilith then. A spoiled Eden. Now, instead of Warden organisms and mathematical constructs, chemical catalysts and the other stuff of science we take so much for granted, replace it with the word *magic.* The upper classes, those with the power, then become magicians, wizards, sorcerers. Utilizing the Warden organism as you tell me you did, on that chair for example. A thing of nature? How about a 'magic spell' instead? *You* know what runs this world, and how, and *I* know, but do most people? Without that knowledge, isn't it a world of wizards and magic spells?"

I saw his point, although it didn't cheer me. "So we're being placed in the hands of people who believe all this?"

He nodded. "So watch your step. They're doing this mostly because it gives 'em a kick to have a priest ask a favor of Satanists. But *they* believe it, and they don't have much of a sense of humor about it, either. Some of 'em can fry you, too, so watch that sharp tongue."

I shut up. Whatever craziness these people believed, no matter how absurd it might be, they were the only hope I had.

We waited for the Satanist party.

They appeared without our having ever detected their presence. At one moment we were just lounging by the cart, relaxing and hoping that one of Lilith's frequent and violent thunderstorms, which was looming close on the horizon, would not hit where we were when I was suddenly aware of a number of people standing around us. I jumped up and turned in fighting posture, but quickly relaxed when Bronz seemed less concerned.

They were all women, about a dozen of them, some with the look of the civilized worlds about them—but certainly different-looking in this context. Their hair was cut very, very short, and their faces and skins had that rough, weathered look pawns get, although these women were not pawns. All wore some sort of breechclout that as nearly as I could tell was made of some tough and weathered leaf, held on by carefully braided and tied ropelike vines. On a loop of that vine, each bore some sort of weapon—a stone axe, some kind of mineral-carved knife, or in at least two cases, bows and flint-tipped arrows.

One of them, a large woman who was tall and imposing, was the exception to the hair rule, her long, silky-black hair reaching down past her buttocks. She was obviously the leader and radiated a charismatic confidence you could almost feel. Not that she could fail to dominate any scene she was in; at more than two meters in height, she was almost as big as I was.

"Well, well, Father Bronz," she said, her voice deep and rich. "So this is the fugitive in trouble." She looked at me and I felt as if I were being examined by some scientist unpleased with the odor and look of her specimen. She turned back to the priest. "You said something about a girl. Was that just a papist lie?"

"Oh, stow it, Sumiko," Bronz growled. "You know me better than that. She's in the cart."

A flick of the leader's head and three of the other

women rushed to the cart, pulled the straw off Ti, and gently removed her.

"Sons of bitches," the leader snorted in genuine anger and stalked over to the comatose girl. She repeated what Bronz had done when he'd first seen her, placing her hands on Ti's forehead and concentrating hard. After a moment she drew back, opened her eyes, and turned again to face us. "What bastard did this?" she almost snarled.

"Pohn, over at Zeis," Bronz responded wearily. "You've heard the stories, and now you know they're true."

She nodded gravely. "Someday, I promise you, I will get that worm in my hands and I will slowly, very slowly, dissect him as he watches."

"Can you do anything for her?" I put in, both concerned and piqued at being ignored.

She nodded thoughtfully. "I think so. A little. At least I can bring her out of it, but there's the danger of clotting or brain damage if she's not gotten to a doctor—a real one who knows just what repairs to make. From what I can see of the spell, Pohn is less powerful than I am, but he's damned tricky and clever." She gestured to us and started walking. The other women put Ti back in the cart, and one jumped up behind Sheeba, saying nothing. The cart started, and so did the witch queen—that was the only way I could think of her. We followed off into the bush of the wild.

As we walked, Bronz turned to me and said, softly, "Well, now you've met her. Sumiko O'Higgins, chief witch and a regular loving charmer."

"She is—ah—formidable," I returned.

"That she is," he agreed. "Still, she's strong. If anybody can help Ti and you, she can."

"I don't think I made a good first impression or something," I noted. "She certainly seemed less than pleased with me."

He chuckled. "Sumiko doesn't like men very much. But don't worry. This is strictly business."

I didn't feel reassured. "Will she really help me?"

I pressed. "I mean, all things considered, she's got us where she wants us."

"Don't worry," he responded, "you're perfectly safe. Satanists pride themselves, oddly, on their honor. They simply don't break agreements and commitments once made. Besides, she hates the keeps more than anyone I know, and you're a refugee wanted by the higher-ups. That gives you status here."

"I hope so," I said dubiously. "Who *is* she, anyway? She's at least a Master herself."

He nodded. "Probably more. And with no formal training whatsoever. If she'd gotten some, she might have been ripe for Lord, but that wouldn't fit her personality."

We walked along for some time, losing sight of the cart and of any trace of the road or anything remotely familiar. We were in fact prisoners of the witch-queen's whims. I hoped fervently that Bronz was right about her, but I still remembered his cross and prayer. This was definitely the first human being I'd seen that Father Bronz feared.

We walked on for some time—how long I couldn't tell, since the life on Lilith and the abnormally long days and nights had played hell with what little time sense I retained. Finally, though, we arrived at our host's encampment, a jungle enclave that was quite different from any of the Keeps that I'd seen. The houses were made not from *bunti* but from strong wood and bamboolike reeds, the pointed thatched roofs from some woven straw. The arrangement was a bit odd: thirteen such "houses" were arranged in a large circle around a clearing in the center of which was a pit, a fireplace for central cooking, and some sort of stone cairn. The inhabitants of the village seemed most active in the dark; they were going about their tasks as we entered the village, and I noticed that the population was larger than I'd expected— sixty, perhaps more—and that all were women. The lack of men anywhere only served to increase my nervousness.

The cart had already arrived by some other route. The women doing whatever they were doing by the flickering light of the low central fire and a number of gourd lanterns filled with the flammable juices of several plants paid us no real mind as we entered. A few glances up of obvious idle curiosity, but no more. Clearly we were not only expected but weren't even big news. I noticed that most of the women were naked and unadorned, marking them as pawns. Apparently the ranking members of the tribe, Supervisor level and above, had *all* come out to meet us. That told me that they felt their village secure but hadn't been any too trusting of us.

The leader called out to a couple of women, and instructions started flying all over the place. Father Bronz and I decided that we were somehow redundant at the moment and just stood back out of the way, watching.

A covering was removed from the central area near the fire, revealing a large stone slab with what might have been a carved recess in it. It looked like a cross between a birdbath and one of those damned tables in Pohn's chamber of horrors. The fire was being stoked, and now Ti's inert form was brought from the cart and placed in the recess in the stone. Twelve women, ten of them apparently pawns, formed a circle around the comatose girl, almost blocking her from view.

I turned to Bronz and asked, "What the hell is going on here?"

"That's what it is, all right—hell," he sighed. "They're going to try and bring Ti out of the state she is in, but being Satanists, they will do it as a religious ceremony. This is hard on me, understand, but these women are deluded rather than evil and I'm a pragmatist. Sumiko was the only one I knew with this much power and some medical knowledge who wasn't on the other side or too far away to do us any good."

I shrugged. Satanism and Catholicism were one and the same to me, both remnants of ancient superstitions and power structures no longer relevant to modern times. Still, I conceded to myself, if this mumbo jumbo allowed them to concentrate and focus their powers to help Ti, well, so be it.

The twelve started chanting. I couldn't really catch

the words, but if they *were* words, I think it was a language I didn't know.

They chanted for some time, until it started to get boring, but just when I'd settled down to relax, Sumiko O'Higgins entered from one of the huts. She was something to see, draped in black robes and a cape, wearing what appeared to be a carved upside-down cross on some sort of vine necklace.

As she approached the circle of chanting women, the fire, which had almost died out, burst back into explosive life with a force all its own, an action that startled me. It was an eerie effect, all the more so since I knew that the Warden organism died in fire just as all others I'd ever known did, and thus that fire business couldn't be a Warden power trick.

O'Higgins closed the circle by her presence and joined the chant, then dominated it, eyes seemingly closed, arms stretched out to the sky, appearing almost in a trancelike state. Suddenly the chant was stilled, leaving only the sounds of the massive insects of Lilith. I didn't even hear anybody breathe or cough.

"Oh, Satan, Lord of Darkness, hear our prayer!" she chanted.

"Gather, darkness!" the others responded.

"Oh, great one who combats the totalitarianism of church and government, work within us and hear our plea!"

"Hear our plea," echoed the others.

She opened her eyes and lowered her arms slowly, then placed both hands on Ti's unmoving head. "Give us strength to heal this girl," she prayed, then closed her eyes again, still touching Ti's head, apparently reentering the trancelike state. It was difficult to tell if she was faking it or was really in a trance. I began to have some doubts about this procedure, but there really was no alternative. I glanced over at Father Bonz and saw him just looking on and sadly shaking his head.

The tableau in the center court seemed frozen for some time, and I understood that, no matter what their odd beliefs, O'Higgins and maybe some of the others were probing, analyzing, perhaps even making repairs.

Suddenly the witch queen let go and stepped back, raising her arms once again. "Oh, Satan, Prince of Darkness, rightful King of the Universe, we give thanks!" she almost shouted, and the litany was repeated by the others. The fire flared again into near-blinding brilliance, then almost died, causing the strong impression of a tangible darkness closing in, embracing all of us there in the village. I felt a little chill despite the heat and humidity, I have to admit. I could well understand how this sort of thing could attract followers.

"From light into darkness, from dark knowledge the final victory," she intoned, and then it was broken, as if by some signal. All thirteen of the women stood a little unsteadily, appearing to have gone through some strenuous physical labor.

O'Higgins recovered quickly, though, and walked back to the still unmoving form of Ti, placing hands again on her head. She nodded to herself, then called for others to bear Ti to one of the huts. As they were carrying out her orders, she turned and walked over to us.

"Well, Bronz, your side couldn't do a damned thing," she noted.

Bronz shrugged. "You did what was necessary?"

"I undid what I could," she admitted, "but I told you that that butchering bastard was really good and really clever. She'll be all right for a while, though— in fact better than all right, since I had to bypass a lot of Pohn's knots and create alternate routes that might not hold up. There'll be a rush, though—she'll probably feel like she can topple mountains, even though in reality she'll be quite weak until she gets a lot more exercise and regular food, and I fear the repair job won't hold forever."

"You mean," I put in, "that she'll eventually lapse back into that state?"

She nodded. "Remember the way the system works," she said. "The Warden organisms have a single idea of what is natural. Those with the power can convince Wardens that something else is what they want to do—and that's what Pohn did. Her Wardens

want to put her back into that state because he's
fooled them into thinking that it's normal. I bypassed
the nerve blocks by using parts of the brain not normally used at all, but the Wardens will perceive my
meddling as an injury, like a broken arm. They will
rush to fix it, put it right. They'll be battling my own
work with some localized Wardens, but the barriers will
eventually break down. It'll take somebody as expert
in cranial medicine *and*/or more powerful than Dr.
Pohn to put her completely right, although that could
be accomplished in a matter of minutes by such a person."

I frowned. "How long, then, will she—wake up?"

She shrugged. "A few days, maybe a week. No
more. It'll go slowly, so there's no sure way to tell."

I groaned in frustration. "Then what the hell was
the use of all this? Who could really heal her in that
length of time?"

She looked at me, slightly surprised at my tone.
"You really care? About a small female?"

"He cares," Bronz put in, saving me from making
nasty comments to my host. "He escaped from Zeis
and he could have done it a lot easier without bringing her. Instead he's lugged her with him everywhere,
fed her, cleaned her—you name it."

She looked at me again, this time nodding slightly,
and for the first time I felt like I'd attained the status
of human being in her eyes. "If she means that much
to you," she said to me, "then perhaps something *can*
be done. There's only one place I know of for sure,
though, that could do the job, and it's pretty far
away."

"Moab Keep," Father Bronz added, nodding. "I
suspected as much. But four thousand kilometers,
Sumiko! How in God's name can we possibly get her
there in under a year? Let alone Tremon here, who
needs to take the full treatment."

She grinned evilly. "Not in *God's* name, Augie. But
the answer's obvious—we fly. A *besil* can do three,
maybe four hundred kilometers a night, resting days,
so we're talking ten days at the outside. That sound a
lot more possible?"

"Besils!" Bronz scoffed. "Since when do you have access to any domesticated *besils* capable of carrying passengers?"

"I don't—now," she admitted. "I expect that if we need *besils,* though, we can get them pretty easily courtesy of Zeis Keep."

I jumped. "What!"

She shrugged. "Either you slipped up somewhere, Augie, or *he* did. It doesn't matter. We're partially surrounded by Zeis troopers right now, and I expect them to come in at sunup, when they can see what they're doing."

I whirled around, staring at the darkness in nervous anticipation. When I realized that neither of the other two seemed in any way concerned by that news, I just grew a little more paranoid about them.

I turned to Father Bronz, who was cocking his head slightly, as if listening for something. Finally he said, "How many do you make them?"

"No more than twenty or thirty, all on *besils,*" she responded casually. "I'd suppose somebody's gone back for more, but he's not about to commit more than a fraction of his force. Some of the other knights might get the idea to exploit the weakness and attack Zeis."

Bronz nodded agreement. "Then we'll face no more than forty, a fifth or so of his force. I agree. Okay, forty people at arms, with Artur almost a certainty and, say, two other masters?"

She nodded. "That's about it."

"Wait a minute!" I exploded. "It may not be important to *you,* but they're after the girl and me! You can't fight a force like that!"

Sumiko O'Higgins shook her head slowly in disgust. "Now, isn't that just like a man! Look, you just go cower someplace and maybe get some sleep and leave the worrying to me."

"But—but—they're all highly trained soldiers, all of 'em at least supervisors and with more masters than you've got here!" I sputtered. "How do you expect to defeat them?"

"Just don't you worry about it," she replied condescendingly. "We—Father Bronz and I—have a lot of work to do between now and dawn. A good thing the God-lovers and we Satanists can get together and agree on one sort of cooperative venture," she added. "*Atheists! Pgh!*"

Father Bronz added, "She knows what she's doing, Cal," in his most reassuring tone. If it hadn't been for the under-the-breath addition of "I hope" to his statement I just might have believed him.

As it was, I just stayed there, not feeling at all asleep, seeing Master Artur's fierce mustachioed gaze behind every darkness-shielded bush and tree in the jungle.

Chapter Seventeen

I Do Believe in Witches—I Do, I Do!

Needless to say, I got very little sleep that night. Of course nobody in the witch village seemed to sleep at night, although they were all rather expert at ignoring anybody they didn't want to see and I was a nonperson in their eyes.

The best I could do was occasionally check on Ti, who when I peeked in for the third or fourth time was not only breathing deeply and regularly, as if in normal sleep, but actually gave out a moan and turned over by herself. That sight alone made this whole business all worthwhile—provided, of course, I lived through the next day.

Although I knew little about witchcraft and remembered less, from the village itself I made a few deductions. Thirteen, the unlucky number because it was the number at the Christians' Last Supper, was naturally a positive number for devil-worshipers. Thirteen women in the coven, then, which explained the number at the ceremony. Thirteen large huts, too, although there were far more than that number living here communally. I never could get an exact count, but I was willing to wager that whatever it was, the number was a multiple of thirteen.

Witch, of course, was a female term. If my old children's stories meant anything, a male witch would be called a warlock, but for some reason you just about never heard about them. They were more mischievous, less powerful, somehow. I remembered that Father Bronz's faith limited the priesthood to males in most cases, which might explain female dominance in Satanism, but it also occurred to me that Dr. Pohn had said that women tended to have more of the power than men, particularly wild talents. I wondered about the hierarchy itself on Lilith now. How many of the knights were female? I wondered. Half? Or a majority? Despite the fact that Tiel was the knight at Zeis, it was Vola who taught me, as she had taught Artur and Marek Kreegan. Artur, Dr. Pohn, and Father Bronz not withstanding, it suddenly seemed to me that an extraordinary number of the staff of the Castle had been female, and the first master I'd met after arriving on Lilith had been a woman, as had at least half of Artur's soldiers.

Even in my statistically small sample, then, the women were numerically superior to the men. Perhaps Pohn had more reason to confine his experiments to young women than just perversion.

I looked around again at these—witches. Dismiss the religious cultism, the "savage" label, all the rest, and reduce it to what was known. Their chief was one who had the power in spades—Bronz had said she might be in Kreegan's class had she had training, but as I knew only too well, such power even untrained can be enormous if emotionally aroused, and hate was one of the best emotions for that sort of thing. Sumiko O'Higgins hated Zeis, if only for the principle of the thing—Zeis had Pohn, and Pohn had done a number on Ti, a woman.

These others . . . Even though most *looked* like pawns, were they? There was something here I was missing, unless Satan, Prince of Darkness, really had something here. Something had kept this tempting target for Keeps all around safe and secure—so secure O'Higgins dared bring her most powerful personnel to collect us.

It was getting close to dawn, and I was becoming more and more nervous. O'Higgins and Father Bronz had been at it all night, making plans of some kind or another—an odd couple if there ever was one, I decided—and finally the priest emerged from a hut and came over to me. "You look lousy," he said.

"You don't look so bright and eager either," I responded glumly. "But how'd you expect me to sleep through something like *this?*"

He sat down wearily. "I need some strong tea to wake me up," he muttered, more to himself than to me. "She's really got something here. I have to hand it to her. I don't know if it'll work or not, but if it does, it's almost revolutionary. No, it *is* revolutionary."

I stared at him. "Give. What are you talking about?"

"You remember our talks on the balance on Lilith? Well, she seems to have something that upsets that balance, at least a little."

I frowned. "What do you mean?"

"You see these women? All virgins, believe it or not, at least with men. All exhibited strong wild talents at puberty, although most subsided to pawn status, as per normal, after a few months to a year."

"You can't tell me O'Higgins is a virgin," I commented.

He chuckled. "Hard to say. I doubt if she's ever been to bed with a man, if that's what you mean, and that's all that seems to count in this business. There may be something to the old legend of virgins having more power in magical things—in a purely biological sense, Lilith style, I mean. Perhaps some very tiny chemical changes were not introduced. I don't know. But Sumiko got this idea, after combing the savages of the wild, that it was so. She may be crazy but she's not stupid. She was once a pretty good biochemist Outside, so don't sell her short no matter what her crazy beliefs now. At any rate, when she got sent to Lilith she didn't stay a pawn very long. Hot-blooded. Got so damned mad she not only fried her supervisor but stalked angrily out of a Keep to the west of here, glowing, it's said, like a firecracker from the Warden power, injuring or killing anybody who even tried to get in her way."

"None of that catalyst?" I responded unbelievingly.

He shook his head. "None. Now you see what I mean. She was in the wild for a while before she even found out about the stuff. She wasn't just a biochemist, Cal—she was a botanist. It took her months, but she found out what the catalyst was and worked out her own methods for distilling it. How she did it without tools, without a lab, and without even the facilities of a Keep we'll never know—sheer guts and willpower, I'd say. Cal, I don't know what she's come up with, but it isn't quite the nice, pure stuff you and I got, so it isn't as effective, but it works. She recruited all these women when they were very young, just for their wild-talent potential—and, I suspect, their sexual orientation. For short periods of time—I don't know duration —she can dose every woman here with the stuff. Awaken all their old wild talents. Use the cult beliefs and discipline to shape and direct them." He sighed. "You know, in an hour or two I think old Artur may be in for a big surprise."

I thought about what he said and it gave me some immediate hope, but the more I thought about it the more I realized its long-term implications.

Pawns were hardly celibate—Ti, for example, would never make a witch for *this* group—but if O'Higgins really *did* have this stuff it was the equivalent of a fusion bomb to Lilith.

"Bronz, how many women does she have here?"

He was resting, and for a moment I thought he was asleep. But one eye opened. "Thirteen times thirteen. What did you expect?"

One hundred and sixty-nine women, I thought. All handpicked by somebody who knew exactly what she was doing and what she was looking for. All with demonstrated wild talents of major proportions, and with a little chemical aid to awaken those locked-away powers; all fiercely loyal to their leader and mother figure.

"She hasn't got a Satanist nut cult here," I said aloud, "she's got the kernel of a revolutionary army."

"So it took you that long to figure all that out?" Father Bronz muttered sleepily.

The facts weren't all that reassuring. I really wasn't quite sure if I'd like a world fashioned by Sumiko O'Higgins as well as I liked the one run by Marek Kreegan. I wondered idly what the witch-queen's offense had been to have her sent here. Nothing pleasant, that was for sure.

As the sun rose the entire company of witches went through what appeared to be a solemn ceremony that involved, as far as I could see, cursing the sun for rising and spoiling the lovely night and asking for Satan's aid in the coming fight. In the center area, over the restoked fire, a giant gourd caldron bubbled and hissed.

After morning "prayers," each and every one of the women approached the caldron and, with an incantation, drank the hot, foul-smelling liquid from a crudely fashioned dipper. I felt helpless in the coming fight and wished for some of that brew, but Bronz would have none of it.

"Sumiko says the stuff would play hell with your nervous system," he told me. "I'm not sure I believe it, but we're the guests here. You just stay back and watch what happens—and keep out of the way. They'll have spears, poison darts, blowguns, bows and arrows, and even crossbows. Your duty is to stay down and out of the way. If you get killed, then all this will have been for nothing."

I started to argue, but his logic was unassailable. I went to Ti's hut, now emptied of its other occupants, and looked down at her.

She moaned, turned over, and opened her eyes, seeing me. "Hi," she muttered weakly.

"Hi, yourself," I responded, not bothering to hide my big grin. "You know where you are?"

She groaned and tried to sit up, failed the first time,

then managed it. "Sort of," she told me. "It was—kinda like a crazy dream. I was sound asleep, and I knew I was sound asleep, but I could hear stuff when there was stuff to hear and see stuff when my eyes were open. It was all dreamy like, though, not real." She hesitated a second, looking puzzled and serious. "But it *was* real, wasn't it, Cal? All of it? That creepy doctor, that horrible room, you rescuing me, Father Bronz, witches—they really *are* witches, aren't they, Cal?"

I nodded. "Sort of. At least *they* think they are."

She stared at me with the kind of expression I had never seen anyone give me before. "You could've got out real easy, but you took me," she whispered, low and almost to herself. Her voice broke slightly and she said, "Oh, Cal, hold me! Hug me! Please!"

I went to her and gently squeezed, but she grabbed on to me and hugged and kissed me as hard and strong as she could. Finally she gasped and I saw tears in her eyes. "I love you, Cal," she almost sobbed, and hugged me again.

I looked at her strangely for a moment, not quite comprehending her actions nor my reactions. "I—I love you too, my little Ti," I replied, then held her close and hugged her, a sense of wonder and amazement coming over me at the realization that, incredibly, what I'd just said was true.

The village seemed deserted. I could see only the smoking remains of the fire and an empty gourd-pot. Not a sign of life, although all around I could hear the ever-present insect chorus.

And then the sound stopped.

It was eerie, incredible. For a moment I thought I had gone deaf, so absolute was the silence in contrast with what I was used to. Not a sound, not a whisper. Even the wind had stopped.

Suddenly, from all around came the sound of incredibly loud, piercing screeches, and a sudden wind whipped the trees from all over. I remained in the hut, conscious that I could do no more, but I was damned well going to see what I could see. Ti, although still very weak, was equally determined once the situation was explained to her, and when I objected to her nearness to the doorway she objected to *my* being too exposed. I surrendered and we both watched, cautiously.

The *besils* rose effortlessly from cover a hundred meters or so from the witch village. Although I couldn't see anything in back of me, I was aware from how they were deployed that they must have the place encircled.

I marveled at how the creatures seemed to rise incredibly smoothly as if on some invisible hoist, then hover there, nearly motionless, about twenty meters up, just beyond the treetops.

One *besil* glided slowly out of the formation and approached the center of the village, almost over the caldron, then descended to a point only four or five meters above the ground. I was marveling at how effortlessly the creature moved, but then the rider drew my attention.

"Artur," I heard Ti gasp. And in fact it *was* the Sergeant at Arms of Zeis Keep, his icy power radiating like a living thing.

"Witches!" he shouted gruffly. "I wish to speak with your leader! We have no need to do battle here today!"

Suddenly, as if popping up from nowhere, Sumiko O'Higgins stood there in full robes and regalia, facing him. I had no idea how she got there without being seen.

"Speak, armsman!" she called back. "Speak and begone! You have no right or business here!"

Artur laughed evilly, although I could tell he was slightly disconcerted by her sudden appearance and defiant tone. "Right? *Might* makes right, madam, as well you know. You and your colony exist here at the sufferance of the Grand Duke because you do us occasional service, but it is for that reason alone that I might spare you. You err, too, madam, in saying I have no business here. No less than my Lord Marek Kreegan has charged me to return with Cal Tremon, the fugitive who is now in your charge. Surrender him to me and we will depart in peace. All will be as it has been."

"*Just* Tremon? You don't wish the girl as well?" the witch queen responded, and I had a sudden queasy feeling that she was striking a deal to her liking but definitely not to mine.

Artur laughed again. "Keep the girl if you wish," he responded airily. "We will even make certain she is fully restored. It is Tremon we must have, and it is Tremon we *will* have."

"I don't like your tone, armsman," O'Higgins responded. "You are so used to wielding absolute power that your arrogance will be your undoing. We do *not* exist here at the sufferance of Grand Duke Kobé or anyone else. Marek Kreegan is *your* Lord, but mine is Satan Mafkrieg, Prince of Darkness, King of the Underworld, and no other."

He ignored the commentary, but I heard Ti mutter under her breath, "Atta girl, witchie! Give him a taste of his own big mouth!"

Artur shrugged, looking very formidable and splendid on his great black beast. "I take it, then, that you will not voluntarily surrender the fugitive?"

"I have no love for him," the witch responded, "but I have far less for you and your masters. If you attack, you will be utterly and completely destroyed. The choice is yours."

Artur just glared at her a moment. Then with an almost imperceptible nudge of the big man's foot, the *besil* floated back to its place in the waiting formation. Sumiko O'Higgins just stood there, and while I marveled at her courage I thought she had acted in a pretty stupid fashion, all things considered.

Suddenly, as mysteriously as Sumiko had appeared, the rest of the witches were all there, spread out in an almost unbroken circle around the perimeter of the village, facing outward toward the attackers. None appeared to have any weapons.

Artur gave a hand gesture, and the two *besils* on either side of him glided forward, their riders aiming pretty nasty-looking fixed crossbows, like artillery pieces, mounted in front of them on their saddles. All four, by their positioning, fixed on Sumiko O'Higgins as they closed in, then fired almost in unison, the arrows flying with enormous force toward the black-garbed figure below.

I started to cry out, but instantly the witch queen waved her hand idly and all four arrows landed in the grass, neatly framing her. Then suddenly every third or fourth woman in the long human circle turned inward, and O'Higgins gestured again with her right arm at the four soldiers.

What followed was incredible. Although the men were bound in by thick, secure straps, they were hurled from their saddles as if plucked by a giant hand, then dashed to the ground below with a force far in excess of gravity. None of them moved.

Artur roared in anger, and the other soldiers closed in and started letting loose their terrible arsenal—spears, arrows, and all sorts of other stuff rapidly flew back and forth across the field—taking point-blank aim at the circle of women. An incredible hail of lethal stuff rained down upon the witches.

It all missed.

Now Sumiko was gesturing again, making some sort of symbol with her hands. *Besils* screamed, and several dropped out of the sky like stones, crashing to earth and taking their riders with them.

I was beginning to admit that the woman had something here.

Artur was fit to be tied, of course, but he gestured for his troops to regroup. It had occurred to him, as it had to me, that nothing nasty happened to you unless you broke that circle of human bodies, and he was reorganizing to meet that fact.

"Fire at the circle from the outside!" I heard him yell. "Knock 'em down!"

Now all the witches were turned outward once again, and Sumiko O'Higgins moved to the center of the open space, practically atop the altar or whatever it was. She shouted a single command and all the women turned inward, facing her, fixing their gazes upon her. I was puzzled but a lot less worried. Artur, I thought, was learning even more than I was today,

"Oh, Satan, King of All!" she shouted, and seemed to assume that trancelike state once more. "Mass thy power in thy servant's hands, that these unbelievers be brought to heel!"

Artur's troops formed a circle outside the witches' circle and prepared to let loose again. I braced for whatever would happen and watched as the witch-queen's head suddenly shot skyward, eyes open but still in some sort of hypnotic state; her arms were out-stretched, as if they were weapons aimed at the *besils*. She started to turn now, opposite the circling beasts and soldiers, and while I could see nothing, heat began crackling around that flying circle, the kind of odd internal fire I'd seen once before, when Kron-lon had fried. I looked briefly at the circle of women and saw their equally hypnotic gaze resting entirely on their leader.

"They're transmitting through her!" I gasped. "They're channeling their fear and hatred into O'Hig-gins!"

A number of missiles from the enemy were loosed and some reached their targets. A few women were struck and fell, bleeding, unconscious, or perhaps dead, but the rest never wavered, never even looked at their fallen sisters. The concentration was absolute.

One by one, as her invisible touch reached them, the soldiers of Zeis Keep were fried to dust in their saddles, or in some cases knocked completely out of the air. I saw that Artur himself had fallen back and was now shouting for the others to break rank and join him. It was all of three or four minutes since the attack had started, and less than half of his company remained.

"All right, witch!" he shouted. "As I said, might is all, and right now it is on your side! But when word of this reaches the Keeps, the force raised against you will be more powerful than this world has ever known! Enjoy your victory—for what it is worth!" And with that he was gone.

The witch-queen's arms came down and made an-other sign; then the spell or whatever was broken.

Women staggered, some fell, and others now bent down to attend to their fallen comrades.

O'Higgins snapped out of her trance in an instant and was all command. "See to the wounded!" she shouted. "I want a fatality count as quick as possible!" She turned and stalked over toward the hut in which Ti and I were hidden.

"Wow!" Ti breathed. "I never saw or heard anything like *that* before." She giggled. "That look on Artur's face was worth all of it, too! Many's the pawn at Zeis would've given his life to see this whippin'!"

"Don't sell him short," I told her. "He's lost a battle, not a war. He came up against a weapon he didn't know existed and he paid the price, but he's not licked by any means. He wasn't kidding when he threatened to come back with a super-army. They have to stamp out power like this or they'll never sleep easy again in their castles."

I saw Father Bronz emerge from a nearby hut looking suitably impressed. He and Sumiko O'Higgins quickly joined us in the hut.

"How many did you get?" she asked the priest.

"Six, maybe," he responded. "The rest had to be destroyed. Is it enough?"

"Hardly," she snapped. "But it'll have to do."

"Don't blame *me*," he retorted. "*You* shot 'em down. All I did was pick 'em back up."

I looked at the two in confusion. "What the *hell* are you two talking about?" I wanted to know. "Where *were* you during the battle, Father?"

He laughed. "Picking up the pieces. We needed *besils*. So while Sumiko and her witchy friends got the riders, I was able to grab control of six of them."

O'Higgins nodded. "That's what this was all about. That's why I permitted Artur to find the village in the first place. I'd hoped for more, though—at least a dozen."

"You'd've *had* a dozen if you hadn't fried or smacked down some," Bronz responded. "That was an amazing sight. Sumiko, I really underestimated you. Even when you told me last night I still couldn't believe that what you said was true, not in *that* way. Accumulated broadcasted Warden power! Incredible!"

She shrugged. "There's nothing in the rules against it. The Wardens don't really know the difference between a human cell, a plant cell, and a copper molecule, except that their genetic code or whatever they use for one acts on what they're in to keep it that way. If we can 'talk,' so to speak, to the Warden organism inside anything and tell it to do something it doesn't like to do—reprogram it, as it were—we can tell it to do other things, too. It's just like a computer, Augie. You can program it to do *anything* if you can figure out how."

"You're too modest," he replied sincerely, obviously not just flattering her. "It's a monumental discovery. Something entirely new, entirely different. It'll do for Lilith what the Industrial Revolution did for primitive man!"

She gave what I can only describe as a derisive snigger. "Perhaps," she responded, "*if* I decide to give it to people, and *if* it can be handled and managed on a planetary scale."

I was awestruck by the implications, which made Bronz's arguments against social revolution on Lilith obsolete. "But you have the means here to destroy the hierarchy! The pawns can have the power to run their own affairs!"

She sniffed. "And what makes you think they'll do the job any better than the ones doing it now? Maybe worse."

I shrugged off her cynicism as darker thoughts intruded. "He'll be back, you know. Artur, I mean. With a *hell* of a force. What are you going to do?"

"Nothing, dear boy," she responded. "Absolutely nothing. That surprises you? Well, would you believe that this place can't even be *detected* unless I wish it? Oh, they'll come back, of course. Maybe even with a couple of knights or even the old Duke himself. They'll fly around and around and they'll comb the ground with troops and they'll simply not see us. It will drive them mad, but they can land right in the middle of the heath out there and they won't see the village. How do you think we survived *this* long?"

Bronz himself shook his head in amazement. "Sumiko, the consolidation of Warden power I'm willing to accept, since my mind can at least explain it, but that's impossible!"

She laughed wickedly and tweaked his cheek. "Augie, you're a fine little fellow even if you are everything I can't stand, but keep believing that, won't you? It'll make life a lot simpler."

"But *how,* Sumiko?" he demanded to know. *"How?"*

She just smiled and said, "Well, the only thing I can tell you that'll get you thinking is that the Warden organism is in every single molecule of every cell in your body, the brain included. I haven't discovered any miracle formula here, Augie! All I did was sit down with the little beastie and learn how to talk to it properly."

"Father Bronz!" Ti shouted; he turned, then lit up as he saw her. She ran to him and gave him a big hug, which he returned, smiling. "Well, well, well!" he responded. "So we have our little Ti back with us once again!"

"And that points up the urgency of our getting a move on," Sumiko put in. "I'm going to go check the casualties and see what can be done. You all better get some rest—the defenses are already all reset. We have a long night's ride ahead of us, the first of many, and everybody should be well-rested."

Bronz stared at her. "We?"

She nodded. "I've been meaning for some time to find out what those old fools at Moab know that maybe I don't," she told us. "I think that now the cat's out of the bag about us here I had better find out all I can. Besides, I better be along to see that there are no relapses."

I glanced over at Father Bronz. "You're coming too, I hope. I'm not sure I want to face ten days with just the witches for protection."

He chuckled. "Sure. I intended to, in any event. It's been a great many years since I was at Moab, and my curiosity is aroused. But don't expect miracles down there. They know more about the Warden organisms than anybody except maybe Sumiko—now that I've seen her in action—but they are not selfless scientists. There have been some, uh, unfortunate changes over the years down there."

Chapter Eighteen

Moab Keep

The worst part of the journey was riding the *besils* themselves. The creatures were ugly, they stank, and they oozed a really nasty gluelike ichor when under stress—not to mention occasionally giving out with one of those earsplitting shrieks that seemed to come from somewhere deep within them. We were all inexperienced riders, too, and the sensation was much like getting whipped in all directions at once, that apparently seamless, fluid motion of theirs feeling quite different if you were actually on a *besil* back.

Still, the creatures were selectively bred types, born and raised for this sort of work, and they seemed never to tire. They were also easy to care for, since they foraged for themselves in the jungle below, eating almost anything that wouldn't eat them first, plant or animal. Being large animals, though, they ate often, and that slowed us down. They needed three times their considerable weight per day to keep going at any reasonable pace.

Still, the kilometers passed swiftly beneath us, although I saw less of the countryside than I would have liked. In order to maintain security, and to avoid meeting a lot of possibly bad company, we headed almost due east to the coast and skirted it, somewhat out from land, heading in for an encampment only when and where the wild reached the sea and gave us cover. The ocean was dotted with numerous uninhabited islands, but none provided the large amount of food our *besils* required, so some risk was necessary.

Our witches afforded us some protection, of course. I suspect that was the only reason we encountered so little in the way of other traffic on the way south. But though we could take care of individuals who might chance upon us we had nothing like the massed force to withstand an assault of the type Artur had mounted on the witch village. Sumiko couldn't even take her full "core" coven, since the most we could safely fit on and strap into a *besil* saddle was two, and Ti and I had one, O'Higgins and Bronz each had one of their own, and the other three held two of the aproned witches apiece. We had no control over the *besils* ourselves, either; Bronz and O'Higgins did the driving for all of us.

Days were spent in foraging, resting, and checking bearings. It was not a totally friendly group, with the witches paying little mind or heed to Ti or me and Father Bronz devoting most of his time, apparently without success, to trying to discover the nature of Sumiko O'Higgins's remarkable discoveries about the Warden organism.

I confess I was never really sure about the witch queen. A genius, certainly, with the single-mindedness to set herself impossible problems and then work them out. A pragmatist, too, who was putting her discoveries to use building up some sort of superior army—for what it was hard to say. Discussing the plants and animals of Lilith, the Warden organism, and some rather odd ideas about the relationships between plant and animal biochemistry, she was as expert and as dry as a university professor. But whenever you started feeling that her Satanism was a sham, a device to accomplish some kind of psychological goal with her followers, or simply a means to an end, she would drop into a discussion of it with an unmistakable fervor and sincerity. Ti and I talked about her at length, and both of us were convinced that either she was one of the truly great actresses of all times or she really believed that junk.

I was able to pump Father Bronz a bit more on her, although he admitted his own knowledge was sketchy. She was the daughter of scientists, experts in the biological aspects of terraforming, and from what little we could gather, was something of an experiment herself, having been genetically manipulated in some way in an attempt to produce a superior being, an alternative to the civilized worlds for a rougher, frontier life. They had certainly produced *someone* unique, but I wondered what the psychological effects of growing up knowing you were just experiment 77-A in Mommy and Daddy's lab might be. Exactly what the crime was that got her sent to Lilith was unknown, but it was of truly major proportions and left inside her a legacy of hatred and revenge directed toward the civilized worlds. In point of fact, she was the quintessential Lord of the Diamond personality I'd come to expect, yet she disdained even that. To her, Marek Kreegan and the Confederacy were two sides of the same coin.

The relationship between Ti and me continued to develop, and I felt things within me that I had never known were there. In some ways it disturbed me— that a man of pure intellect could form such strong emotional attachments seemed somehow an admission of my weakness, an internal accusation that I was human when I had always clung to the notion that I was a superior human being above all those animalistic drives affecting the common herd. She was certainly not the type of woman I had ever thought myself attracted to. Bright, yes, but totally uneducated, highly emotional, and in some sense very vulnerable.

Still, I felt better with her here, awake, laughing and oohing and aahing and having fun like a kid with a new toy. It was as if I'd had a painful hole inside me, one that had been there so long that I wasn't even aware of it, had considered the ache and emptiness normal and not at all unusual, but now the hole was filled. The relief, the feeling of health and wholeness, was indescribably good. We were complementary in some ways, too—she was my hold, my perspective, on Lilith, where I would live out my life, and I was her window to a wider and far different universe than she could now comprehend.

It took eleven days to reach Moab, with a little dodging of congested areas, neither pushing ourselves or taking chances. Moab Keep itself was below us now, a huge island in a great, broad tropical bay. Almost on the equator, it was insufferably hot and humid; but, looking down upon it, I could see why it had been selected.

The first manned expedition to Lilith had no idea what it would be getting itself into. It needed a base, one that would provide a good sample of the flora and fauna of Lilith without exposing the group to unknown dangers. The huge island of Moab was their choice, a place large and lush enough to provide a small lab and base for travel to other parts of the world but isolated enough with its high cliff walls and broad expanse of bay all around to be defensible against attack.

Time and knowledge had reshaped it only slightly. You could see cleared areas for agriculture, and lines of fruit trees too straight and regular to be haphazard. On a bluff almost in the center of the island was the headquarters for those who still lived and worked on the island. The hard rock of the bluff itself had been hewn out by the most primitive labor methods to build what was needed, a great rock temple that looked neither crude nor uncomfortable. In fact, it made Zeis's Castle seem like a small and fragile structure, although Moab had none of the fanciful design of Sir Tiel's edifice. It was straight, modern, utilitarian, functional—and huge.

Still, Father Bronz had warned us that this was not exactly all it seemed. The science of the founders was still here, for sure, and there was no authoritarian hierarchy such as the other Keeps maintained, but the purpose for the enclave had drastically changed as it became more isolated from the outside world. Today the thousands of men and women below carried on their work in the name of some odd mystical religion that seemed anachronistically out of the dawn of man. In their years of studying Lilith they had come not merely to anthropomorphize it, as Father Bronz tended to do, but actually to regard it as a living, thinking creature, a god now sleeping that would someday awaken.

In other words, here was another nut cult, although one not formed from the history of humanity but rather by the conditions of Lilith itself.

We landed atop the great bluff and immediately attendants came from stairwells to attend to the *besils*. For a moment I thought we were being attacked, so rapidly did they come forth, but it quickly became obvious that we were on the Moab equivalent of a helipad.

I took note of the appearance of the attendants. Many were of civilized worlds standards, and all had some of the look within them. Many were naked, others lightly dressed, and all seemed young, yet none of them had the look or bearing of pawns. All were neatly groomed and had that scrubbed look.

Father Bronz, the only one of us who had been here before, took the lead, and we followed him to one of the nearby stairwells.

"I have to say that they don't seem at all worried or even curious about us," I noted to him. "It's almost as if we were expected."

"We probably are," he replied. "Remember, these people know all we've been able to find out about this crazy world. Their grandparents were the original colonists, and they and their children discovered the Warden organism, the Warden powers, the various drugs and potions we all use. They designed and perfected the methods by which anything can be done here." He glanced over at Sumiko O'Higgins. "They're unassailable and they know it. Even from you, my dear, I think."

She just looked at him expressionlessly and didn't reply. Even though I owed my life and my existence here to her I would never feel comfortable around her and would certainly never completely trust her.

We were met at the bottom of the long, winding stone stairs by a woman in flowing pure-white robes. She didn't look very old, but her billowing hair was snow white and her eyes a deep blue, while her complexion showed that she just about never ventured out into the sunlight. It was an odd appearance, sort of like one of Father Bronz's angels.

"I bid you greetings, Father Bronz, you and your friends," she said, her voice soft and musical.

Bronz gave a slight bow. "My lady, I am happy to see that I am remembered," he responded somewhat formally. "May I present my companions to you?"

She turned and looked at us, not critically, but not curiously, either. "I already know them all. I am Director Komu. I will see you all to quarters that have already been prepared for you where you may rest and refresh yourselves. Later on today I will arrange for a tour of the Institute, and tomorrow is soon enough to get down to business."

I looked at her, then at Ti. "Lady Komu, I thank you for your hospitality," I said, trying to be as politely formal as seemed required here, "but my own young lady here has need of medical assistance. She's already been feeling particularly sleepy and numb."

The director went over to Ti and looked at her thoughtfully for a moment, not touching or doing anything we could see. Finally she said, "Yes, I see. Please don't worry about it—we will fix you up in no time at all." She turned. "Now, if you will follow me."

The place inside was, if anything, more impressive than outside. The walls and floors were all tiled in light, micalike panels that seemed slightly translucent and behind which some light source glowed. It wasn't electrical, of course, but neither was it the kind of localized and flickering light that oil lanterns would give off. In fact the place looked as if it were back in the Outside. I was about to ask about it when Sumiko O'Higgins beat me to it.

"This is most impressive, particularly the lighting," she noted. "How do you do it?"

"Oh, a simple matter, really," the director responded airily. "The light source is a lumen distilled from various self-illuminating insects common to Lilith. The power source is somewhat complex, but based very much on the same principle the insects themselves use to brighten the material. The basis of the power is friction, fed by water power. Whoever told you such things were impossible on Lilith, dear?"

There was no reply to that, and I was beginning to see that I would have to revise my world picture once again. There certainly *wasn't* anything in the rules governing Lilith to prohibit a lot of classical power sources; the limitation was that there were very few people who could talk the Warden organism into holding in new shapes of waterwheels and the like.

Our rooms were luxurious, furnished with fine hand-carved wood and a large bed that was as close to a stuffed mattress as I had seen on Lilith. The common baths were similar to those at the Castle, large tile-lined troughs filled with very hot, bubbly water that soothed as well as cleaned. I felt both more human and totally relaxed at the finish, and Ti had quite a time with the first bath she'd ever experienced other than those in pools of rainwater or rivers. She was tired, though, and I just about had to carry her back to the room. She was awake enough to find the bed too soft and strange for her liking and for a while considered sleeping on the floor, which she finally did. As soon as she was asleep, though, I placed her on the satiny sheets and stretched out beside her. I hadn't realized what sort of tension I'd been under the past almost two weeks, though, and I was soon out cold.

Chapter Nineteen

The Wizards of Moab Keep

We toured the huge Institute, as they called it, as evening fell. Not Ti—she was still tired and her body was continuing to fight Dr. Pohn's handiwork, so I decided to let her sleep.

Everyone at the Institute seemed to live well, in Lilith terms. They seemed bright, alive, highly civilized, and happy. We saw the laboratories used by plant and animal experts to study all they could, revealing cleverly fashioned if primitive tools of the trade, including wooden microscopes whose lenses were actually quite good, and to my surprise, even a limited number of metal tools that looked like they'd been manufactured in major factories. I remarked on them, and was reminded that Lords such as Kreegan could actually stabilize a limited amount of alien matter, making it resistant to the Warden organism's attack. The intrasystem shuttlecraft, for example, that had landed me on Lilith and carried me to Zeis Keep was one such example, and a pretty hairy and delicate one at that.

The food prepared for us was also excellent, although I recognized almost nothing except the melons. I was told that the meat was from certain kinds of domesticated large insects; specially bred types of plants and plant products provided many of the other dishes and a variety of beverages that, if not really beer and wine, served as excellent substitutes.

It seemed to me that the full potential of Lilith was exercised only here, at the Institute. Comfort, civilization, worthwhile work—all were possible here. This world didn't need to be the horror house it primarily was, not if those with the power were to use it more wisely and well.

Why, I began to wonder, wasn't it, then?

The next morning Ti was taken down to their Medical Section, which was a much more complex setup than Dr. Pohn's, although the doctors there used some of the same techniques for a lot of the routine measurements. The doctor, a woman named Telar who frankly didn't look much older than Ti, let alone old enough to be a doctor, placed Ti on a comfortable but rigid table, felt key points all over her body, then touched her patient's forehead in that classic manner and closed her eyes briefly. Less than thirty seconds later she nodded, opened her eyes again, and smiled. Ti, who was neither drugged nor instructed to do anything more than lie still, looked puzzled. "When will you start?" she asked nervously.

Telar laughed. "I've finished. That's it."

We both stared. "That's *it?*" I echoed.

She nodded. "Oh, I'd like to take a quick look at you as well. You never know."

"That's all right," I told her. "I'm fine." I started making all sorts of excuses at that point, since I was just reminded that there was something extra up there somewhere in my brain, an organic transmitter I might not have worried about if it had been anywhere else —but this doctor would spot it for sure.

Frankly, I hadn't really thought of it much since the early days. I don't even know why I didn't take advantage at that point of the opportunity to have it removed, to make myself a totally free and private agent. Perhaps, after thinking of you up there for a while as an enemy, I was now reluctant to cut this last umbilical to my former life and self. To cast it out, and you with it, would be the final and absolute rejection of everything I'd lived for all my life, and I wasn't quite willing to do that as yet. Not yet. If the information went directly to Intelligence, that would be one thing, but it went to me—that other me sitting up there somewhere, looking in. My Siamese twin.

Not yet, I decided. Not yet.

Classes started shortly after. They decided that both Ti and I would undergo as much training as we could take, although separately, of course. Only the basic stuff could be group-administered, and I'd already had that. I was curious to see what Ti might come up with, and hopeful, too.

I had been somewhat nervous when told that they were a religious cult, but aside from a few offhand references and the fact that there were occasional prayers, like before meals, and temple hours, when the staff went off somewhere and did whatever they did, there was no pushing of the faith, no mumbo-jumbo, and no attempt either to convert us or to indoctrinate us with their beliefs. Their religion interested me no more than the faiths of Bronz or

O'Higgins did, and I was thankful for its lack of intrusiveness.

Of the others who had come with us I saw nothing. About two weeks into the training I was informed that the witches had gone, returning to their strange village, but Father Bronz was said to be involved in some project of his own at the Institute, something that required the use of their massive handwritten library scrolls and some of their lab facilities. I wondered idly whether he, now seeing that it was possible, was trying to crack the O'Higgins secret.

I made easy progress in the use of the power itself, but I began to realize that things would still be very slow, since, as Ti's example had so graphically pointed out, just having the power to do something wasn't enough. You needed the knowledge to apply it properly, and *that* could take years.

Still, a lot could be done in general terms, and it became absurdly easy for me to do so. Weaving patterns, duplicating patterns as I had with the chair, were simple as long as we were talking inanimate objects. O'Higgins had likened the Warden organism to some sort of alien organic computer, and that was a pretty good analogy. But not a lot of little computers, all components in a single, massively preprogrammed organism.

"Think of them," one of my instructors said, "as cells of Mother Lilith. Your own cells all contain DNA spirals encoded with your entire genetic make-up. Also, one part of that complex code tells that particular cell how to behave, how to form and grow and act and react as part of the whole. The Warden cells, as we call them, are like those in your own body. They are preprogrammed with an impossibly complex picture of how this planet should be, and each one knows its own place or part in that whole. What we do is slightly mutate the Warden cell. Essentially, we feed it false data and fool it into doing what *we* want instead of what *it* wants. Because our action is extremely localized when compared to the whole of Lilith, and because we can concentrate our willpower on such a tiny spot, we are able to do so. Not on a large scale, of course, but on a relatively localized scale."

I looked around at the sumptuous surroundings of the Institute. "Localized?"

My instructor just nodded. "Consider the mass of the planet. Consider the number of molecules that go into its composition. A colony of Wardens for every molecule. Now, do you think this is more than a tiny aberration, a benign cancer, as it were?"

I saw the point.

The more I practiced, the easier everything became. Although I was a little put off when I discovered that most of the silky cloth I'd seen was made from worm spit, I soon dismissed that as another cultural prejudice and had my own clothing with the option and ability to make more. Burning holes in rock and shaping those holes to suit my design also proved very easy: you just told the Wardens governing the molecules to disengage. Unfortunately, the skill aspect again came into play here, and I decided that I was cut out to be neither an engineer nor an architect. What I had done to Kronlon, the Institute considered an abuse of power, since what it seemed to amount to was an overloading of the Warden input circuits. They burned themselves out in some manner.

Classes in combat emphasized defense, but took a lot of the mystery out of what I'd seen. Knowing the proper points in an opponent's nervous system was as important in the mental combat of Warden cells as in physical stuff like judo. The trick was to keep total control over your own Wardens while knocking out those of your opponent, a really nasty task requiring not only that you have more willpower and self-control than your opponent but also that you have an enormous ability to concentrate on several things at once.

I learned as much as I could learn, and although I felt elated when they no longer gave me the potion and I grew stronger still, I realized that only experience could fine-tune my skills. The key test of my power was when they brought two small steel rods from Medusa, which, though containing Warden organisms as well, was a thing alien to our Lilith parent strain and beyond my ability to communicate with.

I was aware, though, that Warden cells were already attacking the alien matter, much as antibodies attacked a virus in the bloodstream, trying to break it down, even eat it, in some mysterious way.

Here there was no pattern to solve or imitate. I somehow had to work out a form of protection, some sort of message that would keep this metal from corroding to dust under the Warden cell onslaught. I failed miserably time after time. There seemed nothing to grab on to, nothing I could even reprogram to protect the alien matter, which even to me had a somewhat dark, dead appearance in contrast to all of the Warden-alive matter around me.

After two days the stuff crumbled into dust.

I was discouraged, feeling somehow inadequate. To have come so far and not to go the last little bit to rank me near the top in potential on this world was tremendously depressing. If I could not solve this last problem, I knew I would be no match for the Dukes, let alone for Marek Kreegan.

Ti tried to console me. But, living here at the Institute at a higher level than she'd ever dreamed of or known was possible, she had a more limited ambition than I. Her own lessons had helped somewhat; as both Sumiko O'Higgins and Dr. Pohn had intimated, the power was at least latent in everyone. But even with all the training, her power was limited more to the Supervisor level, although she certainly could use it more discriminatingly and effectively than the Supervisors I'd known. The only thing they could offer beyond that was something of the witch methods: if she were truly consumed with emotion toward something, her power could be multiplied; but to make it controlled and effective she'd need temporary augmentation from the potion. Even then it would be only a destructive power and very limited.

This aspect worried me a bit at first, since she *was* highly emotional and I was more than a little concerned that lovemaking would cause problems. Occasionally it did, but not anything serious, since she would never aim anything destructive, even subconsciously, at me. If ever we had a falling out, I was strong enough on reflex alone to protect myself. Still, occasionally when we *did* make love and her power ran a bit wild, the earth really *did* move.

Her powers, particularly with my help, allowed her to create her own clothes, which was particularly important to one brought up in the pawn world of the Keeps, where clothing was status. Still, she had enough of an understanding of the Warden power to understand my problem and my frustration, and did think of it. In fact she came up with part of the solution.

"Look," she said to me one day, "the problem is that Warden cells ridin' dust and everything else in the air just rush in to eat this metal stuff, right?"

I nodded glumly. "And I can't stop it because that metal stuff, as you call it, doesn't have anything I can talk to, let alone control."

"Why not talk to the attacking stuff, then?" she wanted to know. "Why not talk them out of it?"

I was about to respond that that was a ridiculous idea when I suddenly realized it wasn't crazy at all. Not in the way she meant, of course, but suddenly I saw the key; it was so ridiculously simple I didn't know why I hadn't thought of it before.

Talk to the attacking cells . . . Sure. But since the attack was continuous and from all quarters, just protecting something the size of a nail would be a full-time job. But if the metal was coated in some Lilith substance and the Warden cells in that coating were told not to attack . . . Accomplishing that would not be all that easy. In fact, the process was hideously complex, but it was the right answer. When you extended the concept to a really complex piece of machinery, it became a nightmare, clearly, a lot of practice and hard thought was needed.

The Institute people were pleased, and so was I, though. Few were ever able to master the stabilization of metals on *any* scale, and I felt as if the Confederacy had certainly made its point about me. I knew now that what they'd done was feed Marek

Kreegan's entire file into their computers, and that alone was why I had been selected. My life, profession, outlook, you name it, had most paralleled his —therefore I was most likely to attain the potential of Lord.

I *had* learned, though, that I was not the only one with that power and potential besides Kreegan. A number of people, as many as forty or fifty, would qualify. Kreegan simply embodied not only the greatest single power on the planet but also the greatest single power who had the will and capacity to rule and the skills to pull it off. And that, of course, was what it all boiled down to—not power, but skill. The question was brought home to me by one of my most advanced instructors when she asked, "Well, now that you have joined the circle of the elect, what will you do with your powers?"

It was a good question. I now had the power, all right, all of it. I didn't have to fear this planet and its petty leadership any longer, and I had a good deal to live for, embodied in Ti and my hopes for a comfortable future.

But just what *were* our skills? Ti was trained mostly to run a nursery, to look after small children, and I certainly intended her to exercise that skill with our own children. But what *could* I do? What was I trained to do? Kill people efficiently. Solve sophisticated technological crimes—here on a planet where the technology was not at issue. In point of fact, the only jobs on a world like this I was in any way qualified for were ones like Artur's, but the challenge of fighting for the sport of my employers didn't appeal to me. In defense of employers or for a cause, yes, but not just to let out aggressions and give the violent folks something to do.

It was the same problem that had faced Marek Kreegan at this stage in his own life, I reflected, and his own conclusion was the only one that I, too, could reach. We were more alike than even I had realized, and our fates somehow seemed bound up together. What in fact did he have that I did not? Experience, of course. He'd worked his way up. I was already a

Master, although a Master of nothing in particular. The next step, administratively speaking, was Knight. From Knight to Duke. And finally, with all that experience behind me, from Duke to Lord.

For the first time I understood a bit of Marek Kreegan. He hadn't necessarily come to Lilith to take over and run it. He had become the Lord of Lilith, one of the Four Lords of the Diamond, simply because he wasn't qualified to do anything else. It was absurd, but there it was. Kronlon's own words came echoing back once more. None of us has any choice.

It had been twelve weeks since we'd come to Moab Keep, and I was beginning to realize there was nothing more they could teach me here. The next step was up to me, and my own destiny lay elsewhere. So far I'd learned a great deal about myself but almost nothing that I'd been sent here for. I knew nothing at all about the aliens, nor did I even know what Marek Kreegan looked like these days. To go further I would have to take a knighthood, and to do that I'd need an army and some advisors closer to the scene of things.

Once again I sought out Father Bronz.

The priest looked fit and well-rested and seemed happy to see me. We shook hands and then embraced warmly. I realized that, although he'd kept his distance from me, he nonetheless had kept careful track of my progress.

"So—a Master now, with the potential of a Lord!" he laughed. "I told you I wanted to be remembered when you took over!"

I returned the laughter. "But that's a long way off," I responded. "Marek Kreegan must be getting old now, so he might not even be around by the time I feel confident enough to take him on. Still, I have to take the first step, and for that I'll need help."

"You're going to try for a knighthood, then," he said matter-of-factly. "I could have guessed as much. But your normal channel is denied you. You can't apprentice yourself to some Knight as a Master and bide your time. Nobody's going to take you on."

"I thought of that," I told him. "No, I'll have to go

for it in one stroke. I'll have to take on a force, defeat it, and then face down the Knight."

"A good trick," Bronz admitted. "And where are you going to get the fighting force to get in the front door?"

"I've thought about that. It seems to me that I've only got one avenue to take there, and I'll need your help. You and I watched, many long weeks ago, a relatively small and unarmed force take on and defeat an elite corps. I think the whole bunch of them could take an army."

"Perhaps," he replied thoughtfully, "but she'd never go for it. Her whole force to take a Keep so a *man* could rule? You saw Sumiko."

"I saw her. Saw her and studied her. I think she's itching for a fight. I think that's why she came here, to perfect her methods. I think she'd welcome such a test."

"At random, yes," he said. "Just for the hell of it, or to prove her theories. But not for you, Cal me boy. Not for you."

"If her test is Zeis Keep?"

He stood there, dumbstruck at the idea. Finally he said, "You don't want to take the easy way out, do you? Zeis isn't a small, weak nothing of a Keep—it's one of the big ones. Important enough to be designated a shuttle landing point, which is why all the bigwigs pass through there. And you've got Artur fighting defense on his home ground. Remember the *geography* of that place?"

"I remember," I told him. "Still, it *has* to be Zeis. I think Dr. Pohn is the one individual object of her hatred that would tempt her, don't you? And from the point of view of location, it's close enough for her without a lot of logistical problems."

He considered the proposal. "She might buy it," he admitted, "but are you sure you can take *her?* Once she fights for Zeis and wins, if she *can* take it, do you think she's going to hand the place over to you?"

"I don't know," I responded honestly. "I don't even know if I can take Boss Tiel. I've never even met him. But I think I have to try."

"I think you do," Bronz concluded, more to himself than to me. "I don't know. I'll send out some feelers to Sumiko and see if she'll buy it, or at least agree to talk about it. And I think I can reach Duke Kisorn, at least. Talk him into letting you try."

"But what about Marek Kreegan? Will *he* stay out of it? After all, he's the man who put the price on my head to begin with."

"'Oh, I'm sure Kreegan will keep hands off," Father Bronz told me confidently. "He'll want to see just what you can do at this stage, in order to evaluate the true threat to himself and his own power. But *if* we talk Sumiko into this, and *if* you or she beats Tiel, and *if* you can beat her, *then* you will have to worry about Kreegan. You sure you want to start this? That's a lot of ifs, and once you start, you aren't going to be able to stop. You'll be the initiator, and responsible."

"You think I'm nuts, don't you?" I asked him. "You think I should just settle down here and read all the books and raise a family and say to hell with it, don't you?"

"*I* didn't say that," Bronz replied in a tone that implied exactly that.

"I can't," I told him. "I'm just not made that way."

"We'll see." Father Bronz sighed deeply. "I'll start the wheels in motion. May God have mercy on your soul."

Chapter Twenty

Council of War

It all came together so easily and quickly that I was almost suspicious about it.

The witch's village seemed to have changed not at all from the last time I'd been there, although now I was far more sensitized to the entire Warden environment and everything looked a little new and different. I felt a mild, discomforting dizziness that I couldn't really put my finger on. Father Bronz explained to me that he'd felt it from the first visit, an aftereffect of the process by which Sumiko O'Higgins stayed hidden from the outside world.

"They take turns," he told me. "One of them at Master grade and a coven of twelve others, all satiated with Sumiko's juice, standing ever vigilant. Nothing short of a planetary satellite photo would be able to see what's down here, and even that doesn't seem to work—the place is well camouflaged from the air, and a couple of distorting inversion layers add to the effect. That's why she chose the place."

She'd been confident that Artur would not be able to return and find it after his defeat, and she'd been right. Basically, it was a message sent by that particular guardian pack of thirteen to all around simply not to notice the place. It was neither invisibility nor any form of telepathy, but it was a formidable mental barrier all the same.

From what Father Bronz was able to tell me, O'Higgins seemed more than delighted with the idea. She said something about needing a "test piece" anyway. Furthermore, she held particular grudges against Zeis Keep not only because Dr. Pohn was there but also because Artur had killed two of her witches in the attack.

But even though she had replaced the two dead ones, there was still a strong numerical problem in going against Zeis. Many of her procedures were far more effective defensively than offensively, since techniques such as the circle, which I'd seen in operation, and the "mind clouding" were not really much use to a mobile, advancing force. They would be able to take out *some* of Artur's forces, but not all; in close quarters her pawns, even amplified slightly, would be no match for Artur's trained and experienced Supervisors and Masters. Their strength was a group strength. Artur now knew this, having been bloodied, and would take measures to counter it. With perhaps a thousand witches Sumiko was invulnerable, but with a hundred and sixty-nine she needed support.

Again it was Father Bronz, showing a most interesting bent for Machiavellian political maneuvering, to the rescue. At our final meeting were not only the priest, the witches, and myself but also three strange women wearing colorful, flowing garb. Except for their manners and dress they looked rather ordinary, with common backgrounds of the civilized worlds in their features. Nonetheless, the immediate impression was that these were no ordinary inhabitants of Lilith, not even Masters. They were . . . something else.

As we sat around eating small, tasty pastries and drinking mild local wine, Father Bronz made the introductions. First Sumiko, then me; then he turned to the three strange women.

"May I introduce Boss Rognival of Lakk Keep," he said, pointing to the most overdressed of the women, "and her administrative assistant, the Lady Tona, and her sergeant-at-arms, the Lady Kysil."

Although they were all fighting for their own interests rather than for mine, I never really felt so left out of an operation that would decide my future as I did at this one. I stared at the three women in curiosity not only as to what they were doing here but also because I'd never seen a knight before. Except for the slight fur trim and a small jewel on a headband of some kind, she didn't look so superhuman. I had to admit, though, that the Warden power burned and shone a little brighter inside her. The map in my head clicked in again, and I saw that Lakk Keep was a very small one several kilometers due west of Zeis—across that formidable-looking swamp.

"Let's get down to business," Rognival said sharply, her tone tough and crisp. "We are going to attack and take Zeis Keep. The witch here has her own reasons and some old grudges to settle; the young man over there has ambition, and I—well, let's just say that Lakk is a very small Keep almost surrounded by a pretty lousy swamp. It wasn't always that way. I used to have four kilometers square of choice *vai* cropland on what is now the Zeis side of the swamp. Tiel and

Artur took it as well as the pawns that worked it from me over nine years ago, reducing me to the island of Lakk, which though it has several melon orchards and some *snark* pastureland, is hardly self-sufficient. I became, in effect, Tiel's vassal, and I've hated him for it. Until now, though, I've had insufficient forces to attack across the swamp, and I no longer have the clout necessary to get allies. You're my chance to get back my land, my self-sufficiency, and my self-respect."

O'Higgins warmed a little to her. I could see Father Bronz's thinking in all this—a female knight who hated Zeis. Perfect.

Too perfect, I decided instantly. Something smelled wrong about this. *Very* wrong. It seemed all too convenient, all too pat. I felt uneasily that somebody was setting me up, and that somebody had to be Father Bronz.

Ever since I'd escaped from Zeis and found him, he had been in total charge of my life, a charge he seemed willing and eager to accept. As much as anything the Cal Tremon who sat in the council here was by now a product of Bronz's own machinations, as was this whole carefully orchestrated exercise. What the hell *was* his game, anyway?

I'd done what checking I could given my limited contacts with others on this world, and they'd all borne out the image of a roving Master, a priest not merely deposed but defrocked by his church, who had been around as long as everybody could remember. And yet it was that last that bothered me. Nobody ever remembered the priest saying a service or a mass or whatever it was they did, nor carrying out any real priest-type functions at all. I certainly had never seen him do so, nor did we have anything but his word as to his life Outside, his background and reason for being here.

Still, if he were with Boss Tiel and Kreegan and that bunch, why had he gone to so much trouble over me? Why not just turn me in and get on with it? If he was someone high up on the social scale masquerading as a lowly priest, why make certain I reached the Institute and received the best training and experience

possible on Lilith? If he had his own ambitions I
would be a threat to him, if not at this point then
some time in the future.

But if indeed he was what he said he was, what
were his motives? A staunch defender of the system
on Lilith, he nonetheless was using its greatest threat,
the witches, to put into power a man who hated that
system, mainly me.

I looked around at their faces as they earnestly dis-
cussed the coming campaign. I paid only slight attention to what they were saying, as, ironically, I was the
least important person at this council of war in terms
of the outcome, although of course I would fight.
O'Higgins, the possibly Lord-class psychopath with the
power to amplify, combine, and direct Warden power
at will. Rognival, who wanted revenge for her earlier
loss and her territory back. Bronz . . .

In thinking of him I'd once used the term Machiavellian. If I remembered my studies at all, that ancient mind was never the leader himself but merely
an advisor—an advisor who was the *real* ruler while
his prince took all the heat and did all the dirty work.
Was I perhaps his prince-designate? Or were all three
of us somehow in that category? With patience and almost diabolical cleverness, could he perhaps dream of
controlling the whole sector indirectly through its rulers, then, perhaps with O'Higgins' discoveries, going
on to take the whole planet? What could even a
Marek Kreegan do about it? He would only strike at
princes, never at the wandering priest and advisor.

It was a good plan, perhaps a brilliant one. I told
myself that if I survived all this and attained the
knighthood, I wouldn't be quite the pawn in his game
that he counted on.

The council broke up in seemingly good spirits,
having arrived at a plan that looked pretty good—at
least in theory. We would see how well it worked out
when human beings faced down each other.

Returning to the hut where Ti and I were spending
our time until the dawn of battle, I was surprised not
to find her there. She had little interest in or understanding of the battle strategy, and the witches were

only mildly communicative, but she'd certainly gone somewhere and all I could do was wait.

It was close to dark when she returned, looking a little haggard and worried. "What's wrong?" I asked, concerned. "Where have you been?"

"Spying," she sighed and sank down.

"Huh? How's that?"

She nodded. "I don't like these women," she told me. "There's something creepy about 'em." She looked up at me, concerned. "When is the battle?"

"Three days from now," I told her. "At dawn."

She shook her head. "This O'Higgins may've been nice an' all, but she's real crazy, Cal. I went over an' got real close to one group havin' a meeting of some kind. They never saw me, don't worry. Anyways, I had to listen real hard, but I heard most of it." She shivered.

I frowned. "What did you hear that upset you so much?"

She leaned forward, whispering as low as she could. "They ain't gonna keep to their side, Cal. Once they win, they're gonna kill you *and* Father Bronz. They'll give that lady knight whatever she wants to keep her off their backs for a while, but they mean to take Zeis for themselves. They were talkin' about the beginnin' of the purge. What's a purge, Cal?"

I told her.

She nodded. "That's kinda what I thought. The purge of Lilith, they said. Near as I can make out, it means they're gonna kill all the men in Zeis and turn it into a witch's keep."

I had the sinking feeling I'd known most of this all along. I just hadn't wanted to admit it. "Don't worry." I tried to console her with a confidence I didn't feel. "Father Bronz and I aren't going to allow ourselves to get cornered like that. And that old witch couldn't do it, anyway. Marek Kreegan and the other top bosses would close in before she could get started."

Ti shook her head violently from side to side. "You think so, but they know that, too. They're nuts, not stupid. They say O'Higgins is already more powerful than Lord Kreegan, and with the power juice—potion of Satan, they called it—stronger than any army that could come against them. They say she's so strong she's already stabilized two laster guns or something like that from Outside."

Laster guns . . . "Laser pistols?" I prompted, sounding a little weak despite my false front.

She nodded. "Yeah. That's it. Oh, Cal, what're we gonna *do?*"

All I knew to do at that moment was hold her tight and hug her and try and make her worry fade just a little. But sometime in the next two days I would have to have a long talk with Father Bronz.

The priest frowned. "She can stabilize laser pistols, huh? Then she *is* as strong as Kreegan. That poses a problem." We were far outside the witch's camp, officially in the danger zone but out of it as far as our current needs went.

"That's not the half of it," I told him. "On a world like Lilith, a simple small stungun would make you a king. A pawn could knock off a Lord if there was the element of surprise. I know *I* could, and this world's full of expert killers."

Bronz nodded thoughtfully. "It's a little late to change our game plan, and I'm not sure she would allow it to be changed now. Still, we're not without resources." His eyes brightened a bit and a ghost of a smile came to his lips. "I have to say that I am not totally shocked or surprised by any of this. I anticipated something like it, and I planned for it."

Instead of cheering me, his comment worried me a little more. "Just who *are* you, Bronz? What's your game in all this?"

He sighed. "Cal, you have no reason to believe me, but several to trust me. I could have killed you at any time, particularly in the early days when you were ignorant and helpless. I didn't. I helped you and Ti, too, as much as it was in my power to do so. Will you concede that?"

I nodded, not quite conceding the point.

"Then I must ask you to trust me until the battle's done," he went on. "You must stay as far away from

O'Higgins as possible. She's the only person that one of your power has to fear. Wait. When it's all over, all worked out, you'll know everything, I promise. Know and understand everything, and profit by it." ⌐

"Whose side are you on, Father Bronz?" I asked suspiciously. "Can't you at least tell me that?"

He smiled. "I'm on my side, Cal. You must understand that. But it is fortunate that your side and my side do not conflict but rather converge here. You have my solemn word on that. Trust me now, this one time more, and all will be clear."

"I'll try," I sighed, "because there's not much else I can do."

He laughed easily and slapped me on the back. "Come, let's go back. Why don't you go in and try to make a baby with that pretty mate of yours? It may be your last chance for a while. In two days' time that mind of yours will tell *you* the answer. I won't even have to explain it, I suspect. Just remember that I really *do* like you, son. You're going to be Lord of Lilith one day if you watch your back."

I just stared back at him and did not reply, but I couldn't help wondering if by that time the Lordship would be worth taking.

Chapter Twenty-One

The Battle of Zeis Keep

A prince does not fight commoners. His own battle is reserved for those of equal or superior rank. As a result, my initial job in all this was to stand and watch. Only after the armies had done their worst and the battle decided would I myself face the challenge of entering the Castle through the front door and walking down that forbidden central hallway. Oddly, I would have preferred to have participated in the battle, since this was the sort of thing I'd devoted my life to. As much as it might shock some of the soft elements of the civilized worlds, I enjoyed it. But I'd graduated now, beyond being the lone assassin, beyond the foot soldier and cavalry. Now those others, the soldiers and fighters, sallied forth in my name.

We walked, Ti and I, down the cloud-covered path where, a short time ago that somehow seemed a lifetime, I had borne her still body past the guards and out of Zeis Keep. We were returning, under our own power and of our own free will, dressed as Master and Supervisor in the same color and design material, indicating we were a wedded pair.

Just after emerging from the clouds on the downslope, the whole of Zeis Keep was illuminated in the dawn-lit sky. It was the same impressive, fairy-talelike place I remembered.

I heard Ti give a sharp intake of breath. "It's *beautiful!*" she gasped, then looked over at me, apparently concerned that she was sounding too childlike. Finally she decided that she didn't *care.* "I was born down there," she said, pointing to the area of our old village. "There was a lot of bad there, but I'm part of *it* and it's part of *me.* Can you understand?"

I nodded, although there was no place that could claim my own soul as Zeis claimed hers. I was the product of an alien society of strange forms and structures made by computer design and formed and shaped by plastic. Still, I had a reaction as close to hers as I could come, and one that was totally alien to my old nature and lifelong philosophy. I pulled her against my side and hugged her. "This can all be ours," I breathed, wondering as I said it whether in that moment I had ceased to be what I had been and joined the race of Lilith.

We sat on a high ledge and relaxed. Ti was holding a woven basket made of some strawlike material, and she now pulled out its contents—a gourd pot, two smaller gourds, a flint, some of Father Bronz's *quar* leaves, which would burn hot but slow, and some of his tea. Runoff from the mountains caused small waterfalls all along, so water was no problem. Also in the basket were some of the small pastries and a cheeselike substance made from some insects in a manner I didn't ever want to know.

I had to chuckle. It seemed absurd to have a picnic while watching a battle.

An advance guard of witches had "swept" the trails prior to sunrise, so we weren't due for any unpleasant surprises—not, at least, until the battle started. We could see the whole area, from the swamps to the Castle, a perfect vantage point. Still, everything seemed very tiny and far away. I wished we were closer.

Ti rummaged in her basket and came up with two collapsing wooden tubes. I stared at them in wonder, then turned them over in my hands. They were small telescopes, actually monoculars.

"Where did these come from?" I asked her wonderingly.

She gave me a satisfied smirk. "I made friends with a supervisor from Lakk, the Lady Tona's *besil* pilot. When I spotted one on his belt, I asked about 'em, and got two. Thought we might need 'em."

I was impressed. I had the bad habit of continually underestimating Ti and mentally kicking myself for it later. I'd actually tried to get her to stay behind, but that proved impossible. I was beginning to think she deliberately cultivated that childlike vulnerability so that she'd have an edge on everybody else, Warden power or not.

I put one to my right eye and studied the field. "Things should be popping any moment now," I said tensely.

"Things are popping already," she responded. "Look down there, near Artur's fort. See?"

I trained my monocular on the spot, wishing I had something with better focusing and a stronger glass. "I don't see—wait! Yes, I do too!"

They were there, already lined up in a neat formation, the great hopping *wuks,* their huge bulks almost invisible at this distance against the green of the valley. Behind them a formidable array of foot soldiers stood in perfect military formation.

I shifted my glass to the *besil* pens cut in the mountain above the stockade and saw signs of frantic movement. They would come shooting out of there, I knew, at some signal from the ground. Idly I wondered where Artur would be.

Next I looked at the Castle. The great door was shut, I could see, and red flags were flying from the pointed towers. I thought I could see figures on those towers, but it was pretty far to be sure. What was certain was that no pawns were in the fields or anywhere to be seen. They had been withdrawn to the base of the mountains, as far from battle as possible, to await the outcome.

I studied the trail heads next, down on the valley floor below. During the night the witches had infiltrated and now they stood, linked in a line rather than a circle, facing inward, at each point.

There was no way to carry out any movements of this sort without your enemy knowing about it, so nobody had made much of a secret of their movements. The witches had dispatched the guard and stood in such a way that they might reinforce each other if necessary, but though Artur could probably wipe out any coven of thirteen with his forces, this would be an open invitation for the coming Lakk forces to overrun his rear. Artur, I decided, would take his chances with the divided witches until he met and defeated the Lakks. The way his forces were now moving, I was sure he intended to meet the invader as close to the swamps as possible, fighting in the air over the dank and treacherous terrain and forcing the Lakks to land on solid ground piecemeal. There they could be mopped up in small batches before they could regroup into a major fighting force.

What we'd seen in front of the stockade had merely been the reserves, a bit more than half his force that could be thrown in where needed or committed against individual groups of witches if need be. It was really good military thinking, and I could see at a glance why Artur was held in such respect and why Zeis was considered unassailable by Lakk.

But there were only seven roads into the Keep, and

each was blocked by thirteen witches. That left seventy-eight witches, and those seventy-eight were a tremendous amplified and coalesced Warden force. Zeis was the model of what you'd want to defend in a military sense, but its strength lay in the impossibility of establishing a beachhead against it. If a large enough force could be landed on solid ground, it would be the defenders who would be rolled back into a trap, totally surrounded by mountains.

"There go the *besils*!" Ti shouted excitedly. I didn't need the monocular to see the great dark shapes flow out of their mountain stable lair. The riders were braced in special combat saddles that also supported long, pointed wooden lances. I looked out over the fog-shrouded swamp, seeing nothing for a moment. Then, out of the murky grayness, a long, slow line of *besils* appeared. Unlike Artur's *besils,* whose underbellies were dyed a reddish color, these were yellow underneath, the color of Lakk.

They came in slow and low, cautious until they had a full field of vision. Inside the valley, despite some wisps of ground fog, the eternal clouds had retreated past the thousand-meter mark, plenty of room for an aerial duel.

The Zeis *besils* neared the swamp, then stopped, their great wings beating so fast to keep them in place they were totally invisible. I never understood how anything that big flew, anyway.

The attacking formation split now, one-third going left, another third right, while the center column pushed ahead, accelerating suddenly and with great speed. Hundreds of black, swift shapes weaved in and out, parrying and thrusting, lances attempting to score a hit either at the underbelly of the enemy *besils* or at the riders atop them. It was a battle in three dimensions at crazy angles and speeds and with sudden whiplike motions.

While the vanguard of Zeis *besils* were occupied, the swamp itself seemed to come alive, eerie shapes moving to and fro in the fog. Emerging now were the great twelve-legged, hairy *snarks*, raised for fur and used in stews by the people of Lilith. These creatures of that swamplike terrain were somehow able to avoid sinking into the muck and mire by shifting their centers of gravity at will. Herbivores, they were totally harmless to people, but they made effective troop carriers when a swamp was to be the battleground, and Lakk Keep had bred them for just that purpose.

The great, hopping, green *wuks* leaped into action from the Zeis side, aiming at going so high and landing so exactly that they would come down right on top of the fragile *snarks,* spilling them and their contents into the swamp. It should have worked, had the *snarks* contained combat soldiers, but this time was different.

The *snarks* stopped suddenly, as if waiting for certain death, but the proud and lordly *wuks* were the ones that seemed to reel in mid-hop as if struck by gunfire and topple over, out of control, to the ground below.

The *snarks* contained not soldiers but chemically enhanced witches, all concentrated on the center *snark,* where the leader was knocking *wuks* out of the air with a gesture. Seeing what was happening, Artur quickly shifted. Realizing from the pattern in which his *wuks* were falling that a central and single power was picking them off, he committed a section of his reserves to fan out across the entire basin, to keep a great distance from one another and to fan out over a wide enough front to divide the witches' fire. Their concentrated power had only one metaphorical barrel, and it couldn't point everywhere at once.

Besils, too, were screeching and falling all over the place, unable to help either side in the battle below but keeping the other from also doing so. It was bloody carnage all around, and Artur's plan was working to an extent. A *wuk* struck one of the witch-laden *snarks,* pulling up incredibly at the last minute so that it hit with its powerful hind legs out. The great spiderlike creature collapsed as if made of thin sticks, dragging its complement of passengers into the muddy quagmire—and diminishing Sumiko O'Higgins' power by a small amount. From where we were, it was impossible to see how many were on any given snark, but considering the number of the beasts it had to be four or five at least. The whole scene was stunning, an eerie ballet of death and destruction as it might have been centuries ago on mother Earth.

The *wuk* maneuver had weakened the witch force, but most of them had made solid land and were quickly descending and assembling into their groups. Some would not have their full complement, but since all worked with, through, and at the direction of Sumiko O'Higgins, however many managed to land would have impressive force indeed.

Suddenly the grass blazed in front of the landing witches, a huge wall of fire across the entire field, blinding everyone for a moment.

Warden power was being used against Warden power now, I knew.

After a moment's panic, the witches regrouped. Then, incredibly, a whirlwind of dirt like a great, gigantic plow shot up along the fire line, damping the fire, although small patches continued to burn. The witches advanced now, in a broad semicircle. I didn't know exactly how many there were, but it was fifty or more, I was sure. Sumiko had bragged that she could level the Castle with less.

Now fire was turned against the defenders. A terribly thin, bright wall of flame shot out from beyond the firebreak they'd just created, then started moving, widening out in an ever-increasing semicircle, pushing ground forces back and revealing large, dark holes that were obviously pits to trap invaders who advanced that far.

I frowned and turned my tiny telescope on the reserves, still sitting in front of the stockade. "He's going to lose," I muttered, more to myself than to Ti, "unless he sends those reserves in fast. They've got their beachhead. Why don't they move?"

Ti didn't answer, and I couldn't keep my eyes off the unfolding spectacle.

I turned again to the swamp, where hordes of *snarks* were now appearing, landing troops of Lakk behind the witches' screen. I looked again to the reserves, still poised but unmoving, and shook my head.

"They can't be this incompetent," I told myself. "Why the hell doesn't he move before the beachhead is totally established?"

I heard Ti gasp. "The *besils* have stopped fighting!" she cried. "Look!"

I turned my gaze in that direction and saw that it was true. The survivors of the initial encounter, perhaps forty or so out of an initial hundred or more, had disengaged, but neither side was retreating.

"They—they're regrouping together!" I rasped, amazed. "What the hell . . . ?"

I heard the sound of a tremendous explosion below, its roar echoing back and forth across the mountains, its very existence so jarring that I was forced to look for it. An explosion? Here?

I looked at a great puff of smoke near the front of the witch line, then saw soldiers *behind* the witches wading into them and attacking them! Suddenly the reserves moved, the explosion an apparent cue. The reserve *besils* flew out of their mountainside nests and the *wuks* and ground troops started deploying— but not toward the invaders.

"Look, they're going after the witch groups guarding the trails!" I yelled, mouth agape. Still, I forced my attention back to the beachhead, only to see the unmistakable signs of slaughter. A wall of fire now trapped the witches between their own defensive wall and the attackers, formed and started to close in on them.

Disorganized and confused, the witches dropped their own firebreak and started forward into Zeis proper, on the run. Now the *besils,* both yellow and red-colored, started moving in on them, dividing them. Bright flashes told me that Warden power was being used on them, killing them as they ran, as they tried to comprehend what was happening.

Below, the reserves were taking something of a beating from the power of the covens, but it wasn't a hundred and sixty-nine witches to forty *besils* now, as it had been back in the witch village. It was more like twenty *besils* plus a dozen *wuks* and running, well-armed ground troops against thirteen witches in each case. It was costly to take them out, but even though they took half the attackers with them, the witches went down—went down and were mercilessly hacked to death.

I put down the monocular and looked at Ti for a moment. She seemed to sense it and turned to look at me, the stricken and confused look on her face mirroring, I'm sure, my own.

"The Lakks attacked the witches," she said wonderingly. "The two sides joined up. Cal, what's going *on* here? Have we been taken for *suckers?*"

I shook my head dully. "No, honey. Well, yes, I guess we *have*. It's kind of crushing, though, finally to understand all this. *Damn!*" I smacked my fist in my other hand. "I don't know why I didn't figure it out from the start—at least from a few days ago, when I had all the pieces."

"But they were fightin' for us, weren't they? They were gonna get us Zeis Keep!"

I shook my head slowly and sadly and squeezed her hand. "Baby, I doubt if *anybody* down there gives a damn about us one way or the other. I doubt if they have since the decision was made to fight." I let her go and smacked my fist in my left hand again. "Pawns!" I muttered. "God damn it! All this way, all this far —and still pawns!"

She looked at me uncomprehendingly. "Wha . . .?"

I sighed and got up. "Come on. Let's take a nice long walk down to the Castle. Don't worry. Nobody's going to stop us or probably even notice our existence."

With Ti still confused, we started on down.

Chapter Twenty-Two

First Lord of the Diamond

The extent of the carnage was enormous. The massacre of the witches had been most thorough, more gruesome than any autopsy.

It took over two hours to reach the Castle, and by that time even the mop-up had been completed. Yellow and red forces were methodically surveying the field, helping those who could be helped, cleaning up the debris. It would be a long, tough job.

As I expected, Father Bronz and a number of others were sitting in wicker chairs outside the Castle's gates, relaxing, eating, and drinking. I recognized Vola and her sister, Dola, Boss Rognival and the Ladies Tona and Kysil, and Master Artur. The others were not familiar to me but wore designs indicating they were of Zeis. One of them—a small, frail-looking man, bald and wizened—was dressed as elaborately in ornate silken tunic, heavy boots; he wore atop his head a tiara with a single large blue gem similar to, but not identical to, the one Rognival wore. Another man, dressed in a manner similar to the older, thin one but wearing mostly gold colors, as well as a wide-brimmed hat, relaxed nearby. He was an older man, with neatly trimmed gray beard, certainly once of the civilized worlds. Although he was many years my senior he looked to be in nearly perfect physical condition.

Father Bronz spotted us. "Cal! Ti! Please come over!" he called pleasantly, and we did. Up close Bronz looked dead tired, and very, very old. He's put on at least ten years this morning, I thought. Still, he rose wearily from his chair, took my hand warmly, then kissed Ti on the forehead. Only then did he turn and nod toward the others.

"Some of these fine people you know," he began, "but I don't think you ever met Sir Honlon Tiel." The thin old man nodded in my direction, and I could only stare at him. So *that* was the knight I was to take on, I thought glumly. The Boss of Zeis Keep. The Warden cells glowed more in Artur than in him.

"The gentleman in gold there is Grand Duke Kobé," Bronz continued, and the other also nodded. He also introduced the others, but they were all of Zeis's ruling group. Then he turned back to me. "I assume you understand everything now?"

"Pretty much," I told him. "I can't say it makes me happy to be used in such a way, though. I feel like the child promised the new toy he's always wanted for his birthday, only to have nobody even come to his party, let alone getting the gift."

Bronz laughed. "Oh, come now! It's not all that bad."

"Will somebody," Ti interrupted in an even but slightly angry voice, "*please* tell me what the hell is going on here?"

I looked at her and sighed. "Ti, may I present Marek Kreegan, Lord of Lilith, First Lord of the Diamond?"

The fact that she gasped when Father Bronz bowed indicated she still had a lot to learn.

The full explanation came later, after we'd bathed, changed, and sat down to a sumptuous feast in the great hall of the Castle. Ti still hadn't recovered from the shock of Father Bronz's true identity, but given that, she *had* managed to figure out the basics, I'll give her that. And she was mad as hell.

Still, I wanted to hear the tale from the man who had planned it all.

"From the top, then," agreed Marek Kreegan. "Of course, we had a problem. Lilith, as I told you long ago, is a rigid ecosystem in which we humans play no part. Its economy is fragile, its ability to support a large population in the wild very much in doubt with-

out Warden protection of the masses. The pawns
don't enjoy a wonderful life—but who does? The ruling class, always, that's who. Because while everybody
would love to be king, if everybody *was* a king there'd
be no labor to support this monarch. The civilized
worlds are no different, only thanks to technology on
a massive scale the standard of living for their pawns
is higher than is currently possible on Lilith."

"I still can't see the masses on the civilized worlds
as pawns with a privileged class," I responded.

His eyebrows rose. "Oh? Were you born in that
body?"

"You know I wasn't," I growled.

"Exactly. The Merton Process, right? Potential im-
morality for anybody and everybody, right? But will
the masses get it? Of course not! For the same reason
that cures for the big three diseases that kill people
have been withheld. We are at maximum and the
frontier can expand only so fast. New planets take
decades to develop, particularly to the point of self-
sufficiency. Cal, no system can survive if its population doesn't die. Nor is the Merton Process any
cure-all, since you need a body for it. That means
massive cloning—a couple of *trillion* clones. Ridiculous. They have to be raised and supported by some
biomechanical means until needed. But the *leaders*
of the Confederacy, now—that's a different matter.
They're already immunized against diseases people
don't even know are killing them. They get age-
retardant processes like mad. And when they finally
do wear out, they now have the Merton Process to
keep 'em going for an infinite number of cycles. The
masses count, in Confederacy society, only in the
plural. Masses. Averages. Everything's an average.
Only the elite get the plums. Exactly the same as
here."

"I'll agree with you to a point," I admitted, "but
leadership is available to those who wish it."

Again he laughed. "Really? You think so? You
think you got where you were because of willpower
and dedication? Hell, man, you were *bred* for it. They
designed and manufactured you as they would any

tool they needed, because they needed it. The same as they did me."

"But you crossed them up," I noted. "That's why *you're* here."

He shrugged good-naturedly. "The trouble with their system is that their human tools have to be smart guys and they have to be thrown out into the cold, cruel world to do their jobs. Eventually we wise up and have to be eliminated ourselves before we become a threat. That's done by promotion to the inner circle—if they can fit you someplace—or sometimes by just having a junior knock you off. Hell, they can do it just by having you show up at the Security Clinic for normal processing, then instead of feeding you your past and what you need, reducing you to the common pawn vegetable with a nice little job as a widget monitor or something. I discovered this fact almost too late and mostly by accident, and I ran like hell."

"To Lilith," I noted. "Why in heaven's name *Lilith?*" Everybody at the table laughed at that, except of course the native-born.

"I'm not going to tell you," he responded. "At least not until we've gotten that damned organic transmitter removed from your skull and until you've been around enough to know whose side you're really on."

"The aliens," I muttered, feeling like my last secrets were being stripped from me. He even knew about the transmitter.

He grinned and shrugged. "Let's just say, ah, powerful friends of mine—of all Warden citizens, but mostly of the Four Lords of the Diamond. Anyway, it must surely have occurred to you that any civilization able to penetrate the security chamber of Military Systems Command would have no trouble at all finding out about the Merton Process. And report same to me, who knows better than anybody how the great minds of the Confederacy run. I know they'd zero in on Lilith because I was running the place, and that the only logical person to send would be someone whose own past and career matched mine as closely as possible."

I said nothing to this because I'd been a lot slower than he was giving me credit for, a fact I didn't like at all.

"Well, anyway, we knew you were coming," continued the Lord of Lilith, "and, Confederacy Intelligence being what it is, I had to figure that any agent sent down here would most logically duplicate my own initial situation as closely as possible, since they were setting one assassin to catch another. That meant Zeis Keep, since I had started here. That meant I just had to wait until Zeis got a new prisoner. Then you turned up. After your seasoning, I stepped in to size you up a bit and tantalize you as well. It was pretty clear to me that you were somewhat in the doldrums and needed a swift kick in the pants you couldn't wear then to get moving. Ti was the all-too-obvious leverage."

I glanced over at Ti, and she bristled. The full implications of what a "pawn" really was were dawning on her, and she didn't like it one bit.

"So, anyway," he went on, "I had already established myself in your mind as the only independent spirit on Lilith and told you pretty much where I was heading. Then I came back here and ordered Dr. Pohn to take Ti. I figured that, if you were anything like me, you'd get so damned mad you'd come after her, and that meant you'd have to have a Warden explosion. You were already ripe—I could see it in you."

"And if it hadn't happened?"

He smiled. "Then you weren't any good to me *or* to the Confederacy and you would have been abandoned to plant beans for the rest of your life. But of course it *did* happen, the night of the banquet. When Dola came and told us here, we immediately made plans on what we'd do next. We had to expose you to Dr. Pohn at his worst, for example, and Ti in that totally helpless condition at his villainous mercy. We had to show you not only Master Artur but his troops and beasts as well—Artur usually doesn't show newcomers around personally, you know—so you'd realize it'd take an armed force to come after Zeis

Keep. And of course we had to test you for Warden potential and give you a taste of what that power is like without actually giving you that power right off. Vola took care of that, then also got you on the run with that wonderful piece of midnight theatrics. I of course was nowhere near at the time, since I already had to be far to the south to lay my trail for you to follow."

"But I heard a voice . . ."

"Duke Kobé, I'm afraid, using a reed tube," he responded. Kobé shrugged apologetically. "It was important that natural early suspicions about me be allayed. I *couldn't* be Kreegan in the hallways and also have gone to several Keeps in the time allowed, not without you finding out about it. I counted on you to file that away in your mind. On the other hand, I had to be the only person to whom you could turn for help."

"You took a chance there," I noted, nettled by his manner. "I could just have gone to the wild."

"I *never* took a chance with you," he replied. "If at any time you hadn't been up to the job for one reason or another I could simply quit and find somebody else. But I had some insurance in Ti, here."

She shot him a glance that, had she had my Warden power, would have demolished the hall.

"Remember," Kreegan said, "I'm forty years your senior, but we came out of the same background, went through the same training, did the same job for the same bosses. Oh, the faces and names change occasionally, but it's always the same bosses. It's a stratified and static society with a system it believes works. As a result, *I knew how you thought*. I could simply put myself in your place, decide what I'd have done, and act accordingly."

"How were you so sure I'd take Ti, though?"

Again he grinned. "Well, first of all, your reaction to Ti had been strong enough to trigger the Warden effect and get you to the Castle. So you *had* to be emotionally attached to her. Additionally, Dr. Pohn was an inducement if you cared anything about her. However, just in case you suddenly turned into the

total pragmatist of your self-image, Vola mixed a
mild hypnotic herb in with the first batch of juice; this
—reinforced your tendencies, shall we say. I needed
Ti. She was essential. You *had* to take her, since
she was the only possible inducement for Sumiko
O'Higgins to get involved."

"Did you get her?" I asked.

He nodded. "But that's getting ahead of things.
You must understand the threat she represented. She
was a psychopath such as comes along only once in a
century or more, thank heavens. There are some monsters who, when caught, deserve to be exterminated
and had better be. Sumiko was one such. Had she not
been caught in a fluke accident, she'd have accomplished the actual genetic code of the Institute for
Biological Stability that determines the future look of
the civilized worlds. Not just the look—well, you
know how much genetics can really determine."

"You just got through telling me that the civilized
worlds needed changing," I pointed out.

"Change, perhaps," he replied, "but—monsters,
Cal. Monsters in standard civilized world guise. They
should have gotten rid of her, wiped her, vaporized
her—but instead they sent her to Lilith, on the theory
that anybody that smart might come up with something unusual. And she sure did!"

I nodded. "I got a whiff of her plans, thanks to Ti."

"Not the half of it," Kreegan told me. "You have
no idea what a brilliance that twisted mind had. To
tailor-made mutations in existing organisms. Mental
genetic engineering! We had word of her activities,
of course. She was hardly quiet about her recruiting of
young women, that sort of thing. They performed human sacrifices, too, there in that village common. The
same stone on which Ti rested was designed to hold a
living human being; the grooves there were to drain
off the blood, which they would all then drink. She
was sick, Cal. Sick and enough of a genius to pull it
all off. We had to stop her—but thanks to her brilliance, we couldn't even find her."

I nodded again, seeing it all. "And, as Artur proved,

she was unassailable even if you *had* been able to find her."

The sergeant-at-arms grumbled to himself.

"That's about it," Kreegan agreed. "Understand, she had discovered nothing that the Institute didn't already know about, but the Institute goes to a lot of trouble to keep things stable here. Using you and particularly Ti, I was able to get us all to her village. There I could tantalize her enough that I felt sure she'd come with us to the Institute—and come she did. A lot of evaluation went on there, without her knowledge, although she also learned from the library things she needed to know. Shortcuts, so to speak. We had to give her crumbs just to keep her as long as we could. Afterward, we had long discussions on what to do, the extent of her power, that sort of thing. We felt we'd given her enough new material for her to grow overconfident, and so it only remained to play the trump card—offer her a chance to find out how strong she really was. We made the bait as irresistible as possible."

"The object, in other words, was to create a situation by which Sumiko would leave her protective haven, split her forces, and not suspect that the enemy was not merely Zeis but everyone else."

"That is true," Boss Rognival put in. "And the cost was great. We truly had to fight one another until they all landed on the beachhead. That was difficult but unavoidable. Regardless, we deployed sufficiently to allow *some* Zeis forces to get through and knock out as many witches as possible. Weaken her. But we could not close in on her forces and destroy them until the bitch herself was dead."

"Just out of curiosity, Kreegan, how *did* you kill her?" I asked.

"Oh, I had several options," he replied. "As a last resort we had, thanks to the Institute, enough of the amplifier potion to mass me, the Duke, here, two knights, and about forty Masters against her—but we didn't have to, for which I'm thankful. I had no idea how powerful she really was—still don't—and I didn't want to find out. It was you, Cal, who gave me the idea."

I started. "Me?"

He nodded. "When you told me about her laser pistol. I figured she'd have it with her for insurance, and particularly for afterward. Look, only a Lord can stabilize offworld metal. You know that. That gives you some idea of her power."

I frowned. "But what does that . . . ?"

"Come on, Cal! If *you* were in my shoes, and had my power, and if *you* knew she had a laser pistol on her, what would *you* do? Particularly knowing that her entire mind, her whole concentration, was elsewhere?"

My mouth fell open in surprise as I realized what he had done. "You concentrated on nothing but that pistol," I told him. "You undid the Warden pattern on the insulating coating. The Warden cells in the area would start immediately attacking the pistol."

He smiled and nodded. "Yep. It exposed the power supply, which overloaded and exploded. She had it tucked in her belt at the time. I'll tell you, I sweated blood waiting for that to happen. I was only going to give it another few minutes before we switched to a mass attack and damn the consequences. But it blew, praise God, and the bang was the signal for everybody to stop fighting, join hands, and take those witches from all quarters."

"You still took a terrible chance," I noted. "It could have gone off any time—maybe hours later. And you yourself said your mass attack might not have been strong enough."

"I'll admit I had a third backup," he said tiredly. "The Wardens act fast, but not *that* fast. If all else had failed, my orbital satellite would have released a null-missile right into Zeis. Everyone and everything would have been atomized, but of course so would all the witches. That's how seriously I took the threat."

That answered all the questions.

"What about this Father Bronz act?" I asked him. "You couldn't just invent the character."

"Oh, I've been Father Bronz for ten years," he told us. "It's the easiest way to get around inconspicuously." He paused. "Of course I'll have to undergo some physical changes now and find a new persona." He sighed. "Too bad, too. Old Father Bronz really did some good. I've been considering asking for some real clergy here."

I let the topic go and finally asked him the most important question. "What about me?" I asked. "What happens now?"

"You'll do fine," he assured me. "Stay here as a Master for a while and get some experience, then either outlive the Boss, here, or go find yourself a weak Knight and start it all. You're going to be at least a Duke someday, maybe even Lord. I told you. It took me seventeen years."

"I'll beat your record," I told him, not at all jokingly.

He stared at me hard. "I think you might at that."

Dinner broke up soon after that, with Kreegan saying that he was catching the shuttle when it put down the next day. "Business," he told us. "Four Lords business."

And Boss Tiel, to my surprise, had a few words for me as well. "I'd like you to stay here," he told me sincerely. "I'm an old man now, Tremon. You could take me out right now, as you originally planned. But a number of the Masters, Artur in particular, are strong, and you might take *me* out only to find yourself losing, on experience alone, to somebody else. Maybe even Rognival, who'd love to swap that island for Zeis. A couple of years here, though, learning technique and the full use of your power, making contacts, doing the proper politics, and you'll have the knighthood by acclamation. You're the best qualified. Artur's a great soldier but a lousy administrator. The others are pretty much the same. No talent or no ambition. It's up to you, of course, but you've impressed me."

I told him I'd think about it, but I knew the answer. I would stay, of course, because that was the path to my own ambition most open to me and because of Ti. She'd never like or forgive many of these people, but as she said, she was a part of Zeis.

Finally, I sought out Dr. Pohn. I still didn't like the little son of a bitch, and I knew that he'd be one of the first to go in the Tremon regime that was coming. Still, now I needed him.

The next afternoon he would undertake a little Warden-style operation. Okay, my twin and counterpart up there somewhere—I failed miserably. I got played for a sucker. I learned nothing about your precious aliens, and Lord Marek Kreegan, curse his black soul, remains Lord of Lilith and First Lord of the Diamond. But that's it. I've done all I can do for now and I find myself less and less anxious to do you any more favors. Up yours, Confederacy! Maybe when I become Lord of Lilith I won't like those aliens; but then again, maybe I will. But whether or not I feed you any information will be based on my own assessment at the time, from the viewpoint of my own interests.

Cal Tremon, none too respectfully, resigns.

Chapter Twenty-Three

A Little Unfinished Business

The air was warm and moist. We'd just had another of Lilith's nasty little thunderstorms, and the cloud ceiling was extremely low. Nonetheless, the shuttle arrived right on schedule—as if it would stand up Lord Marek Kreegan.

I had spent most of the night calming Ti down. "I hate that man," she kept saying over and over. In a sense, she'd lost as much as I had, and her world picture now included bitterness. As much as Sumiko O'Higgins had upset her, she could not forgive the man who had caused her to fall into the hands of Dr. Pohn, to degrade her so much for somebody else's cause. She felt as if she'd been raped by Marek Kreegan, more so than if he'd assaulted her sexually. It was a total violation, and she'd be a long time getting the stain off her soul.

Still, she was learning. She was there with me when the shuttlecraft landed to the west of the Castle as it always did, appearing out of the clouds and settling to the ground. The elaborate set of airlocks and safeguards came into play, although they were less necessary with Kreegan on board.

Kreegan still wore his old priest's robe, but I knew it would soon be exchanged for something else. I might not even know him the next time I saw him, although I felt sure I'd recognize that man anywhere. And one day, Kreegan, I told myself, we'd have more than a little chat.

Duke Kobé remained behind, although usually he was the one who used the shuttle. I wondered idly if Kreegan hadn't made one mistake this time after all, since he knew that the broadcaster had been in place until this afternoon. It was entirely possible that the orbiting Confederacy troops would blast his little shuttle. But no, I told myself. They wouldn't do it because that would involve a choice of record. That's why they hired—created—people like me. Nobody up there would want to take the open responsibility without clearing it back to the Confederacy itself, and by that time Kreegan would have vanished to who knew where?

Besides, he had powerful friends. Would they permit him to be blown to bits? I doubted it. He was their most valuable ally, the man who knew how the Confederacy establishment thought. The aliens wouldn't want to lose him.

He waved, smiled, and entered the shuttle, and the stairway retracted. I heard the soft whir of the engines starting up again, and, slowly at first, it started to lift.

"Cal," I heard Ti say beside me.

"Yes, hon?" I responded and looked at her.

In that moment something in my head seemed to

explode. My Warden cells seemed to flare, and the
energy flowed from me, maximum energy, beyond my
control, flowing straight at Ti! But she didn't burn,
nor even do more than shake slightly. Instead she
turned and looked directly at that lifting body, heading slowly up into the clouds, cautiously trying to
clear the mountains before full thrust.

I stood transfixed, unable to move, think, breathe.

The sound of the shuttle engines varied slightly,
coughed, then sounded very, very wrong.

There was a sudden explosion, and a brightness in
the clouds, and then, tumbling down, crashing again
and again against the rocky mountainside, the shuttle plunged. It struck bottom with a thunderous roar
and suddenly was bathed in a terrible glow, too bright
to look at. Ti turned away, and I felt myself abruptly
freed from that mysterious, terrible hold.

I turned, stunned, first in the direction of the shuttle, but it was now just a smoldering, bubbling and
hissing mass of molten metal. Soon it, too, would be
gone. When it cooled enough, I knew, the Warden cells
would begin their relentless attack on the alien matter,
reducing it to dust in a matter of days.

I turned back to Ti in shock. "Wha— What the
hell did you *do?*"

She smiled, as evil and self-satisfied a smile as I had
ever seen on another human being.

"Back at the witch village a few days ago—you remember?"

I could only nod dully.

"I swiped some of that potion. I drank it *all* this
morning, just before coming down here. I was lucky.
I was hopin' to surprise you and be able to use your
power before you could stop me. And I did."

"But—but *how?*"

"Last night after dinner I talked a lot with Duke
Kobé and Boss Tiel," she told me. "I asked 'em a
few simple questions. One of 'em was how they kept
the shuttle level. Kobé was particularly nice about
showin' me. Drew me a picture of somethin' called
a geoscope or some such. I asked him if the shuttle
had a thing like that and he told me it did, but not

like that. He told me what it looked like. And using your power, I just did the same thing to the shuttle that Kreegan did to Sumiko's gun. I just took the spell off."

"But—but it would be in a vacuum chamber!" I protested. "It shouldn't have made any difference."

"She did more than that, young man," said a voice behind me. I whirled and saw Duke Kobé standing there, looking more thoughtful than angry. "You sure as *hell* have some power, son, and she hated old Marek worse than anybody should be hated by anybody, that's for sure. I could see it, feel it, but I couldn't do a damned thing about it."

"What do you mean?" I asked, feeling suddenly totally drained.

He shook his head in wonder. "The gyros didn't get him, no matter what she thinks. She punched a hole with Warden cell material clear through the outer hull and right through the power supply!"

I sat down on the grass. "Oh, my God!"

"If nothing else, you can see now that even Sumiko didn't have an idea of just what the power of a Lord could do," the Duke noted.

I thought he was taking the death of Marek Kreegan pretty lightly and told him so.

He just smiled. "It's the way of Lilith," he said philosophically. "I did all the administrative work for the whole damned planet plus, yet I was still his toady. No, son, I had no love for Marek Kreegan."

"Cal is Lord now!" Ti exclaimed forcefully. I could still feel her tug on me, but knowing what was going on, I found I could block it.

Kobé shook his head slowly from side to side. "No, little clever and ambitious one. He's not. *He* didn't kill Marek Kreegan—you did. I doubt if he could muster that much hate on his own. No, the position is open, pending someone claiming it and being able to hold on to it. That'll take weeks, at least. In the meantime, I'll act in his stead." He sighed. "Damn. Guess I'll have to attend that damned conference now myself."

Ti flared at him, but I was now able to dampen her rage. In a few hours, I knew, the effect would wear off. In the meantime, I had to keep a really close watch on her.

I looked up at her, still a little stunned. "You don't have any more of that juice, do you?"

She looked a little hurt at the question and stared down at me. "Would *I* lie to you?"

Epilogue

The man came out of it slowly, only vaguely aware of who and where he was. He removed the headset almost idly and rubbed his temples. He had a headache that was killing him.

He looked around the control cubicle for some time, as if not believing that he was really here, on the picket ship, in his own lab, and not down there somewhere, on Lilith.

Finally he managed something of a recovery. "Computer?"

"Responding," a calm, male voice responded.

"You now have the raw data and the data filtered through me," he noted. "Any conclusions?"

"For the first time the connection between the aliens and the Lords of the Diamond is confirmed," the computer responded. "I also have an awful lot of data that asks more questions than it answers. Not enough now—but we do have another report in. I might also point out, sir, that Marek Kreegan knew only about Cal Tremon, so this might well mean that they do not suspect the other three."

"That's something," he admitted grumpily. "Did you say we had another?"

"Yes, sir. Cerberus. Because of the peculiar nature of the Warden cell there it was not possible to do the organic mind-link, but we imposed a command on that subject agent to report when able and then forget he reported. It is a technological culture, sir, so that was possible. I believe we have a full accounting. Would you like me to play it for you?"

"Yes—*no!*" he shot back, a little angry. "Give me a little bit, will you?"

"If you have a headache and natural fatigue, sir, I can provide the needed counters in window slot number two."

He nodded. "All right, do it. But give me a little."

He couldn't tell the computer that the headache didn't matter, that the fatigue didn't matter, that none of that mattered. What troubled him was far deeper and far more upsetting.

Cal Tremon, he wondered, are you really *me?* Would I have acted that way, would I have done things that way? Why are you a stranger to me, Cal Tremon? Are you not my twin?

Marek Kreegan's account and version of the Confederacy bothered him, too, if not as much. It was unthinkable to believe that way. It would make all this a lie, a joke. It was unacceptable.

Still, he told himself, perhaps this was an aberration. Cal Tremon's body, his hormones, whatever, affected the mind. It *had* to.

Suddenly, instead of fearing the Cerberus report, he needed it, and badly. He *had* to know. Was Cal Tremon the aberration—or was he truly seeing himself?

If so, could he face the stranger in these four mirrors?

He settled back in the chair and sipped a drink. Finally, he sighed. "All right. Run Cerberus."

"Acknowledged," the computer responded. "Recorders on. But if I may say so, sir, it would be of great help if you would put on your headset."

He sighed, picked up the fragile crown, put it on and adjusted it for maximum comfort, then settled back, wondering why his hands seemed to be shaking so.

Mirror, mirror, in the mind . . .
Would I lie to you?

Thus concludes LILITH, Book One of *The
Four Lords of the Diamond*. The story will
continue in CERBERUS: A Wolf in the
Fold, available in 1982.

About the Author

JACK L. CHALKER was born in Norfolk, Virginia, on December 17, 1944, but was raised and has spent most of his life in Baltimore, Maryland. He learned to read almost from the moment of entering school, and by working odd jobs had amassed a large book collection by the time he was in junior high school, a collection now too large for containment in his quarters. Science fiction, history, and geography all fascinated him early on, interests that continue.

Chalker joined the Washington Science Fiction Association in 1958 and began publishing an amateur SF journal, *Mirage,* in 1960, After high school he decided to be a trial lawyer, but money problems and the lack of a firm caused him to switch to teaching. He holds bachelor degrees in history and English, and an M.L.A. from the Johns Hopkins University. He taught history and geography in the Baltimore public schools between 1966 and 1978, and now makes his living as a freelance writer. Additionally, out of the amateur journals he founded a publishing house, The Mirage Press, Ltd., devoted to nonfiction and bibliographic works on science fiction and fantasy. This company has produced more than twenty books in the last nine years. His hobbies include esoteric audio, travel, working on science-fiction convention committees, and guest lecturing on SF to institutions such as the Smithsonian. He is an active conservationist and National Parks supporter, and he has an intensive love of ferryboats, with the avowed goal of riding every ferry in the world. In fact, in 1978 he was married to Eva Whitley on an ancient ferryboat in mid-river. They live in the Catoctin Mountain region of western Maryland.

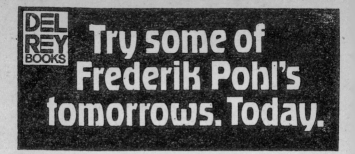